THE WEALTHY WHITES OF WILLIAMSBURG

Cover design by Mumblers Press LLC.

Cover art: "Williamsburg Bridge at Twilight & Manhattan View at Blue Hour from Domino Park Williamsburg Brooklyn New York City NY P00628 DSC_0481" by incognito7nyc is licensed under CC BY-NC 2.0.

Author photo © Thomas J. Duffy Jr.

Published by Mumblers Press LLC, San Francisco CA USA

ISBN 978-1-7362444-5-6 (paperback) | 978-1-7362444-4-9 (e-book)

LCCN: 2022920012

THE WEALTHY WHITES OF WILLIAMSBURG

MIKE KARPA

MUMBLERS

For Tom

THE FOG

Casey wandered the Port Authority bus terminal, newly debarked off her bus from Memphis and feeling like midtown Manhattan had punched her in the face. A guy approached her. The man looked like a farmworker who'd wandered in straight off a *granja*—his brown skin weathered and creased, his white straw cowboy hat similarly battered by the elements. He was pushing sixty if he was a day.

"*¿Cómo llego al JFK desde aquí?*" he asked. How do you get to JFK from here?

Casey was surprised to have the question come in Spanish, because she didn't think she looked particularly Spanish-speaking. But it felt like a welcome to New York. She'd spent the last five years studying language and applied linguistics at the Universidad de las Américas Puebla, UDLAP, in Cholula, Mexico, achieving professional competence in Spanish, and maybe that had revealed itself in her choice of clothing, or the way she walked. Or maybe the old fellow just couldn't see.

Casey had noticed plenty of signs for JFK plastered high on the walls of the Port Authority, so she told him he could take the subway from there or get a train from Penn Station, a ten-minute walk or so, which was faster and the same price.

"*No mires tanto hacia arriba. Parecerás una turista. Es lo que alguien me dijo.*" Someone had told him looking up makes you look like a tourist, he said. He tipped his hat as he left, in the direction of Penn Station.

Fifteen minutes in New York City and already she was getting advice.

Looking up is how I know how to get to JFK, she wanted to call after him, but the impulse wasn't a strong one. No impulse was these days. She was grateful that he had wanted to protect her, and wary of being easy prey. Even after her years-long escape to the pulsing new experience of Cholula, part of her remained in an implacable fog. She imagined herself walking the streets of Manhattan and looking up at all the skyscrapers. That kind of aw-shucks naïveté might be an improvement over the fog; most days it was more than she could manage to maintain eye contact. There was more than one way to look vulnerable.

Casey rolled her bag out of the Port Authority onto Eighth Avenue, not knowing where she was going, only that she had to get there. Car horns sounded, people yelled. Video screens were garish red and hot pink. There had been a recent rain and she could hear tires. Somewhere, jackhammers were going. I'm in a movie, she thought.

Crowds approached. Her chest felt tight. Her gaze fell to the sidewalk.

The dirty concrete was a comfortable place to rest her eyes. She avoided oncoming pedestrians by watching for their feet. She'd become quite comfortable out amongst human beings in Cholula, where people had accepted her as another earnest language learner attending UDLAP, but her distrust of strangers, which she'd fled Memphis to heal, had come back in force once she returned to the banks of the muggy Mississippi. Within a month she was on a bus out of there. Now she felt that same distrust in New York.

Coming here was a mistake, she thought. All these miles between her and hell and she didn't feel one bit better.

People jostled her, banged into the bag she rolled behind her, and cursed her as they spilled their coffee. A standing man wearing a sign selling bus tours forced her to a stop. She collapsed the pull handle of her bag into its interior and held the bag by the side handle to reenter the stream of walkers. It was hardly better. She remembered the bag had a shoulder strap, so she dodged a bicycle to step into a urine-scented alley where she unspooled it. Now she held the bag in front of her, as she might have done on a Cholula bus, there out of consideration for fellow passengers though also to guard against thieves. Here, the familiarity of the move helped her breathe.

A book in her bag listed inexpensive places to stay. Exorbitant by Memphis standards, let alone those of Cholula, but she'd had hundreds of miles listening to bus tires hum on asphalt to make her peace with that.

She spotted a diner that looked unexceptional, far more so than the chain coffeehouse next to it, whose jaunty, overly familiar logo promised some kind of reassurance Casey knew it could not deliver. She pushed open the diner door. The bell hanging from it rang. She took a seat at the counter and looped the strap of her bag around her stool as she tucked it where she could rest her feet on it.

An older woman, mid-forties perhaps, approached behind the counter, tossed a menu in front of Casey and continued walking, turning her mop of thick red hair back toward Casey just long enough to utter, "Coffee?"

"Yes ma'am," Casey said. "Thank you." A busboy slid a clattering white ceramic saucer and cup in front of her.

"Light?" the waitress asked on the return leg of her *vuelta*.

"Pardon me?"

"Cream, honey," she said, pouring coffee into Casey's cup. "Would you like some cream?"

Pareces una turista, the waitress might as well have said.

Casey nodded. The woman poured a stream of cream into the shimmering black in her cup.

"I must seem like a tourist," Casey said.

"Nah." The woman pitched her voice low, in what sounded simultaneously like scoffing and praise. "New in town, sure, but I saw your maneuver with the bag. You seem like you're here to stay." The woman gave Casey a smile and patted the countertop twice next to Casey's menu. "You're in the right place." She moved on to another customer.

Casey's chest muscles relaxed further, allowing her to draw the first deep breath of her new life. A mild sort of terror had gripped her in Memphis, a terror she'd earned. Now it was gone.

The fog remained.

Casey took a sip of coffee. She knew she was not okay. But for the first time since she'd returned to the US, she thought maybe someday she would be.

PART I

CHAPTER 1

R oger White watched from his lectern as the new crop of shockingly young students filed into his lecture hall, ready to unmask him for the fraud he was. They filtered down the curving, carpeted stairs on either side of the hall and chose their comfortable, fold-down seats deliberately—near friends, near the door, or near him, the celebrity prof, screenwriter of *The Fix*. A skinny one locked eyes on him, preparing for combat. Jesus, another September.

I'm getting pretty old if I can think that, was his first reaction, although forty-eight was not ancient, comparatively speaking. He thought, immediately, of sharing this inner dialog with his students, but decided it wasn't funny enough. Also, it was August, not September. School years hadn't started in September for decades now. And he *was* ancient, in teacher psychology terms, at least as measured by numbers of students taught. Thousands, all because of *The Fix*. His only produced script, *The Fix* had won Sundance praise (but no award), then Oscar buzz (but no nominations) and finally selection for *Un certain regard* at Cannes, where he, director Bill, and cinematographer Elżbieta had floated off the closing-night stage in a sea of victorious giggles, carrying the *Priz d'interprétation masculine du jury*.

"Welcome to Film Studies 345, Hyperlink Cinema, people."

The hall was packed. There had to be well over a hundred young things out there, more than anyone in his department got for an upper-level NYU course and more than he could handle these days. Classes where students got to sit in the dark doing nothing always had a high yield ratio. Or yield. Yield *was* a ratio. It was important to be precise with language if he was ever going to win a MacArthur.

"So . . ." (he hated sentences beginning with *so*, but there it was) ". . . what brings you here today?" No one laughed. "Kidding. I know what brings you here. Hyperlink cinema, a scriptwriting style that fractures the structure to gradually reveal connection between seemingly disparate storylines." That sounded reasonably authoritative. "Name me examples of hyperlink cinema. Let's see who's read the course description. Hands?"

The palms went up, fingers wiggling here and there. Who to choose? Whom. Whom to choose? He pointed at a girl, her blue eyes and freckled skin reminiscent of a long-ago girlfriend, from his hot-shit phase when he was a twenty-three-year-old doing a Fulbright at Oxbridge, the first of his two books already brewing in manuscript form.

"*Syriana*?" Her rising tone showed that up-talk was not dead.

"You're not sure?" He sensed she might rise to his challenge.

"*Syriana*," she said more robustly, displaying a gravelly smidge of vocal fry. Good for her.

"Yes. Others?"

He pointed to the boy next to her. They looked like a

couple. They weren't matching, except for the curliness of their hair, but they leaned toward each other. Their perches were middle row, center: they wanted to be seen.

"*Babel.*"

"Yep. That was in the course description. How about one that is not?"

"*City of God, Pulp Fiction, Dazed and Confused,*" the same kid spouted.

Roger chuckled. "Someone came prepared." This time the students joined him in laughing. The trick was to be a little mean, but not too mean; he wasn't a drag queen.

Now the class went wild, naming films when he pointed at them, but many not waiting for his OK, just going for it. *Hannah and Her Sisters. Hereafter.* The wretched *Short Cuts.* The more wretched *Love, Actually.* And he was enjoying it, too, reveling for a moment in the fantasy that he could give all hundred plus of them the attention and education they deserved.

"So, you all know how to talk. Our first assignment will show if you can write. I would love to have you write about why *Short Cuts* is *not* hyperlink cinema . . ." somebody out there was blushing, ". . . but it's too fucking long to watch." Laughter. They always loved it when he swore. "Instead, today your dreams come true. Today, we watch an entire film, one hundred minutes, together. For next class, write me three pages about it. Not facts. Thoughts. I want thoughts. So, as you sit here, in the dark, don't fall asleep, don't get caught up in the story. Be thinking. Bright, scintillating thoughts."

He pushed a button on his remote and the lights dimmed. Another button and the screen descended. A third and the film began: *Kanchenjungha.* Black and white. That ought to get rid of the lookie-loos, those drawn by the course description but not actually interested enough to do serious work. About a third of today's lot, maybe. That would give Roger a fighting chance. Instead of just grades from the TA they might get a personal note from him to demonstrate he viewed them as individual intelligences.

The film started. Damn. He'd forgotten it was in color, a mental lapse that set his palms sweating. But never mind. The Bengali dialog and stilted subtitles should scare off an even greater number: he'd not only make them think and write; he'd make them read. Another fucking September. And one way or another, Roger White would survive it.

CHAPTER 2

For the first time ever, Casey doubled-parked. She stopped her gleaming black SUV beneath the old spreading oaks that lined the clogged drop zone in front of The Hartley School. She screamed inside at the illegality of it, the puredee selfishness. But today, her nearly six-year-old daughter Abby had graduated from the safety-seat her peers derided ("it's for babies") in favor of a booster she was technically two pounds too light for. Casey, too, would conform to her peers, especially Frannie, *jefa* of the mothers, now watching Casey from the sidewalk. Casey would show the world a performative entitlement she did not feel. Parking legally was for babies.

Casey set the SUV's hazard lights going. In the back, Abby watched a Lizzo video on the SUV's crisp backseat display. Lizzo's swirling white boas went so far beyond Abby's five-and-three-quarters years in "appropriateness" (as Frannie had noted) that they became perfectly suitable; sensual feathers brushing the exposed skin of a sex-positive breast were transformed into cuddly ducky hugs. Which was perfect. Lizzo's positivity and assertiveness had things to teach that Abby needed to know: Be at home in your body. Be confident. Be you.

Casey turned off the rumbling gas-powered engine of the car (which her seventeen-year-old stepdaughter Demmy had dubbed "the Planetkiller") and braced herself. Abby had been known to refuse to leave her seat until Casey allowed a song to finish. Such back-talk tested Casey. She'd been raised on Ozarkian law-abidingness and courtesy, so negotiating the line between rudeness and effectively articulating your needs was tough. Especially with a five-year-old.

"Come along, sweetie."

As it happened, Lizzo had wrapped up her song and Abby came willingly. In fact, she had unshackled herself before Casey opened the rear door. They walked hand in hand across the lawn to the kindergarten gate at the side of the red brick school. Casey loved this moment of the day, walking with her daughter before they reached the other mother/daughters (and the larger number of nanny/daughters, plus one father/daughter) entering the premises.

Chatter rose from the clot of mothers while nannies squeezed around them. On Casey's first day, she had escorted Abby through the grand front door of the school, and had been corrected. The front door was for the first-through-eighth kids, a separate breed who had survived an admissions process even more grueling than the preschool and kinder-garten gauntlets Abby had passed. Casey had also been corrected on permissible scents. (None.) And there had been a peanut-detecting wand for lunches and a full-body gluten patdown. OK, no, there hadn't, but Frannie, who would have been a knuckle-rapping nun in a previous age, *had* opened up Abby's eco-friendly plant-based snapware and sniffed. It had been all Casey could do not to grab Abby and run.

"Hi, Frannie!" Casey called out, in a peal whose friendliness could not be questioned. Some skills of rural central Missouri translated well enough in Brooklyn.

Frannie had teased out the highlighted dishwater blond locks that hung past her shoulders. "Abby, you look lovely," she cooed.

Abby did, Casey thought: her clean, matching clothes were picked out every morning by their nanny Constanza; her shiny hair was washed, conditioned, and untangled by Casey, hanging not too limp, not too full bodied; she had sweet features that she'd grow into nicely. Abby would never look white trash, thanks to the upbringing Casey had secured for her. Casey would ensure that Abby could survive and prosper in the world, without Casey if need be, a lesson Casey had learned the hard way. Ah, so many thoughts she could not share, the accent she'd shed but a minor secret compared to the ex-husband—could be dead, should be dead—who even current husband Roger, bless his heart, didn't really know anything about.

"Is that your Explorer, with the flashing lights?" Frannie asked.

"Porsche Cayenne," Casey corrected her, wishing immediately she hadn't said "Porsche." That was *extra*, as Demmy would say. But dammit, Casey was sending out the outrageous bank transfers each month, and the car was in her name. It was one glorious possession that was hers.

"Aren't you worried about getting towed?" Frannie took a sip from a mottled green beverage.

Casey was indeed worried—she could not afford a ticket, much less the Cayenne—but recognized this as a trick question. Frannie was merely noting that Casey had at last taken her place in the hive mind of the Hartley mom. Part of the appeal of The Hartley School was the presumption that one would get a free pass on such mundanities. For these parents, hazard lights canceled all traffic laws. Casey wondered what message lay behind Frannie's ploy. That all the other mothers lived in Park Slope, not Williamsburg, and thus walked (or hired someone to walk) their progeny to school? The other mothers had their own language, and despite Casey's linguist profession, fluency stubbornly eluded her.

Casey glanced back at the SUV. The Planetkiller. "I'll just be there a minute." She laughed. Among these parents, every inconvenience to others was "just a minute." In Park Slope, *ahorita* generally lasted an hour.

"Mommy, I need to pee," Abby said, her speech precociously crisp and clear. Casey proudly thought of this provident excuse to get away from Frannie as her little girl doing her part to secure for them the benefits of this existence.

"Nice to see you again, Frannie." Casey ran with Abby into the building before the woman could launch another probe. She took her child to the surprisingly institutional bathroom. They conducted their business and Casey got Abby situated in her classroom and herself back out to the Cayenne.

Her gleaming black ferrier of children sat tall and heavy in the middle of the stream of cars, as imposing as if a president might step out of it. What lesson was it teaching Abby? Casey wanted Abby to obey the law, but also to be naïve about its power to destroy when it turned on you. As she walked to the driver-side door, Casey waved cheerily at the dispirited drivers flowing uncomplainingly around the Planetkiller, as though a mother dropping off a child had every right to be there. And the Cayenne's sparkling windshield bore no ticket.

Of course it didn't. This was The Hartley.

CHAPTER 3

Delaney-sensei leaned toward Demmy, clearly intent on reprimanding her. "*Tenkou shitain desu ka?*"

Demmy registered the overly earnest emphasis on *tenkou* right off the bat—oh joy, being on the receiving end of a teachable moment—but what the fuck did *tenkou* mean? It wasn't "weather," though that was *tenkou* too. Why had she ever begged her parents to put her in an all-girls Japanese immersion school? *Tenkou, tenkou.* What was that, and why should she *want* it? Of course: change schools. Her teacher was asking her if she wanted to transfer. It was a threat of punishment for talking to her friends in class. But last class of the day, it was kinda hard to keep quiet.

She looked straight at Delaney-sensei. "*Mochiron sou demo nai.*" Of course not. Obvi. Although the idea was becoming more appealing as she sat there, holding his gaze.

"...*demo nai?*" He peered down at her.

Now Demmy's friends snickered. What linguistic flaw was he calling her on now? Delaney-sensei: Young. Tall. Well, tall*ish*. Skinny, potentially good looking if he got contacts and either cut his hair or learned how to use product. He was barely older than she, just back from a couple years of govern-ment-sponsored small-town English teaching in Japan and soooooo full of himself. Ah, now she had it: politeness. Respect for teacher. She'd been too casual.

". . . *demo nai desu!*" She leaned heavily on the *desu*, trying for the saccharine tone her stepmother could deploy so wickedly, though failing. "*Sensei*," she added.

That seemed to mollify him. He smiled, and now looked genuinely pleased. Perhaps he just wanted her to learn. Perhaps she should go easier on him.

After the bell, she and her friends made for the strip of dried-up grass they'd dubbed "No Woman's Land," between the prisonlike high-school building and Ninety-Fourth Street, for surreptitious vaping.

"*Tenkou shitain desu ka?*" Jodee asked Demmy in teasing tones. Delaney-sensei's seriousness took effort not to mock.

"You bet your sweet ass I'm *tenkou shitai*," Demmy shot back, pretending the idea of leaving her friends didn't fill her with horror.

"You and me both," Lainie drawled. And while Demmy knew Lainie and Jodee were equally attached to being there, there was a grain of truth to it: all three were *over* it. *It* being the school, Delaney-sensei, being seniors applying to colleges and seventeen/eighteen in general.

"I wish Delaney-sensei would just let us call him Martin. He has to be, what, twenty-five?" Demmy's dad was ten years older than her stepmom Casey; a seven-year age gap wasn't a generation, meriting such rigorous politeness.

"Don't you just wanna sit him down for a haircut?" Lainie asked.

Demmy laughed. She did.

"Oh my god," Jodee squealed. "Lainie's hot for teacher!"

Lainie shuddered ostentatiously, but Demmy wondered.

Truth was, she looked forward to Delaney-sensei's class. Yes, he could be soooooo . . . what was the word for someone who did things cringingly wrong but was never embarrassed because he was too clueless to know? If he behaved the way he did on purpose, he'd be brave, or a free spirit or something, but instead he was just an ineluctably (an SAT word) sincere, bad-hair guy. Neckbeard without the actual beard?

"You seriously want to transfer?" Jodee asked Demmy.

"*Chao,*" Demmy responded—nuh uh—in the Kansai slang Jodee taught them. It was just talk. She would hate to change schools. Her friends kept her sane amidst the stress of this final year, devoted as it was to the standardized tests and college applications that would determine their fates in life. "*Moo soro soro,*" she added. I have to get moving. "My mom, I mean my stepmom, is meeting me at Seventh Ave, on the F. How did I let myself get talked into ballet of all things? Not hip-hop. Ballet."

Her friends said nothing. They did not get it either. And yet, of course, they did. Hip-hop was fun; ballet got you into Yale. Like going to a Japanese-immersion school. Like acing entrance exams, earning at least a four point oh. She had to be well rounded, contribute to society, model altruistic behavior. And since her father, grandmother, and grandfather had graduated from Yale, Demmy had better at least get admitted. And then *not* go, in a grand statement against privilege.

Demmy snorted to herself as they walked to the subway. Like Nana would let her not go. Like any of them would.

CHAPTER 4

Maude rocked her tall chair slightly at the hotel bar where she and Roger had arranged an after-work drink, their first in some time. She wasn't normally fidgety, but he'd proposed this little adventure out in the world and she had no idea why. Nothing untoward on the face of it—she and Roger had been pals for years—but Sherbeam had made a hurtful crack when Maude mentioned it, about Maude now being single. Typical. Maude refused to give Sherbeam any more room in her head. Maude was fifty-nine; what need had she of a mentor?

She looked up at the whoosh of the revolving door but it wasn't Roger. Should she motion the bartender for a refill? She loved the way the bartender made a Negroni and Maude didn't have anyone to arrive home sober for. She beckoned the girl with her stemmed glass. The girl nodded, maybe smiled behind her face mask.

And then there was Roger, looking around for her, spotting her. She smiled back. He wasn't that much to look at anymore, but only in the way that forty-eight wasn't twenty-eight. What nerve Sherbeam had to imply an adulterous romance could develop between them. Roger pressed his cheek against hers in the semblance of a kiss. The brush of his beard calmed her immediately.

"How was class?" She hoped he'd want to talk about something innocuous.

He produced a wry smile. "I have reasons to be optimistic . . ." He glanced warily downward before placing his oxblood leather briefcase flat on the bar. It wasn't a considerate move, but she said nothing. She wasn't his mother. Sherbeam was his mother. And if it was clean you were after, the bar wasn't a vast improvement on the floor.

Roger ordered a whisky through an exchange of gestures with the bartender punctuated only by the word "Talisker."

He turned to Maude. "Truth is, I'm drowning. I can remember about forty names, but then there are seventy more." He looked horrified. "I want to give each one personal attention, but increasingly, I have nothing to say to them, even if I had the time."

"Nothing like the young folk to keep you on your toes," she said.

"We were the young folk, five minutes ago."

The bartender placed Roger's drink on a coaster. He nodded his thanks, took a sip and ran a hand dewy with the condensation of the lowball glass over his silvering hair. He was just young enough that Maude might call his few white hairs "premature." Roger would like that, puff up a bit. Everyone needs puffing up, once in a while.

"I suppose we were," Maude belatedly replied. She remembered him hanging around Sherbeam's master classes in his early twenties, before Roger had married his first wife. Maude had been thirty-one, so not one of the young folk, even then, but she'd take the implicit compliment on her former looks. Kind words came less frequently as one aged, even for one's younger self, which faded from collective consciousness as babies became adults, wave after wave.

Maude laid a hand on his arm. "When was the last time I saw you? Like this, I mean." She waved a hand around at the absence of Sherbeam, Casey, Demmy, the usual enveloping entourage of family. "Tell me why we're here. Not that catching up isn't a good enough reason."

He squinted, as though concentrating. "I tried all summer to come up with a lesson plan, and here I am, the first week, with nothing. We watched *Kanchenjungha* today and will watch *City of God* next week. I've asked them to think, and I'll make them do group presentations, which is just a way of pushing the work onto them. That's all I've got. The well has run dry." He grimaced briefly, then sighed. "I'll change that to a fresher metaphor when I write my memoirs."

"Lazy and unscrupulous," she cackled. "I love it."

"But I don't, Maude. I've never been lazy. *Persistently point-less*, perhaps . . ." Maude knew this to be a quote from a two-star review of his second book. Decades later, it apparently still touched a nerve, despite the book's critical, if not commercial, success. "I've never phoned it in. What the hell am I doing? I teach at NY fucking U and I . . ."

"Roger, it's the creative process: you have nothing, so you bang your head against the wall, and then you read what's written there in blood."

"That is the most twisted description of the creative process I have ever heard." Maude could tell he liked that she implied lesson-planning was a creative process.

"Good enough for gallery show copy?" she asked.

They both laughed. Anything with blood and violence would be catchy in that way art galleries loved—needed, in fact—but her own process was nothing like that: she had ideas and she worked them, on canvas, in oils. No agony was involved, although there might be, on occasion, a welling tear (though she'd never tell).

"Thing is, Maude, now when I bang my head against the wall, there's no blood. Something's wrong with me."

Maude took his hand. "Roger, there is nothing wrong with you." Maude hoped this was true, but her well had never run dry. After her husband Frank's death, she'd found herself with time and a substantial trust fund and never looked back. She was painting full time, and her work was selling. She even had a solo show coming up.

A pause reigned, as though someone should be smoking a cigarette or checking a fact on a phone. The bar was starting to fill with the chatter of evenings being launched.

"Maybe you're trying too hard," Maude continued.

He shook his head. "Nothing I start ever goes anywhere. If you do a Google search of me, every image is of me posing in front of the backdrop from this festival or that two decades ago. I am literally *posing*. I mean, I love teaching, but without practicing the craft, it's empty. And those two nothing screenplays I wrote after *The Fix*? Talk about no blood."

Maude let herself remember accompanying him, Bill, and Elż to their Tribeca premiere. That evening had been fun, exclamation point. And Roger had photographed well in those days; there were worse ways to be remembered. This set her thinking. Her own recent work had been fueled by a sense of closeness to Frank and the bond with her two sons that had strengthened and matured during Frank's decline. Was that why Roger had reached out to her: did he need friends? He'd kept in touch throughout the years she'd been secluded, attending to Frank, in her brownstone. Roger had phoned regularly. They'd had one memorable visit on the freezing porch, masked up to protect Frank from contagion. It was time to repay the favor. "I have an idea, about the creative part," she whispered, aiming for mystery. "Wait here."

Maude hopped off her bar chair and went to the other corner of the room, where Roger wouldn't be able to hear her if this didn't work out. She pulled out her phone and found the number for The Leary, a boutique hotel frequented by Elż, as Maude remembered it.

The phone rang. Both she and Roger had blossomed in the artistic upwelling of the Bill and Elż era. The best part about it had been that Sherbeam had owned no piece of it. Sherbeam had been squirreled away in her Chelsea studio painting portrait after portrait of neighborhood denizens, a hermitage that had given Maude and Roger room to breathe.

Someone picked up.

"Can you put me through to Elżbieta Gomolka?" Outlandish requests worked best if you assumed the other person would comply.

It worked. Another phone rang.

Maude was excited. She hadn't spoken to Elż in over a decade, but had read on Page Six that she was in town to give a TED talk. It would do Roger good to be around people not from his family or school. But Elż didn't pick up. An artificial voice instead invited Maude to leave a message.

"Hi Elż." Maude whispered, glancing back at Roger. "It's Maude. I want to see you. Can you please call me back? The number's the same."

Maude hung up and wondered if the message was too vague to entice. She'd give it a few days to work its magic. Best not to seem needy. Maude returned to Roger, her loyal friend.

"My diabolical plan to flint your creative spark is now underway. So now let's turn to the not-trying-too-hard part. We haven't seen each other in yonks. Here we are in this beautiful, *beautiful* room, all swirly, fine-grained oak and sumptuous velour that hasn't seen the harsh light of day in a hundred years . . ."

". . . or a steam cleaner."

"Hush, you. This place is a work of art. That's a Berenice Arbus, the abstract upward sweep of capitalist civilization unfettered by labor. And that's an original Rockwell Hart Benton on the wall; and there's another. We might as well be in a museum. Let's enjoy these gorgeous celebrations of the nobility of work enshrined for the benefit of those who don't have to do any."

"*I* have to. *Do* any. *Work*, that is. Casey bought a Cayenne."

"A pepper?"

"A Porsche."

"On your salaries? Maybe there *is* something wrong with you." Now her laugh was lighter, a breeze not a cackle.

He acknowledged his foolishness with a neither-here-nor-there expression, all eyes and tilting neck, the kind of thing you practiced if you needed more people to like you.

She thought of Frank; he'd never need to do that again. Loss could bring you to a goddamned halt, if you gave it free rein. She didn't. "We're neither of us skating through life, Roger, but let's pretend for an hour that we are."

Maude raised her Negroni toward the bartender and held up two fingers. "Try one, Roger," she ordered. "It's sweet, then bitter, then sweet again. Layers of flavor. And it's colorful. Roger, clink my glass. Remember we're alive. Have a fucking drink with me and let's pretend that all this is easy and beautiful and will be ours forever."

CHAPTER 5

As Roger had expected, Constanza was feeding Abby dinner when he walked into the apartment. He was tipsy, but firmly resolved not to show it. He'd had the train ride home to sober up, so . . . piece of cake.

"Good evening, Mr. White." Constanza's formality reminded him of someone from pre-streaming TV. Not a particular someone, but all the someones, the way people who were portrayed for the entertainment-consuming public were soothingly consistent and nothing like real people. And yet Constanza was real enough, calling him Mr. White. Never Roger, no matter how many times he gave her permission to, ordered her to, begged her to.

"Good evening, Mrs. Anzaldua," he chirped back at her. He could be a TV character, too: the bearded, good-natured, latte-liberal employer of a domestic just brownish enough in the right light; he, for his part, looked as white as his surname, going to seed a bit with his expanding waistline, checking the crown of his head in the mirror for a bald spot that wasn't there. Yet.

Constanza maneuvered a fork of purple vegetable toward Abby's mouth.

"I'm not a baby," Abby protested.

"And yet here we are," Constanza replied. "Open wiiiiiiide."

Abby pouted, with pursed, muscular lips.

Roger filled a plate for himself from the pots on the stove, food Constanza had made. He sat at the kitchen table, a speckled, pistachio-green, Formica-topped straight-out-of-a-diner thing Casey had found at Brooklyn Flea.

"Shall I take over?" he offered.

"Have at it." Constanza placed the fork on Abby's plate and took off her apron. She'd be going home momentarily, to her own kids, twins Demmy's age who were grown enough not to need mom home when they returned from school but still appreciated a parent or two in the evening. So she'd said.

Roger sidled up to Abby. "Now shall I do broccoli-airplane flying in on a fork or make them mutant trees that you eat 'cause you're a brontosaurus? Or shall we do a reset and you can show us both how not-a-baby you are?"

Abby grabbed the fork, grunted in exasperation, and started eating, rolling her eyes. Ah, a proper New Yorker, growing up so fast. Being here with her and Constanza in this kitchen he felt no worry about the dryness of his well or curiosity about Maude's mystery plan to "flint his spark."

"Have you ever seen *Babel*, Mrs. Anzaldua?" His buzz had faded but the boozy cheer remained.

She was just shrugging on her coat, which looked definitely too heavy for the globally warmed fall. "The movie? It was OK. Too much jumping around."

"Ah. You've answered my question before I asked it."

"I thought your question was going to be about the Mexican nanny and her thoughtless, rich, Anglo employers."

Constanza had a PhD in comp-crit and could probably land an adjunct position upstate, but being a nanny paid better and her husband's Wall Street employer had forbidden work-from-home, now that corona positivity rates were so low.

"Sure. Tell me about that. Although I do want to hear more about your reaction to the *jumping around*, since my class is on story structure."

She stood there, coat on, the sturdy strap of her handbag across her chest so a mugger would have to pull off her head and one shoulder to snatch it. "I need to get home, Mr. White. The L is so packed this time of day. But I'll leave you with this: Was the nanny so naïve as to think she could casually cross the border with two minor kids, not her own, and no papers? Even for the time, that struck me as unbelievable. Two decades living here illegally and she thinks she can just waltz across the border like it's not even there?" She leaned over to kiss Abby goodbye. "Didn't buy it."

"Ooh. A new lesson plan is appearing in my head even now."

"Although what do I know, illegal? My family has been in this country longer than yours."

"Oh, I doubt that," Roger said, smugly, relishing the response that was sure to come. He liked debating Constanza.

"We can compare notes next time, Mr. White, but you won't win this one. I come from a long and venerable line. That's why you pay me the big bucks."

Constanza waved and backed into the hallway. He heard the front door open and close as she left. It was now just Roger and Abby at home.

"So, Mommy dropped you off and is picking up Demmy?" Roger asked Abby, the two of them not feeling to Roger quite enough for the slender, four-story building, which sometimes felt like one giant staircase.

Abby nodded, broccoli gone. She did not seem anxious to make a prison break for the Lizzo videos. Roger loved that she enjoyed spending time together. Maybe she'd even delayed dinner so she could eat with him. He'd wondered about the wisdom of having another kid at forty-two, but Casey was ten years younger and had wanted a kid of her own. They'd barely known each other when they'd gotten her pregnant and then married, leaving him no decent interval between first wife and second. Roger ran his hand over Abby's head. Rash but good call, Abby had been.

"I'm not a dog," Abby said.

"Oh, am I petting you?"

"Kinda."

"Hey, is that why you didn't want to eat your dinner? It wasn't in a dish on the floor?"

"Not a dog," Abby protested.

This was a little dangerous, this game. Tomorrow she might decide she *was* a dog and insist on having her dinner in a bowl on the floor. Wasn't there a film that happened in?

The front door opened. "We're home!" Casey called out.

Roger heard Demmy amidst the sounds of bags being offloaded, shoes removed, clothing being hung from the hooks, but only Casey came into the kitchen. She gave Abby and Roger kisses as heavy feet tramped up the stairs. Demmy would grab food at her leisure.

"Trouble in paradise?"

"The ballet school didn't let her audition for even the tiniest solo in the holiday performance, and now her teacher warned her she's not likely to get into the corps. That means no performance credit, rendering ballet useless for getting into college. 'Nearly two years wasted,' as Demmy put it."

"Well, she is a beginner." These things took time.

Casey shrugged agreement and plated herself dinner from

the stove, arranging her meal into long foods and round foods. The result was not in OCD territory, but thoughtful. You'd think she was the one with the artist mother.

Casey took a seat on the other side of Abby. "Constanza is a treasure."

Roger nodded, though he liked Constanza more than *treasure*—perhaps only garden-variety Southern hyperbole, but nonetheless touched with a smidge of condescension—seemed to imply. Although, yeah, he loved anyone who cooked for him, given that preparing meals had been his chore for his first wife and Demmy. And in the house he'd grown up in as well, after his dad had moved out.

He was proud that this family was nothing like the one he'd grown up in. He didn't think he took after either his tortured artiste mother, nor the self-indulgent but now respectable man, bordering on bully, that his dad was. Although, if forced to, he'd choose his dad. Roger definitely wasn't a bully, but self-indulgent? Check. Respectable? Magazines salivated over tastemaker articles from prize-winning former-Fulbright script-writing professors, whose flair for critique made others noddingly think they'd devised these thoughts themselves. Whole industries depended on his cohort to define the desires of the high-flying financiers who clogged Manhattan. The academy had put one over on that vastly wealthier mob, getting them to defer to professorial tastes. The world, it seemed, had an endless appetite for the experts it despised. Roger began to envision a think-piece for *Politico*, something to help keep that scam going while also checking off one of the publications he was required to produce. (*Medium* wouldn't cut it anymore, if it ever had.)

The lack of an actual idea for said article suddenly smacked him in the face. He'd so far evaded formal censure by his department chair for his seat-of-the-pants methods, but stringing together lines of facile bullshit wouldn't cut it anymore.

How would his family manage if he lost his job? He had tenure, so fat chance of that, but shouldn't the prospect inspire more horror than it did? He watched his daughter watch her mother eat and ran his hand over his head, searching for the bald spot he felt forming—he almost felt the wear and tear it represented would qualify as one of the publications the university required—but Roger encountered nothing but hair.

CHAPTER 6

Demmy flopped on her bed. She was quitting ballet. What a mistake. You couldn't start at fifteen-and-a-half and be good enough two years later to mention it on your college applications. You had to start at five. She didn't want her dad to think she was flaky, but she had to cut her losses. Besides, she needed volunteer work to fill the altruism blank in her profile.

She opened her airbook. But before starting in on homework, she checked Insta on her phone. Just this once, she told herself, although when did she not check her phone? Jodee had posted a Reel of some literacy thing she did at a prison, which was literally *insane*. Like, DSM VI–code insane. Their high school was prisonlike enough; why ask for more? But what if Demmy did the same thing at the public library? She could get there by subway, meaning no Planetkiller. Would Jodee feel like Demmy was horning in on her turf? *Soo demo nai desho.* Unlikely. She'd probably feel flattered.

It was frustrating that Demmy couldn't just ask her dad about strategies for her applications. She switched over to the airbook and navigated to the NYU site to look at her dad's classes. He was a professor, he *should* know, but things were too different now; all he could contribute was "check that box where they ask about relatives." Status. Privilege. Every conversation about college eventually circled round to him and Nana and Grandpa all having graduated from Yale, and all the sacrifices that had gone into securing that, yes, *legacy*, for Demmy. And how she should think seriously before spurning that hard-won *entrée*. Although he did understand, he said, her not wanting to check the legacy box; he'd felt the same at her age.

Well, he had *that* right: Demmy did *not* want to be a legacy. The entrenched privilege of systemic racism just wasn't fair. No one liked unfairness. She'd seen a video in a TED talk in which two monkeys earned treats for performing a task. The one angry monkey, flinging away the cucumber slice it had previously been eager for once it saw the other monkey get a grape, provoked roaring laughter of recognition from the audience. *Yappari*, she thought: how could it be anything else? It was bad enough that she went to private school, had long blond hair, and her ripening trust fund would vest when she turned eighteen. She couldn't take even more she hadn't earned.

Her phone chimed. Lainie was messaging her. Demmy pushed the laptop aside and reached for her phone.

LAINIE
so not hot for teacher

OwO! you sure?

don't even

o7 ☺

gtg

Got to go? Demmy grunted in exasperation. She was ready for another good hour of banter, but *gtg* meant Lainie's parents were home. That was the last Demmy would hear from her tonight.

She pulled the laptop back over and looked at her dad's course descriptions. It was so weird he got paid money to watch movies. She knew there was more to it. She'd tried to read one of his books once, but found it hard going. It was essentially in another language, one whose primary purpose seem to be, based on her observation of the conversations he used to have with other professors, to allow you to call out others on its misuse.

She'd heard her parents talking to a bunch of their friends at a dinner party once and heard there was a rumor her dad might get a MacArthur grant, that out-of-the-blue chunk of money for being a supposed *genius*. How did talking incomprehensibly about watching movies make you a genius? Started with being a *legacy*, apparently.

She scrolled down the NYU page. She had seen none of the movies ("films") her dad had listed in the description. What if she skipped the ton of homework she had and watched one? She, too, could be a "genius."

Despite knowing she'd regret it tomorrow, she found one of the films—*Babel*—on Netflix, got herself a plate of food from downstairs, and started the movie. It was hard to follow but interesting enough that the timeline didn't matter. Following was basic anyway. Like most movies, it involved someone getting shot. What was art these days without murder? Formulaic, yes, but murder sure beat the heck out of stories about snagging husbands (*Pride and Prejudice* being the exception; also *Emma*).

She watched the entire thing and loved it—though she thought it should jump around more. Instead of five storylines, it could have one hundred, two hundred, more, like a collection of Reels. As the clock approached midnight, she wondered if there was a genius grant for Reels. *Nara ii kedo sa.* I wish.

CHAPTER 7

Casey climbed out of the Planetkiller to rip Abby from her morning cocoon of safety and distraction, noting in herself more ease about double-parking than the day before. Her transition to genuine Hartley mother had begun.

This time Lizzo was still twerking her way to body inclusivity. Casey knew "Truth Hurts" had a good two minutes to go, but she hit *Off* and let the screaming commence. Actually, *screaming* was too harsh a word. Her five-year-old was *remonstrating* with her. The Hartley had already taught Abby to remonstrate.

"Come quietly and you can watch fifteen minutes of *Ugly-Dolls* tonight."

"Thirty," Abby said.

"Done. And I am holding you to that."

Abby made a face, as if she'd made too light a demand. The next negotiation would not be so easy. But Abby took Casey's hand, went quietly into the kindergarten yard and was delivered to her classroom on time with a minimum of fuss, singing as they walked about never being anybody's sidechick.

On her way out of the yard, Casey ran into Frannie, whom

she would have pretended not to see except that Frannie was engaged in conversation with Kelly. Kelly was doing most of the talking.

Ah, Kelly. That lovely black hair, with a few courageous streaks of premature gray, those sharp, well-proportioned features, cream-colored skin, the lithe torso, ace for yoga. Casey would always stop for Kelly.

"Morning, ladies," Casey said.

Frannie made a face, a hard-to-pin-down frowny-smile thing that would pass as welcoming to the uninitiated. Both Frannie and Casey knew Frannie was noting that Casey had initiated contact, something she never did when Frannie was alone. Casey smiled back, thinking *bless your heart*. Casey was comfortable with where she stood vis-à-vis Frannie, although the struggle could at times feel lonely. She wouldn't mind a rest.

"Morning, Casey. Nice-looking Cayenne," Kelly said.

Had Kelly not seen it before? Surely Casey had mentioned they were getting the car months before. You had to milk the anticipation as much as the possession, especially when thoughts of repossession were floating through your mind.

"Thanks, Kelly."

"I'd forgotten you lived too far to walk," Frannie said. Kelly and Frannie both lived in Park Slope. That was the dream, to live in Park Slope, but someone would have to die first. Someone, of course, being Nick or Sherbeam .

"Maybe when Abby gets older we can race-walk from Williamsburg," Casey said. "Turn Abby into an athlete."

The other mothers laughed. An athlete. The idea. Field hockey was fine, if you needed it to get into one of the lesbian schools like Smith or Wellesley, but that was about it. They were still laughing—or chuckling or giggling, some second-cousin to laughter in the amusement family. Their laughter was going on too long. Had Casey said *athuhlete*? She couldn't have, could she? There would be no coming back from an Ozarkian sin of that order. Not even tossing some French into the conversation would save her. *Quelle horreur.*

"Has Abby been admitted to Hartley for first grade?" Kelly asked.

Casey shook her head, puzzled. "She's being interviewed next year, just before ski week. Isn't everyone?" Lord, it wasn't even Thanksgiving!

"Oh, sure, sure." Frannie's tone said there was some insider thing Casey was missing.

Kelly rolled her eyes. "Don't give Casey the wrong idea, Frannie." Kelly turned to Casey. "Everyone is interviewed next year, Casey. It's just that, well, the first-grade class is noticeably smaller than the kindergarten class, and people seem to believe that—if you listen to talk—you can already get an idea who's in. I've never noticed that to be true, and I am going on kid three, with Joseph."

"Who is a shoo-in," Frannie said.

Casey tried to hide her fear. Was Abby not a shoo-in? After the all-consuming effort Casey had put in over the previous two years to get Abby into pre-K, and then kindergarten? How could Casey have missed this? Casey thought of Abby imitating Lizzo, twerking at YouTube. Surely the school would value a sweet, lively, engaging child who loved body inclusivity so much she didn't even know what it was.

Perhaps some expensive concession would be sought to compensate for not living in Park Slope. A whopping dona-tion? A painting from Sherbeam for the school's silent auction would do it, maybe one of the portraits from her Chelsea period, a couple of which Casey knew Sherbeam had lying around. If only Roger could get that MacArthur. Or maybe Casey could incorporate a remotely hosted localization company in Delaware and sell it for a billion dollars, an unexpected unicorn, before her profession of adapting software to other languages was gutted by technology. That is, before software writing other software put her out of business.

Kelly and Frannie were still talking but Casey spaced most of it as she pondered how she would explain localization to the two of them. The word was opaque even to many in the business. And how could she sell for a billion something that turned such a meager profit? The dot-com era was ancient history.

She glanced at the nearby Planetkiller. She'd had it cleaned again yesterday. Its gleaming black paint job still echoed the pristine hint of blue green in its ticket-free windshield. Casey forced a smile for the other mothers, who were now joined by yet another who resided within walking distance, placing Casey firmly at the bottom in the pecking order. But Casey did have one thing even Kelly—lithe, Lululemon limbs notwithstanding—could not claim: having had Abby at thirty-one, not forty-one, Casey alone was not a *femme de moyen âge*. Casey alone knew basic from ded. Not that she ever thought herself as being from Demmy's generation, even if she did enjoy Demmy and her friends' energy.

"Olivia Rodrigo makes me feel old," she blurted. "At least with k.flay I felt I was the same generation," she found herself saying nonsensically.

The blank looks that came back were at first disconcerting —of course the other mothers couldn't follow her distracted train of thought—but then gratifying: they genuinely had no idea what she was talking about. So there was more than one pecking order, and Casey wasn't at the bottom of all of them.

"I *stan* Olivia," Kelly said, a smile on her face. It was likely a smile of relief at having remembered who Olivia Rodrigo was. Kelly was claiming a place in this other pecking order. It was almost undone by the cringe of "stan" from her glossy rose lips, but then Kelly sang an appropriate line from "Good 4 You." In tune. Casey realized that the smile was free of subtext, and that, just maybe, she had started to make a friend, an actual friend, at The Hartley.

CHAPTER 8

"So, what's the single most important thing about this family we follow in *Kanchenjungha*? Give me one word only." Roger looked at the raised hands. The class had not shrunk as much as anticipated. He had noticed, when he logged into the learning management system before class, that the red square indicating the assignments in the *Needs Grading* queue bore a triple-digit number. He could farm out half to his TA, but it was a short first assignment and he wanted to get a feel for his students. Still, three hundred and fifty pages of reading. And a few more stragglers were sure to submit before the next class, appending sob stories, for which he'd make allowances, against his better judgment.

He spotted the couple from the first session who'd caught his eye, curly red hair and curly brown hair. They were seated again in the center of the middle row of the banked seating. Auditioning for teacher's pets, and so far no reason why they shouldn't land the gig.

He'd given the girl a chance last time. Now he pointed at the boy. "Jason."

"Joshua," he corrected.

"Joshua. Give us a word."

"Wealthy."

Roger nodded. He wouldn't call on the girl yet. His finger moved around the room.

"Dysfunctional." "Annoying." "Irrelevant." "Colonialists." (He liked that take on Indians in Nepal, volunteered for the first time ever. He noted the skinny boy who'd offered it, the same one who'd locked eyes with him that first day.)

He brought his finger back to the redhead, Joshua's perhaps-girlfriend. He remembered her name, obviously, but didn't want to say it before he heard it from her. "Kate."

"Niamh," she said. Well, what she said was "Neeve," but he knew the spelling. Could never forget it, was more like it. That had been the name of The Girl. They'd been so young, both in their early twenties that long-ago summer in Oxbridge. They had boated down the River Yeo under the fabled bridge, looking for oxen, the Brit tolerating the ignorant American, armed with his Fulbright but blithely unaware of his yawningly uninformed assumptions. Lost in the memory, he didn't hear what this new Niamh had said.

"Good," he nonetheless said emphatically, and turned his back on them all to start the discussion of the form.

He followed the lead of the one who'd suggested "irrelevant." He was interested to see who would pretend to not care about the actors, the people. They were always lying when they did that—Bill and Elżbieta had taught him that, through their direction and camerawork, respectively. Elż in particular had steered him away from writing dreamy contemplative Malickian interludes into his script notes.

But he would not unmask his students' caring. He wanted to draw it out, not bludgeon it, their caring. He cared too. It was partly why he and Elż worked so well together. Roger had yet to figure out why people pretended to relate to art in any way other than as gossipy voyeur. You might genuinely enjoy viewing a well-lit Diebenkorn or Rothko in a museum, broad areas of abstract color that aspired to motion, but when it came to the moving image, your lizard brain quickly reached a point where if the image didn't have eyes, a nose, a mouth, the film would not hold your attention.

At least, *he* reached that point quickly.

"Professor," Niamh chirped. "The narrative is quite fragmented, but one hundred minutes of film is presented like one hundred minutes in the lives of these people. And yet, being out of order, how are we to know these moments weren't gathered over several days?"

She looked him straight in the eye. Not in a challenging way, just engaged.

"Astute question." He liked this Niamh, and Joshua as well. They had good taste, choosing each other. Roger turned the discussion to the film's weather, the focus on the eponymous mountain, Kanchenjunga (no aitch for the actual mountain), second tallest mountain in the world, seen by each character in turn. Ray had to have shot enormous quantities of B-roll to have enough to keep them on such a tight timeline once interspliced with the scenes of the characters.

The discussion surged with insights, many new to him, which he loved. The kids were having fun. And so was Roger. He didn't feel like a fraud now. He felt like he might even deserve a MacArthur. He might even have felt that he deserved (were he a hell of a lot younger, and single, and she not his student) a beautiful, smart partner like young Niamh, except that he'd undeservingly had one such in the first Niamh, and again in his first wife, whom he'd married at twenty-five, and now astoundingly he had Casey. How the fuck had that happened? *Un certain regard* prize notwithstanding, he knew he had never deserved any of them.

CHAPTER 9

Maude sat alone at Roger and Casey's kitchen table, using a single finger to spin a print of Sherbeam's work on its Formica top. Maude felt unimportant. Her stealthy phone calls to The Leary had gone unanswered. Maude knew for a fact that Elż was still in town—her TED talk had earned a glowing paragraph on Page Six. Maude's initial message had presumptuously assumed that Elż would remember her; Maude had left several humbler messages since. She'd gushed with her desire to swap stories face to face and was almost more excited for her own sake than Roger's. But Elż apparently did not share that sentiment. Maude imagined herself around sixteenth on Elż's to-do list when Elż could only get to the first ten. It was a bitter pill to have a former close friend be too famous now to bother with you.

A chilled cocktail shaker of aperitif Negronis that Constanza had whipped up was sweating cold rivulets as its ice cubes melted. Maude sipped her drink conservatively, not wanting to get too far ahead of Sherbeam in the alcohol department. She was chilled herself—Roger and Casey kept the house too cold—and glad of the blue Fair Isle sweater she wore. Other prints, nestled also in archival plastic sleeves, were arrayed around the one Maude continued to twirl.

Abby's tiny voice floated in from the street-facing living room, singing along with something about a DNA test that said the singer was a hundred percent that . . . and then the dreaded B-word, which Maude despised. As light filtered through the trees outside, which were making good progress shedding their brittle, drying leaves, other lyrics followed: the Vikings, DMs, the F-word.

Constanza had disappeared into the backyard. Probably for a cigarette, or a joint, or to mainline heroin, which Maude would if she had Constanza's job.

Sherbeam returned from the bathroom, a green scarf wrapped around her throat, listening to her granddaughter sing profanity tunelessly. "I admire the spirit, but even *I* wonder about the wisdom of letting a five-year-old sing *fuck*."

"I suppose they hear it everywhere anyway." Maude knew Constanza had only left Abby under their brief supervision because of Maude's presence—Sherbeam was not to be trusted to keep even a houseplant alive. Maude wondered if contradicting her elder mentor demonstrated the requisite responsibility.

"Are DMs still a thing?" Maude asked as Abby played the song yet again. Sherbeam, under the tutelage of the young assistant she called "social media boy," had become surprisingly astute about such things and Maude wanted to keep tabs. The important thing to know about technology these days was when, like one of Sherbeam's houseplants, it expired.

Sherbeam pulled out her chair and sat. "I suppose we could look that up—we both have phones—but knowing the answer is available is enough for me."

Sherbeam moved prints around the table. Each was an image of a painting she'd done in years past, a mix of chunky portraits and text-heavy message pieces, with a few frank nudes mixed in, including one of Maude. None of it was new. "Pau thinks this show will put me back on the map, but I haven't been painting. No ideas. I'm a dry well."

Like son, like mother. Or perhaps like the culture, in which every work of art seemed to be a remix, remake or sequel.

Maude pulled toward her the familiar image of a protest against the third Iraq war, a march through the streets of the Bronx. Maude had been working in Sherbeam's studio when her mentor had painted it decades ago. The first iteration had been a naturalistic colorscape of browns and blues that had given way to this unearthly version in purple and gold. Maude preferred the earlier one Sherbeam had scraped mercilessly away. What did it mean that the earlier image was preserved in her consciousness—she was envisioning it now—immediately accessible but not at all available, not even as a pentimento? Perhaps Maude should record her description of it and sell it as a non-fungible token.

"Is there enough for a retrospective?" Sherbeam asked. "Enough that my collectors would loan out, I mean? Museums won't send work to a mere gallery, and collectors can be so nervous."

"Are you kidding? They will be *thrilled*!" Maude sipped deeply from her red cocktail, her free hand sliding the print aside to inspect the next. "Just imagine them inviting friends for dinner parties after it's over—they're having drinks on the deck, then going inside to stand in front of the art, page through the catalog to show their friends that their paintings are *famous*. It's like your kid getting into Yale."

Sherbeam picked up a pen. "I am including that in my pitch. Cleaned up to flatter the collectors." She appeared to be writing down what Maude had said, word for word.

"You'll come to the retrospective, won't you? You've met Pau, right?"

Sherbeam sounded genuinely unsure, but yes, Maude had met Pau, the gallery owner. Dozens of times. Had Sherbeam forgotten Maude's presence in her earlier life, just as Elż appeared to have? The curse of the caregiver, erased from reality. Maude would need to make an appearance at the retrospective, if only to get Sherbeam to rehearse the earlier memories in her mind. Maude imagined the scene: bright lights, colorful paintings, the ebullient scent of money in the air, even if most of the work would not be for sale. "Who wouldn't go to Barcelona?" she replied. She had a trust fund, for God's sake. She'd go kiss cheeks with Pau at Galería Les Rambles, buy a painting, even.

Abby sang out from the front room, a clever rhyme of *noncommittal* and *a little* introduced by something about a bad bitch. Maude noticed the language again, but with less outrage. She was becoming inured. She wondered if long Covid had pickled to death that part of her brain devoted to propriety, or if that lobe had shriveled up in protest at living in a proto-fascist state more concerned with juicing the stock market than the fact the planet was on fire.

"Are *you* painting?" Sherbeam mumbled the query.

Sherbeam's show of interest was uncharacteristic. She didn't sound like she was fishing for, say, an overblown excuse from Maude to cover up embarrassment over a lack of activity. Sherbeam would enjoy poking that with a needle to watch Maude squirm. But there was no such lack of activity.

"Every day. I am back to my old self. Ideas are coming. Work is getting finished."

"It's such a shame your career never took off," Sherbeam said.

Maude didn't even blanch. Sherbeam verbally slicing little

bits of flesh off her had no sting because Maude was quite satisfied with her career. (Oh, the horror, satisfied!) Maude knew it wasn't personal—Sherbeam had always needed to tear someone down to feel good about herself. Besides, Sherbeam would repay Maude tenfold for being the only painter in town willing to put up with her: through referrals, blurbs, her presence at Maude's openings, talking up Maude's work to collectors.

"My gallery is including me in another show," Maude said. "Nothing so fancy as a retrospective, but it *is* in Chelsea. Six new pieces, all sizable." None would command Sherbeam's six-figure prices, but so what? She was working.

"Single, with an inheritance. It's what every artist needs."

Now that stung. Frank was rather newly dead, after all. Maude still had days when she struggled to get out of bed or found her coffee mug full, yet cold, with no memory of what she'd done for half an hour. Sherbeam had been through something similar after her divorce, kept alive by meals brought to her by her pre-teen son. Did she not remember?

"It's what *you* needed, anyway." Frank had supported Maude while alive, so the fact she now controlled his family's vast estate was neither here nor there.

"You should move to a Tribeca gallery."

Maude felt herself make a face. "Chelsea is still Chelsea," she said, testily.

Sherbeam raised an eyebrow at the tone.

"Oh, who am I kidding. You're always right about these things." Maude snorted a laugh. "Maybe if I had representation in Tribeca I could get my phone calls returned."

"Who's not returning your phone calls?"

Maude told her.

"Leave it to me, dear." Sherbeam tossed her scarf over her

shoulder so she could scribble a reminder in the notebook she carried everywhere.

Sherbeam knew Elż? That felt like a violation. "Please don't get involved. Another Negroni?"

Sherbeam nodded. Maude filled both their glasses and sipped, well on her way to becoming totally plastered. Constanza came into the kitchen and Maude poured her one too as she accepted the invitation to join them.

They clinked glasses again as the Lizzo video restarted in the front room. Familiar chords bounced along.

Maude sang along with the intro about the DNA test, which she'd heard enough now to know, or at least hum along with.

The other two joined in, Constanza calling out "Abby, no B-word!" before the next instance rolled around, whereupon all four sang about being a "bad girl." More Negronis were sipped. They'd be as lit as a MOMA Lichtenstein by the time Casey, Demmy, and later, Roger, returned.

Between them, the three women had more or less raised five children to financially solvent adulthood, or near enough. Maude's two sons were partnered, employed and settled—Jared and Oric in Nashville and Scott and Eksha in San Francisco, an annoyingly unwalkable town, with its landscape like goosebumps. Maude swilled her cocktail and shoved Sherbeam's plasticky prints toward Constanza.

"What say you? Include in the retrospective? Thumbs up? Thumbs down? Don't think. Just judge." Maude felt more important now, directing the decision-making process.

They went through the prints in rapid fire, drunkenly settling on the lineup for the show that would inaugurate the final stage of Sherbeam's career, passing pictures between them, one by one, three Graeae sharing a single eye.

CHAPTER 10

The bearded guy next to Demmy on the F stank. And was looking at her. Though aware of the protection her privilege brought her, she still gripped her keys in her hand, the longest one facing out.

Force of habit.

Demmy had been coached in school that, despite widespread rumor to the contrary, this was not a good defensive move, since by the time she could use the key, Mr. Stinky would be too close. Instead, she was supposed to attach her keys to a kubaton with a carabiner so she could use the combination as a nunchuck. They'd had a whole assembly on this, passing out kubatons and carabiners. Today, she'd left the bulky contraption at home but remembered she should swing at places with lots of bones, like a hand, because that was more painful. They'd called the assembly "Self-defense," but might just as well have called it "Riding the subway," or maybe "Getting to school," or even "Existing in New York City." For next week's assembly, they'd probably be doing "Getting through metal screeners quickly at school-entry chokepoints," and maybe the week after, "Active shooter."

The train was one stop from the Public Library, main branch, where Demmy was going to volunteer as a tutor and coincidentally get a line to put in the altruism sections of her many applications. Please don't let Mr. Stinky be the one I'm tutoring, she prayed. *Tutees,* they called them on the website, not a word that had previously conjured up *stench* for her. The train was too crowded for Demmy to move away from him, but a grinding creak of brakes and gush of burnt oil smell announced her station. Mr. Stinky's eyes followed her, but he did not.

The left-right-left shuffle of Demmy's leather soles on grimy stairs melted into the crowd trudging upward from the platform. She was nervous about her interview, but they wouldn't turn down a literacy volunteer, would they? Or shunt her to the local branch? She wanted a volunteer opportunity that was on her route to school and was reasonably safe. Did that again reveal her privilege? She found her way to the room assigned her when she'd filled out the form online. She checked in, was told to take a seat, and waited.

Her balding, thirty-something boss-to-be Mark told he they were happy to have Demmy. He seemed tired, but his appearance was reassuring: a plump guy in glasses and wrinkled clothes who put in too many hours in a helping profession was unlikely to be a threat. Demmy looked over Mark's shoulder as he scrolled the primitive green-and-yellow display on his balky desktop through time slots till he found the times Demmy had said she was available. Last night she'd come up with a clever chyron for the reality show that was her life —*Ballet pointe to bullet points*—but there were no bullet points to be seen on his ancient screen. This world was so far from the elegance of her phone interface it was practically analog.

"I'm tutoring someone in ten minutes, if you want to shadow. You know, get your feet wet," Mark said.

Demmy eagerly nodded yes. She accompanied Mark into a small windowless room. A large woman wearing a head wrap sat waiting: middle-aged, Black, very dark skinned with a heavy accent. French? Haitian, turned out to be the correct answer. Marie.

Marie looked Demmy up and down. Demmy was again nervous. Would Marie be less comfortable with a white girl than she was with Mark, who was also Black, though closer to Demmy than Marie in skin tone?

"I like your name," Marie said when Demmy explained it, and they were good.

Marie had brought in homework, neatly handwritten in a spiky, European-style script. She and Mark went over it as Demmy watched from Mark's side. Mark invited Demmy to jump in if she had something to say, but she didn't.

Though Mark was a gentle teacher, he did not hesitate to correct Marie when she stumbled, and Demmy could tell the older woman liked him. Was this perhaps a highlight in her week? The reading was hard for Marie, whose English was good enough for working most jobs, Demmy guessed, but had huge holes in it when it came to reading. She dropped little verbs that indicated tense, her pronunciation took effort to decode, and her vocabulary was more limited than Demmy would have guessed from her fluid conversation skills. But Demmy could see she enjoyed learning.

After Marie left, Demmy asked Mark if all the students were that easy. He shook his head. "Marie is already literate in French as well as Haitian Kreyól," he said, "so this isn't literacy per se but English as a second language. People who are illiterate in their native language more often are deeply stressed by lessons. They might have had bad experiences in schools or have underlying learning difficulties. They carry a sense of shame, and older students find it hard to make progress. But you can help them build confidence, and their sense of accomplishment as they improve is amazing," Mark told her. "You'll love it."

Would she? What Mark described indeed sounded "amazing," but she felt out of place. Tutees here wouldn't be debating whether to check the *Legacy* box. What if she unwittingly insulted someone, like labelling Marie *illiterate* when she wasn't? She would hate that.

Mark sat her down in his office for a five-minute primer on what to do when she had her first tutee on Thursday (the following day), and then that was that: she was a tutor. Tomorrow, she'd jump in solo. Mark said he'd be there to back her up if she had any difficulties, but Demmy wondered if that would be true. Demmy had the feeling that emergencies could occur without warning and plans change. She suspected she and her tutee would sink or swim on their own, together.

CHAPTER 11

Casey heard a street sweeper growl past, gobbling up dead leaves, as she pulled the Cayenne into their neighbor's driveway. She and Roger rented the parking space, for which she was deeply grateful; their street was always parked up. Casey backed and filled, backed and filled. The space was barely large enough to accommodate the Cayenne, matching the only just sufficient sixteen-hundred square feet of her and Roger's badly laid-out rowhouse, half that hallways.

Casey toted two bags of groceries from Whole Foods up the front granite stairs, thinking how she'd get rid of the Planetkiller and its car payment when they moved to Park Slope. If they could swing a large enough place for her to have a home office, she wouldn't need to drive anywhere except the grocery store, and she could Uber that. She had the sudden inspiration to pick Kelly's realtor brain; this would have the added benefit of alerting the network of other mothers that the Whites were contemplating a move upward, the rumor forestalling the need for said move for another year.

She handed off the bags to Constanza, who began putting the food away. Was Constanza a little unsteady? Casey noticed three martini glasses on the table. Sherbeam and Maude gabbed away, a gleaming stainless cocktail shaker between them. Neither offered to help as Casey went back outside for the third and fourth bags. They'd aged out of helping, each had told her on separate occasions, but if either had previously lent a hand with something it had been before Casey arrived on the scene. Possibly during the reign of the first wife, though Casey doubted it. Casey imagined having a heart-to-heart debrief with the first wife and laughed out loud. Everyone looked at her, but she did not explain. Lord, of course she didn't.

Constanza had cooked for them—an arroz con pollo sort of thing—and Demmy could set the table if she got back from the library at a reasonable hour. Was it too soon to press Abby into service? She tried to remember herself at five. Even her mother, a dedicated taskmaster, had not had Casey doing anything more functional at that age than carrying small things to the table, which Casey remembered being eager to do.

What a world apart her current married life was from her first time around, when she and her execrable ex had married as teenagers, excited to have a sweaty little shotgun shack in Memphis to call their very own. No nanny/housekeeper then. No other mothers looking down on her or her parenting. No money, no car, and no subway neither. But damn her man had been hot. She had thought herself lucky. Ha!

"What are all these?" she finally asked Maude and Sherbeam, pointing at the plastic-covered images blanketing the table that Casey needed to clear off for dinner, all to entertain two women who had graduated from being helpful.

"A gallery in Spain . . ." Sherbeam.

". . . Catalonia . . ." Maude.

". . . *Catalunya* wants to organize a retrospective of my

work, so I need to sweet-talk or bully collectors into shipping work." Sherbeam glided a hand over her neat gray waves, gathering the ends into a short, ephemeral ponytail that disappeared upon release.

"The idea will sell itself," Maude said, enthusiastic as ever. The woman seemed half a bubble off plumb to Casey, but she chalked most of that up to her own lack of understanding of New Englanders, especially Mainers—ostensibly liberal but secretly conservative.

"And when does all this happen?" Casey knew Sherbeam would insist on the family all going to the opening, as would Roger. Casey mentally added the cost of plane tickets and lodging to the car payment for the Planetkiller and the rent for its parking spot. A horrifying sum. Sherbeam was generous, allowing them to live in the rowhouse for only the price of property taxes, upkeep and insurance, but Casey knew Sherbeam's generosity wouldn't extend to the frivolous family vacation after the opening that Roger would want to tack onto their stay.

"Pau is thinking mid-May next year, when the weather is still mild but the tourists are arriving, eager to spend."

"Spend on what?" Casey asked. "Isn't art in a retrospective already owned by someone?"

Sherbeam scoffed. "I'll have new work as well. Two to five paintings, if I can pull together some ideas."

"One of each of your granddaughters! That's two paintings right there!" Casey said. "And Roger makes three!"

The expressions of horror from the two painters were priceless. Oh, the sentimentality! Casey decided to work it. "You did all those portraits in Chelsea, and didn't what's-his-name who was married to what's-her-name in New Mexico, you know, the lilies and vulvas—vulvae?—photograph his grandkids?"

"Stieglitz?" Maude said. Casey had fed her the straight line and she'd come up proudly with the boasty factoid.

"That's the one."

"I believe that was his daughter, Kitty, as a young child." Sherbeam sniffed.

"And not naked," Maude added, just to clear that up, apparently.

A hush fell over the room. Were they each now imagining a portrait of Roger, naked, and not as a fresh-faced boy but in his current abdominally spreading incarnation? A giggle rose behind Casey, from Constanza, whom Casey had forgotten was there, and more would have been sure to follow, but just then Abby began singing in the front room again about her DNA test and being "a hundred percent that girl."

Casey mentally translated "girl" to the original lyric. You and me both, Lizzo, thought Casey.

CHAPTER 12

When she arrived home, Demmy could tell her dad was drunk, and maybe her stepmom, too, because neither was glaring at Demmy for being too late for dinner, let alone to set the table. Her weirdo nana was still there, though Constanza and someone else had already gone home, judging from the extra set of dirty dishes abandoned at the end of the table. Her nana's friend Maude, most likely. Maude was the one Demmy would have most liked to talk to (Maude never asked her "how is school?"), but oh well. And at least the rest of them were lubricatedly cheery.

"I'll get those." Demmy grabbed her dad's dirty plate, as well as the unclaimed one, definitely Maude's, since it had an untouched piece of pink-filled pie and her dad tended to ply Maude with desserts she rarely touched. Demmy placed the pie to the side for herself later. Washing up would be her penance for taking her time getting home. She'd dawdled with Lainie and Jodee and then strolled around the block a few times once she got in the neighborhood so she could listen to the rest of the new Billie Eilish.

"Sit, sit," Nana said. She always tried to lure Demmy into

not working. Not doing much of anything, in fact, but Demmy liked to keep busy.

"I can talk to you from here," Demmy said at the sink.

"Whaddya say to Barcelona in May, kiddo?" her dad slurred out at her. He looked happy, his focus shifting between different points in the middle distance.

"May when, exactly?" Demmy cleared her nana and step-mother's plates, scraped the detritus (SAT word) into the compost. She tipped the plates into the sink, which she filled with hot water and suds as she put on rubber gloves to protect her skin. She objected to the waste of energy of the quiet German dishwasher.

"Listen to her?" Nana's voice careened into falsetto, bouncing off the walls. "Too *busy* for Barcelona!"

"I have school."

"Skip it!"

"It's the last month of my senior year of high school!" It might be the last time she would have with her friends before they scattered to points unknown, that point for her being not-Yale. Not to mention she had finals. She shut off the water as it crept up the sink.

"You'd choose high school over Europe?" Her dad sounded seriously incredulous. Was he going to back his mother on this? Typical Dad move: volunteering his family for two weeks of purgatory based on the notion that for the first time ever Nana *wouldn't* drive him nuts.

"It's not just a summer vacation," Casey jumped in. "Your nana is having a retrospective. It's an event you will be sorry to miss. There will be work you've never seen, people you've never met, and these are people you want to meet."

Demmy felt betrayed. Casey, of all people, pushing the *connections* angle? She was the one Demmy could usually rely on not to focus on status. Of *course* Demmy would like to visit

Catalonia again—she loved Iberia in general and had had a stunning summer in Asturias last year—but her last weeks of high school, her graduation? That was not nothing.

Demmy scraped off the last of the dishes. She'd heard that lots of slacking off was done those last couple of months, after everyone had their acceptances, but missing so much time would kill her grades. The only place to overlook a plunge in class ranking like that would be Yale, where legacy status would buy her wiggle room. Just when I thought I was out they pull me back in!

Abby wandered into the room. "I want a DNA test."

"What?" "Why?" "I can tell you all you need to know." The three elders all jumped in. And they didn't stop there. "It's such a fad." "The police could get your data." "Where did we put that family tree?"

Thanks for the diversion, Abby, Demmy said silently. She scrubbed and rinsed, grateful for having a five-year-old sister so unlike anyone else in the family. She tried to ignore her parents and nana being such killjoys. The damn DNA test would be boring—#bleh #tsumaranai—but let the kid have her fun.

CHAPTER 13

R oger could tell from their general twitchiness that his class was antsy about getting back their latest corrected homework. I will email them soon, he mentally promised. His power couple, Niamh and Joshua of the silky tresses, remained in their physical position as nucleus of the class, which surprised him. Yes, people generally stuck to the seats they chose the very first time they sat down, but the center of the center could be a tough choice—making a claim for the spotlight, holding it. Many who did not at first realize that would gradually migrate toward the edges. Not these two.

"You dispatched *Hereafter* in your assignment, admirably I might add, which means our next screening: *Babel*. This is our longest film: one hundred and forty-three minutes of running time, people, one *hundred* and *forty*-three minutes, including credits. Watching every minute is a *must*. So I am going to take pity on you. We will screen the entire film, but when we hit the fifty-minute mark, you may leave and watch the rest on your own. Just be sure to use the class link. None of this Netflix bullshit where the credits are tucked up illegibly in the top corner like an undescended testicle. You *must* watch the credits. All of them. Every second. Film is collaborative and you need to see the names of everyone who worked on the film if you are to understand it. For those of you who *can* stay, do. You'll see more here than at home. *Capisce?*"

Hands flew up.

"No, leaving early will not count against you. That would be a trick. I am not tricky."

All the hands went down save one. Joshua. Roger smiled, nodded.

"Will there be any discussion afterwards?"

Roger shook his head no. "Not fair to those not here. Anything else?"

There wasn't. "So, as you watch, there is one question I'd like you to bear in mind. Not because it's crucially important —or is it?—but simply to focus our discussion." He cleared his throat. "So, as you know, there are three geographical story-lines: Morocco, Tokyo, and L.A./Mexico. My question for you is . . ."

Someone cleared their throat loudly. Joshua. It was one of those cough things to disguise speech, but Roger hadn't caught what Joshua had said.

"Something you'd like to add, Mr. Black?"

Joshua didn't flinch. "It's San Diego, not L.A."

"Same difference."

"Is it?" He didn't hesitate.

Jesus. Who cared? González Iñárritu couldn't be from Tijuana, could he? "Well, everyone can watch and we'll discuss that too. But *my* question for you is, Does the Susan/Richard storyline constitute a fourth locale, independent of location?"

Roger aimed his remote control at the machine. Joshua's hand shot up. Roger pretended not to see it and dimmed the lights. He hit play, hoping it did not matter whether the US parts were in L.A. or San Diego, but already realizing it did because of San Diego's closer ties to Tijuana. He'd been planning on using the screening time to comment further on their assignments, sitting in the back with his tablet (some people so far only had a "good job" or "needs work"), but instead watched the film.

He was glad he did. Early on, he realized he had confused Ahmed and Yussef. As he remembered it, Ahmed shot Susan, but now he saw it was *Yussef* who fired the shot that hit her. And Roger wouldn't have been surprised if he'd referred to Ahmed as Abdullah—the father—or even Abdul—not a character in the film at all. Jesus H. Christ. The misrememberings kept on. He was losing it and uncertain whether Joshua's fact-checking presence was a blessing or a curse. It was days like this that made him wonder what he was doing at NYU. This was one of the top film schools in the country, some said *the* top film school (those people being people who thought there was no difference between Los Angeles and San Diego). Roger sweated as he watched the sweltering skies of Morocco and Baja California, and not because they looked hot. Jesus God, he'd need to rewatch *all* the other films. Those additional comments would never get written.

How did anyone manage this? But his peers did. He knew they did.

Maybe Demmy was onto something, not wanting to be a legacy. Being in over your head was a special kind of hell.

CHAPTER 14

C asey spent the afternoon in the living room corner, where a fold-down/fold-up desk housed the heart of her office. Her business model wasn't struggling; it was failing. The applied linguistics and marketing she had studied at UDLAP was outdated; busy with mothering, she hadn't kept up. To demonstrate to herself she was capable of persistence, she sent off a slew of pointless quotes for jobs listed on an online clearinghouse. She'd lowered her rates repeatedly, but the market was heading down, down, down. More Latin American linguists were entering the online marketplace, forcing Casey to accept smaller jobs, lower rates, and piece-work instead of the localization projects she had positioned her little company to win. Time to give up? She could go back to freelance interpreting at the UN, but she'd need to hire someone to pick Abby up, canceling out the bump in income.

She had barely started on the next set of no-hope RFQs (requests for quotations) on another site when her phone tapped her wrist, telling her it was time to hit the road for The Hartley School. She was more than glad to fold her laptop and paperwork into the desk, out of sight. She said goodbye to

Constanza—they couldn't afford Constanza either—and slipped into the Porsche.

God, she loved the car. It was her sanctuary, which felt self-indulgent, but her need for it was real. Just like realtor Kelly had to stay in shape and keep her hair professionally cut and colored, Casey had to impress the other mothers if solid leads were to come her way. Because one thing you could definitely say about the other mothers: those rich a-hundred-percent-that-girls had connections. Even the ones who didn't work, *had* worked, and *would* work again, if they felt like it, at name-brand firms and nonprofits founded by prominent people they'd shared a house with off-campus at Oberlin or Colby or Middlebury. That's where Kelly had gone, Middlebury College.

She looked for Kelly as she pulled up in front of the school. In the afternoons, Casey waited in the car. Abby clearly felt very competent making her way on her own to the car, so Casey let her, keeping a close eye on her the entire way. She found it nerve-racking, physically painful, to let Abby grow up, even that little bit. But she could not let the fear instilled in her so long ago poison Abby's life. Her daughter was strong and resilient, or, as Sherbeam would put it, a mouthy brat (something her own parents back in Missouri had never called Abby).

She spotted Kelly slinking toward the side-yard gate. As always, Casey was aware of the movement of everyone on the block (or felt she was; never assume you've covered everything). Sometimes she had to feign surprise at people's presence, lest they think she was a stalker. Paying too close attention to one's surroundings could creep people out.

She got out of the car. It would do no harm to chat with Kelly a bit. Casey waved at her, but stayed near the car. She did not want to miss that moment when Abby saw her mother waiting and her face opened in delight.

Casey wanted Kelly to come over, but Frannie had Kelly pinned down. They were talking with Paula. All three looked her way. Crap. Casey always did her parental duty at The Hartley, including that bit more than the minimum needed to not look grudging, even if that meant working till midnight.

Frannie looked Casey's way. What now? Frannie reveled in devising extra duties for slackers. Casey caught Kelly's eye. Casey tried to pull Kelly out of Frannie's orbit. She'd show them who was a hundred percent that girl.

But it wasn't happening. Frannie had her hooks into Kelly, but good. Kelly's looks made people want to be friends with her, which was power, but Frannie was still the one in charge, acting as though she had the goods on everyone.

Kelly edged away from Frannie. She was saying her goodbyes, but the goodbyes weren't taking.

Now Abby appeared at the top of the stairs, spotted Casey, and ran down to her for a hug. Casey kissed her and helped her up into her booster seat. Abby started up Lizzo. "About Damn Time." Casey waved at Kelly, got in the Cayenne and drove off. As with dating, there was no upside to looking desperate. God, that's what this was, wasn't it: dating. Well, fine. She was pretty sure Kelly knew Casey had swiped right. If Kelly wanted to make cookies for the next bake sale together —and there was always a next bake sale—it was now up to her to swipe right, too.

CHAPTER 15

J odee *was* pissed. Literacy was *her* thing, and Demmy was horning in on it. *"Datte,"* she whined, with the authority of a heritage speaker. She wrinkled up her face at Demmy over e-cigarettes in their vaping spot, No Woman's Land. *"Uchi no mono wa uchi no mono da."* What's mine is mine. I saw it first. Etc.

"What I do is *nothing* like what you do," Demmy protested. "You work with murderers; I work with housewives." Her very own personal tutee had turned out to be a Dominican immigrant housewife. Teresa cooked, cleaned, and did childcare, although the kitchen, house, and child were not her own. Like Constanza, and yet nothing like Constanza, who'd grown up speaking English in South Texas and spoke crisp Mexican Spanish (the real kind, they both agreed) with Demmy's stepmom as much for her own practice as for Casey's.

"Stop fighting; you're both pretty," Lainie said. "Aren't you more concerned about the AP kanji list? Why the fuck are they adding to it? It's already too long." Kanji were not Lainie's strong suit. The prospect of learning more characters *was* daunting, but Demmy wasn't sweating the Japanese AP test. It was only one of about twenty they'd taken or would be taking, not to mention the several SAT practice tests behind them and the last gasp SAT she'd signed up for, approaching fast.

"Maybe Martin can give you extra tutoring," Jodee said. "*Kiite mireba?*" Why don't you ask him?

Lainie shuddered. "Can you imagine having to spend extra time with him?"

"He's not that bad." Demmy felt like defending Delaney-sensei, who lately they'd started calling Martin. She was in a good mood.

"Do you think he's gay or straight?"

"Don't forget bi, pan, omni, demi, and asexual," Jodee added.

"Oh, no, he's gay or straight. Not bi or pan, and for definite not ace." Demmy sighed. "I wanted to be bi, but it's just not happening." She thought of *Babel*, which she'd started watching again last night. Gael García Bernal. Sigh. Yeah, Demmy was so straight.

"Me, too!" Lainie said. "Or at least genderqueer. Can you make yourself be genderqueer?"

"How 'bout you try and report back to us?" Jodee asked.

"I wonder if it would help with college apps." Lainie rattled her e-cig. It appeared to be empty. She pocketed it.

"It certainly wouldn't hurt. I think it depends on how good an essay you write. *My Genderqueer Summer in Appalachia.*"

"And be sure to number the paragraphs. That's still in. *Forty Things My Pansexual Gender-fluid Grandparent Taught Me About Life.*"

"Awesome, but it has to be an aunt or uncle. Who's going to believe a gender-fluid grandparent? I mean, that generation? OK, boomer."

Demmy thought of Nana. She'd believe it about her grandmother.

"But there's no gender-neutral word for aunts and uncles. Is there?" Lainie looked pleased with herself. "You can have siblings, parents, and grandparents, but there's nothing for aunts and uncles."

"Or nieces and nephews."

"How about *unt*? Martin, I'd like you to meet my hot, pansexual unt."

"Ded!"

"Is that offensive?"

"Probably," Lainie blurted.

"Hopefully," Demmy added.

They all giggled.

"You're telling me we are all cis-gender heterosexuals?" Demmy asked.

"Well . . ." Jodee said.

"What? What?" Lainie was all ears.

"I do actually kind of like girls, too. Now that you, you know, mention it."

"For reals?"

Jodee shrugged. "You didn't get that about me?"

Demmy shook her head. "I always thought 'butch straight girl,' honestly."

"Nope. Not straight," Jodee said. "You're not weirded out, are you?"

"Oh, fuck no. Are you trans too?"

"No, butch girl, that's it. Cis, but butch."

"I feel cooler already, just sitting here with you."

"What's that in Japanese?"

"Not dyke, because *daiku-san* is a carpenter."

"God, what would Martin do if we asked him. Sensei, what's Japanese for lesbian and bi? Would he even know?"

Jodee shuddered. "Oh, no way. Not ready for that."

"We don't have to make it about you. We can keep it general. I'm sure everyone else is dying to know too."

Lainie swiveled toward Jodee. "So what is *your* college essay going to be?"

"I'm thinking, *Traditions Passed Down: What One Baby Dyke Learned in Prison.*"

"You are so getting in everywhere." Demmy noticed Jodee'd gone from "I kinda like girls" to butch "baby dyke" in about a minute.

"Right?" Lainie gave Jodee a hug.

Jodee smiled, the first smile Demmy had seen in a while, now that she thought of it. Demmy smiled big too. "This doesn't mean I'm not mad at you for stealing my idea," Jodee said, but Demmy didn't believe her.

CHAPTER 16

Roger hadn't been to see his father Nick in long enough that he wasn't sure how long it had been. Probably more than a year. Probably not two. And probably his dad would tell him when he arrived.

The elevator dinged. He was at the top floor of the apartment building where dear old Dad lived. Which was to say that he was in his dad's apartment, because his dad had the entire top floor. If one had the code, the elevator opened into the living room. The floor-to-ceiling windows beyond provided a shockingly good view of the Hudson and cliffs and forests in Jersey beyond.

"I can't stay long," Roger said. He didn't explain about grading, about being a dad.

"What's up Roger? You need money?" His silver-haired dad looked ruddy, trim, healthy. And two inches taller than Roger, just for spite.

"No, I do not *need money*. Wait, what am I saying? I live in New York. Of *course* I need money!"

His dad waved his hand at Roger—what a sense of humor —but truthfully between the two girls' schools, Roger had big bills. He should act like it, watch every dime, but the solid salary he earned and the knowledge that he stood to eventually inherit pots from one or both of his parents helped him sleep like a baby. What he needed was not money.

His dad made his way to the kitchen island—granite, stainless steel dishwasher, and wine chiller, so early two-thousands—where Dad's latest wife was fixing cocktails. OK, yes, his dad had only had two wives in his lifetime, but Roger enjoyed thinking of Shoshana as "his latest."

Shoshana had chosen her own name to replace one so hideously Gentile she refused to disclose it. ("It's my 'dead name'," she said, in what struck Roger as cultural appropriation.) She kept two kitchens, one kosher, one not. She made hamantaschen for Purim, outdoor shelters for Sukkot. She even celebrated Tu BiShvat. She had soft-looking ringlets, dishwater blond going gray, and Roger sometimes wondered if his slender dad had married her because her delicate frame made him look huge.

"What has it been? Just shy of two years?" his dad asked, right on cue.

Shoshana passed them both cocktails. "Roger, you like your martini dirty, right?"

"How else would I get my nutrition?"

"I like this one, Nick," Shoshanna said to his dad, as though his dad had other kids to choose from.

"I haven't been staying away on purpose," Roger said. "I'm shocked it's been so long. I was just thinking of you both earlier today, as I was musing on how I have no time to do anything, and it struck me how long it's been."

"We really should get together for Christmas. Are you in town?"

"Stowe," Roger said. His family had a cabin in Vermont.

"Mauritius for us," Shoshanna said, remindingly.

"Oh, right." His dad sighed. "And another year goes by. Is it supposed to be like this?"

"Is it OK for the answer to be yes?" Roger asked.

Shoshanna shrugged at Nick, Nick at her. It was nice to see them. Why didn't he come over more? Probably because Casey would soon be setting out dinner for his two lovely daughters—he pictured Demmy arriving home right that second—and that was something he found hard to miss.

That and grading. Christ, why had he even come? Maude had also asked if Roger had time that evening. He'd felt an incipient meltdown. She had news about "his condition." Jaundiced outlook? Potbelly? Incipient bald spot? Whatever it was, it would have to wait.

"Come out on the deck, Roger. The air is lovely this high up," his dad said. Shoshanna was still doing something in the kitchen. Roger followed his dad out and took a deep breath. He liked that his dad used words like 'lovely.' He told him that.

His dad nodded. "Do you still miss her?"

Roger flinched. "Don't Dad. Just don't."

His dad nodded. "Sorry." He gestured at the skyline, starting to twinkle, the river. "I waited decades to move here."

Roger thought, As opposed to where? The office, that mythical place where his dad had always been when Roger was young?

"Was it worth it? Being at the office, I mean." Roger tried not to sound bitter.

"If I hadn't been there, I'd have been somewhere else."

Yeah, like at home, getting to know your son, Roger thought, but regrets and grudges could not be his thing, not anymore. One way or another, everyone had to get by, he'd learned. Compromises were made. People survived. He'd survived. But still, it could have been different.

"I missed you," Roger said, "those years."

"I know you did. I'm sorry." Nick looked a bit frightened.

Roger waved away the apology. "I know. Don't worry." Roger laughed. "I'm not going back to the resentful twenties. I got a feature film out of that, so I'm actually kind of grateful."

"*The Fix*."

"And a lot got 'fixed.' You've always been honest with me, pushing back on my bullshit but acknowledging my complaints when they were justified. Do you know how rare that is? Yes, I would have liked you to check in on me when I was growing up, and that absence hurt, and still does sometimes. But not much. And not often. And that's because you haven't pushed my resentment away."

Nick rolled his eyes. "I was so awful even I knew it." He laughed. "Who ever thought that could be a good thing?"

"Well, no one, and it wasn't. Good, that is. But you had compensating bravery."

"I appreciate you saying so. So do you . . ."

"Nope. Not going there. OK? Please?"

Nick nodded. "But you know that I think . . ."

"Nope!"

Nick gave a sigh. "Sorry. I'm so used to . . ."

"Mansplaining?"

"Can a man mansplain to another man?"

"Dad, that's literally what you do for a living!"

"Hmm."

Shoshanna came out with snacks: tapenade, crackers, whitefish. "What did I miss?"

"Just a few needle sticks," Roger said. "Emotional acupuncture. All to the good."

"Sounds like I missed a lot," she said.

"Maybe, maybe not," Roger said. "What do you think of *Mansplaining for a Living* as a movie title." Roger was getting a script idea, the first new one in a while. He would have to jot this down before he got home.

"Dated, too long, not specific enough to spark the imagination. Could be *Medium* essay."

"Don't be mean!"

Shoshana chuckled. "I call 'em as I see 'em. You know me. Are you writing again? And is it about this one?" Shoshana motioned at Nick.

"Not really. Not sure what it's about. And I'm not writing anything anyway."

Shoshana and Nick exchanged knowing glances.

"I'm not!" Roger protested. "How about *Mansplaining to Men*?"

"Better, but no."

"*Women Mansplain Things to Me*?"

Shoshana shook her head. "It's not going to work for you, Roger." She laughed.

Roger chuckled back. This was a feeling he hadn't had in maybe ten years, when he'd written his two previous scripts, now moldering in the proverbial desk drawer, which was actually a folder in the cloud. He was seized with the impulse to douse them with digital lighter fluid and immolate their imagination-less stultification, but instead gave himself fifteen minutes before he said his goodbyes and descended to the sidewalk, where he pulled out his notebook and began scribbling.

CHAPTER 17

C asey idled the Planetkiller in front of Kelly's Park Slope brownstone. Kelly wasn't leaving them enough time to comfortably get there but damn if she hadn't swiped right: Kelly had asked Casey to join her at yoga.

Someone honked at Casey from behind. She hit the hazard button, rolled down her window, and motioned the car to drive around her with an encouraging hand gesture, if such a thing existed. Every such gesture she'd ever been on the receiving end of had felt patronizing at best.

"Asshole," the woman yelled at her as she drove around, offering a gesture of her own.

Casey smiled and waved. She rolled up the window, more amused than angered. Soon after she had arrived in New York, she'd foolishly bought a battered Isuzu pick-up, ticketed regularly at despair-inducing cost. The sound of any street sweeper anywhere would set her heart racing as she struggled to remember where she'd parked. Now, she barely registered the sweepers and never got tickets. A part of her had internalized the rules and knew when and where she could break them. She felt very New York.

Kelly rapped on the passenger side window, her rolled-up powder-blue yoga mat held against her bright yellow spandex, a one-woman Ukraine cheer squad. She got in when Casey unlocked the door.

"I feel so *pampered* getting driven to yoga." Kelly's skin looked fresh and moist.

"It's the least I could do." Casey wondered where she'd stash the Cayenne when they got to the studio, but the alternative had been riding the bus in yoga gear carrying a mat that everyone would bang against, probably more deliberately than not, to let her know she was taking up too much space.

They chatted on the way over about a hatred of baking— yes, another bake sale was coming up, at which the other mothers would buy pastries too fattening to eat that they'd give away, throw away, or fob off on husbands. (Let *them* get fat.) Kelly was describing how she'd allow herself three cookies. It was more than she should eat, but somehow the excess made it easier for her to control herself afterward, "If that makes any kind of sense," she added.

"I get it," Casey replied, though she didn't. Was it something about waste? She thought of how she'd become more frugal since they'd bought the car, but wouldn't dream of exposing that vulnerability to anyone connected to The Hartley. "Any news on whether Joseph has been admitted or approved or whatever the behind-the-scenes term is for getting into first-through-eighth?"

"It's not official, but yes, I think he's in." Kelly rotated her head, stretching her neck muscles. Her breasts lifted and fell as her head made its rounds, despite the stretchy clutch of her lemony top. There was not an ounce of fat on her. Casey wondered if the three-cookies thing was a feint, a way to encourage Casey to eat three—or better, four or five—cookies of her own, gain a pound. But no, that was a Frannie move, not a Kelly move.

"How does that work, exactly? The behind-the-scenes thing. I know I should spend more time talking with everyone when I pick up Abby, but it's such a big deal for her to walk to the car herself."

Kelly shook her head. "It's just a feeling you get. Rumors. The tone in the emails from the school."

People got emails from the school? Casey would have to check her *Junk* folder.

"Will you be at the bake sale? That'll be a good chance to put your ear to the ground," Kelly offered. "Do people still say 'ear to the ground' or is that racist?"

Asking the question seemed more racist than the phrase, but Casey kept quiet. She had initially struggled to learn the latest NYC mores and manners. These days she no longer needed to be silent—having worked so hard on keeping up, she was usually way ahead of everyone else—but the wariness lingered.

The yoga studio street was packed with cars. Alternate-side parking was suspended for Veterans Day, yet here they all were. "Let me drop you off."

"You don't mind?"

Casey shook her head, noting nonetheless the lack of solidarity forthcoming from Kelly, whose tardiness had made them late. As a nondriver, maybe Kelly hadn't realized that the time she'd told Casey to arrive didn't allow for dawdling. Nondrivers sometimes imagined driving took no time, cars magically spiriting themselves over streets clogged with other, presumably non-magical, cars.

Casey dropped Kelly off and circled, realizing that the girl crush she'd had on Kelly for a while now had taken its first real hit. Kelly accepting the drop-off was a jerk move.

But Casey had made the offer, so she could hardly complain. She spotted a few spaces as she drove, but nothing remotely large enough for the Planetkiller. She circled the block and then more blocks, moving farther away from the studio as the start time of the class approached, arrived, and then receded.

A light turned red. Casey stopped. She wasn't that fond of yoga anyway. It was Kelly she was fond of. Or rather drawn to, in a way that bothered her but was too strong not to notice. Casey wanted to touch her. Casey hadn't felt this way in years.

An SUV just like hers was inside the building beside her. Inside a building? How? She turned to look. Ah, a car dealership. The SUV was a Tesla. It looked much like the Cayenne, but somehow better. Inside, a man in a suit noticed Casey staring. Someone honked behind her. The light had turned green. The man in the dealership motioned to her, in broad swings of his arms. Come on in, that was the message.

The car behind her honked again. Casey spotted a sign for the entrance to the service wing of the dealership, just around the corner. She turned right. The honking car floored it, angrily zooming around her. Casey chuckled.

She pulled into the dealership. Her wheels squeaked as she drove into a spacious hall of polished concrete that opened onto repair bays, sales offices. The man from the showroom appeared.

"You can park over here," he told her. She pulled the Cayenne into a slot and left it, following the man into the show room. He was smiling now, as they entered the glass-walled nave, a temple of electric car worship.

Casey needed to get to the yoga studio, but she ran her hand over the Model X, noting the glide of her palm over the flush door handles.

"You like?"

Casey nodded. She spotted the price sticker in the window. $81,000. "Is that really the price?"

The salesman acted a bit abashed. "But worth every penny." He hit a button. Gull-wings rose to reveal a video screen at least the equal of the Cayenne's. Abby would loooove the car.

Casey wasn't shocked at the price; she was angry. It was only one thousand more than what she'd paid for the Cayenne. She imagined arriving at The Hartley in a gleaming black Tesla. Abby would have received those solicitous emails already, consonant chords of welcome bubbling between electronic lines of prosaic prose. So much for keeping up with the latest and greatest.

"Test drive?" the salesman asked her.

Casey shook her head. She'd missed the start of the class, but she still had to give Kelly a ride home. "I'm late for a yoga class." She gestured at her ridiculous outfit—garish leggings, leotard—imagining the mockery it would attract in Eldon, Missouri, where she'd grown up. "I couldn't find parking."

He shrugged. His lush brown hair was neatly combed, expertly styled, and seemed to display tiny shrugs of its own, in moral support of his manly-but-not-too-manly shoulders, a not-accidental one-rung down from the big-shouldered, disagreeable men whom Casey imagined were the typical luxury car buyers.

"Leave your car here," he offered.

Casey winced. "I don't have time for a test drive after either. I'm driving my friend home." She worked a little apologetic smile into her expression.

"That's fine. You can do the test drive next time."

She took him up on the offer and set out on foot for the studio, hurrying as she thought of Kelly's dewy skin and stretched, flexible limbs. She sighed. In a couple of years would Casey be the one unrolling her yoga mat while some yet-to-be-met Hartley-aspirant circled the block for her? Never, she vowed to herself, but part of her wondered if Kelly, whom Casey had put on a pedestal until today, had ever sworn the same.

CHAPTER 18

Maude was surprised to be invited over to the Whites' for Thanksgiving. Since both her sons were spending first holidays with their respective in-laws, she thought a peaceful turkey dinner with her favorite people (except Roger, at the moment) would give her sons time to build their new relationships out west without her butting in.

The Williamsburg street the Whites lived on was in the last throes of fall, color gone from withered leaves fluttering down, the air crisp and biting. Maude shielded her hot dish— a Maine-style apple crisp fresh from the oven—against the cold harshness of a temperature that had once been normal but was now unseasonably low.

"Maude Friendly?" a voice called from behind her.

She turned. She did not recognize the middle-aged woman behind her, blond hair peeking out from her burgundy woolen headscarf. Nor her short, dashing husband, his tuque snug on his head in way that suggested baldness. Nor their three children, barely in tow.

"Hello," she offered. Then, taking a stab, "Yaddo?" Something told her they might have met there during one of Maude's residencies.

The woman looked puzzled.

"Artist colony," Maude heard the husband say in an undisguised Irish whisper that suggested he enjoyed correcting people. She stopped herself from telling him the "colony" part had been dropped due to its oppressive overtones.

"Are you headed to the Whites'?" the woman asked. "Casey mentioned who-all would be coming and I recognized your name. Love your new work at the Flenck."

Maude's gallery. Excellent artist list, but Maude had never cared for the awkward name, indecisive shades of Whitney and Frick with the grace of neither, although it beat her ridiculous surname. Maude noticed the husband was carrying a foil-covered dish as well. She balanced her crisp so she could stick out a mittened hand. "Lovely to meet you."

"I'm Kelly," she said. "And this is my husband, Rich."

"My husband was rich, too." Maude instantly chastised herself both for disclosing her husband was deceased (hey, could be divorced) and for chancing an internal funny. Now she'd have to pretend Frank had been named Rich. She would have explained her joke, but the couple's clothes looked understatedly pricey, and if there was one thing she'd learned being married to Frank it was that if you brought up money around rich people, they'd talk like they were strapped for bus fare for about an hour. But Maude did add, "late husband," clearing up that ambiguity.

"I'm sorry," Kelly said. Rich mumbled something similar.

Maude waved their words away; she was all good on condolences. The subsequent conversation as they neared the door to the Whites' rowhouse began as praise of Maude's work and quickly segued into a discussion of Sherbeam's fabulosity. To her credit, Kelly actually made intelligent

comments on Maude's work first and didn't make the syco-
phantic shift to Sherbeam for a good two minutes. Maude
tried to ask them about themselves, but they were too excited
at the prospect of meeting Sherbeam to respond coherently.

Demmy answered the door, smiling broadly at Maude.
The smile faded as she saw Kelly, the husband, and the three
kids. Now everyone hesitated, the family behind Maude
teetering half-on, half-off the brick landing. "Take their dish,
honey," Maude said to Demmy as she pushed through, trying
to reinforce the lessons of politeness. Maude carried her own
dish into the kitchen, followed by Demmy bearing the
couple's casserole—sweet potatoes, the husband said, his
voice louder now as he spoke to Demmy. Maude felt a
shimmer of proprietary pride at Demmy's nascent hosting
skills. She'd known the kid since birth, after all, having
become friends with Aline, Demmy's mother.

Maude abandoned her cobbler on the stovetop and
cornered Sherbeam, alerting her to Maude's late husband's
new name for the evening—Rich, not Frank—before Sherbeam could start speaking. Sherbeam scoffed. And why
shouldn't she? In what circumstances would Frank come up in
conversation, and who cared, anyway? Maude was still glad, as
she took a gulp of mulled wine, that she'd gotten that off her
to-do list. Her second glogg would soon wipe the issue from
her mind.

"Do you suppose she's serious?" Sherbeam asked.

"Who's serious? About what?"

"Demmy! About not going to the retrospective!"

"She didn't say she wasn't going."

Sherbeam waved her hand at Maude in irritation. "She as
good as said it. She'll be eighteen in January. No one can make
her go."

"Does it matter if she misses it?"

Sherbeam grew silent. Maude wanted to find Roger so he could witness this rare event, but was shocked to see the beginnings of a tear in Sherbeam's eye.

"I want my granddaughters to be there. This could be my last hurrah."

"You're barely seventy. There will be more hurrahs."

"You know that's never guaranteed. Anyway, I'm deciding: I will ask Pau to move it up to spring break. I want Demmy there."

"Problem solved, then."

Sherbeam made an unsatisfied frown. Maude realized this was Sherbeam's way of asking for advice, so she gave Sherbeam what she wanted: "It's a wonderful idea."

"Who's the man with the muscles?"

So that conversation was done. Maude followed Sherbeam's gaze. She had not noticed the husband having muscles, and wondered if Sherbeam had been duped by his bulky clothes—the guy hadn't taken his coat off yet, having gotten embroiled with getting winter wear off the couple's children. But sure enough, once he had his coat off, big arms filled his festive sweater. Score one for Sherbeam's eye for the human form. She might melt bodily contours like candlewax in her paintings, but not because she didn't know what they were.

"Excuse me," Sherbeam said, rushing off.

Maude let her go. "Roger," she said, catching sight of him, smiling.

"Maude," he replied, beaming.

Maude placed her hand on his shoulder as she looked at a stringy brown concoction he was sautéing . "I'm mad at you, Roger." She was more disappointed than angry. He wouldn't have stood her and Elż up, if he'd known.

"Dad," Demmy called to Roger as she reentered the room. "Mom wants me to remind you to baste the geese. Now."

Roger seemed struck dumb for a few seconds. Was it Maude being angry at him or Demmy calling Casey "mom?" Maude hadn't heard Demmy call her anything other than "Casey" before. "Uh, thanks," Roger said, recovering, his powers of speech as he turned to the oven.

"And what's up with you these days?" Maude asked Demmy. The *Mom* moment outranked Maude's petty irritation with Roger.

"My SAT scores should have been up nearly a week ago. It's mean. I missed taking them at the end of junior year when I had Covid, and then I neglected to sign up again until the last minute. I blame brain fog."

"I had no idea you'd had Covid!" Maude said.

"It was mild. I don't really have brain fog."

"I want to take a test," Abby piped up from Demmy's elbow. Metaphorically, not literally; Abby was tall for her age, and easily cleared Demmy's elbow, Demmy being no giant herself.

"Do you have a fever?"

"No, a *DNA* test."

"To see if she's 'a hundred percent that . . .' you-know," Demmy clarified.

Maude had no idea.

"Lizzo," Demmy added.

She'd forgotten that obsession. Maybe Maude had lingering brain fog from her own Covid two years ago.

"Mom says it's a waste of money, because she told me what I am, but I still want to take it," Abby added.

Abby spoke in rather sophisticated sentences, Maude noted. "How old are you again?"

"Five."

She stated it as though it was a moral stance. Not "five and a three quarters" or "nearly six," which she must be, if Demmy was turning eighteen. "I'll put in a good word for you with your mother. I did a DNA test, and found a few surprises. I'm more French than I knew. Are all the kids doing it? I saw three other kids arrive. Did you meet them?"

Abby nodded. "Joseph's in my class." Now Abby seemed younger. And in no hurry to play with the other children.

Maude remembered the look Demmy had given Kelly. "Do you two not like the family?"

Abby shook her head.

Demmy shrugged. "They're fine, Abby."

"But?"

Demmy crossed her arms. Now she, too, seemed younger. "Mom just invites Kelly over a lot."

There it was again: *Mom*. Maude was dying to ask what had changed for Demmy, but recognized this behavior as a deer creeping out from the edge of the woods, easily spooked. Patience was key.

And now Abby ran off, in the direction of Jason, no, Joseph, whom she professed not to like.

"Joseph," Abby commanded in the other room. An unintelligible conversation ensued.

"Kelly taking up too much of your mother's attention?"

Demmy shook her head. "It's just weird."

The doorbell rang. The door was opened to a butch-looking teenager.

"Finally!" Demmy lurched off, but did first say 'excuse me,' Maude noted. Demmy might lurch between child and woman, but she was getting so grown up. Maude watched Demmy trot off, excited to have her friend arrive and drenched in her own immediate experience, entirely unaware that the unrelated adult watching her go, having known her since infancy, would not hesitate to plunge into a burning building for her.

CHAPTER 19

Roger saw Maude tacking to intercept him as he toted a pail brimming with potato peels toward their back-deck compost bin. What could Maude be mad at him for? A cold blast of air as he opened the door reminded him he had nipples. Maude followed him outside. She grabbed his arm and whispered, "When did she start calling Casey 'Mom'?"

"Today!" Roger whispered back, as forcefully as he dared. The shift was a big deal, long awaited, and Demmy might stop if attention were called to it. He dumped the peels. "Though I've felt it coming for some time."

"Does Casey know?"

Roger could hear Casey's voice as she talked to someone in the foyer. The door behind Maude was open, bleeding heat. He asked her to close it. "I haven't talked to her yet."

"I'd be willing to bet she's trying it on you first. Out of respect for your feelings."

"*My* feelings? Maude, that makes me feel bad." That was an understatement. Had Demmy held off embracing Casey because she thought he was too delicate? "I've done nothing to discourage Demmy from thinking of Casey as her mother. I know Casey thinks of Demmy as her daughter. Casey and I have been married for over seven years." Roger stood with his empty compost pail. The door opened again.

Demmy came through with Jodee in tow. "Hi, Jodee," Roger said.

"Hi, Mr. White." Jodee closed the door.

He thought of telling her to call him Roger, but he didn't have a lot of people call him Mr. White. He remembered his first day of teaching as an assistant professor, finally not an adjunct, when a student had asked, "Professor White, what should we call you." What, like *Professor White* was no good? He'd reflexively said, "Roger," but should have said "Professor White will do nicely, young whippersnapper."

The two girls squeezed by them and thudded down the steps into the backyard.

"No vaping!" he called after them.

"Baste, Dad," Demmy called back. "Baste."

Roger stood staring after them, trying to decide if Demmy was being rude or playful. He did need to baste.

"Making goose, then?"

Roger nodded. "Two geese. I get to say things like 'great gobs of goose grease.' I'm in charge, because Casey finds it too much work. You have to lance the skin and duck it—pun intended—in boiling water to melt some fat out before you roast it. Just boiling enough water to dunk a goose is a chore. But so worth it. It's all dark meat."

"They're already vaping," Maude said.

"No vaping, young ladies!" he called after them. They put their e-cigarettes away, but he knew they'd come out as soon as he was gone. Had he and his delicate feelings gone too easy on Demmy, trying to curry favor to ease a stepmother into her life?

He bounded down the stairs after them and held out his palm.

"Dad!"

"I am so serious right now. You too, Jodee."

"But . . ."

"I'll return it when you leave, Jodee."

The two girls heaved heavy, heavy sighs, but turned over their vape pens.

Roger reentered the blissfully warm kitchen as Maude greeted Casey, who was headed upstairs. He drained as much as he could of the crackling layer of hot grease collected under the parallel birds and began filling the metal baster. He carefully squirted the incredibly hot liquid over the goose breasts and drumsticks.

A scream came from the backyard. Demmy! Roger dropped the baster in the pan and ran for the backyard, imagining criminals, freak accidents, exploding vape cartridges. He could not see Demmy through the backdoor window. The doorhandle mechanism caught on something. He smashed the doorknob open. The two girls were looking at a phone with a small Totoro figure dangling from it. Demmy's phone. There appeared to be no bleeding, severed limbs, toxic seizures.

Roger took a breath.

Demmy looked up. She thrust the phone at him.

The screen was open to a scholastic testing website. Demeter White. Her scores. They were excellent. Really excellent.

"You are way smarter than me," Roger said.

The girls hugged. "I am *so* not filling out the section on family members who went to Yale," Demmy said.

Although slightly hurt, Roger was also proud. "You're thinking of Yale?"

Demmy gave him a confused look. Perhaps she had not meant to show a desire to go to his alma mater in his presence. That was fine. He understood. She wanted to make her own way.

"Congratulations, honey," he said, relieved, and now wondering if he had dripped hot grease on the red tile floor.

The two girls were already turning back to the screen. Breaking her scores down. "I can't believe you did better on math," Jodee said.

"The essay score's not quite as strong." Demmy tucked a blond lock in her mouth.

"But top marks for analysis. And, hello, your writing score is nearly perfect."

"Could be better," Demmy said. "*Eigo datta mon ne.*" Whatever that meant. He knew that teenagers had their own language, but this was taking it too far.

They both laughed. "*Ne.*" Jodee stretched the vowel out, but good, as Roger left them to it.

CHAPTER 20

Casey found Kelly upstairs, alone in Casey and Roger's bedroom. Kelly brushed one hand slowly down the lush sea-green velvet drapes as she stared out the window. Her other arm was across her middle, as though hugging herself. Casey cleared her throat.

"It's gorgeous," Kelly said.

The leaves outside the second-floor windows were largely gone, providing a view down the length of the tree-lined street, littered with yellow and red. Park Slope eat your heart out. "Admiring the view?"

There were a range of replies that Casey would have expected, but "I wanted to see where you sleep," had not been one of them.

Was Kelly then drawn to her as well? Casey had made it to yoga twice weekly for the last two weeks, but had sensed from Kelly only hints of interest so slight Casey could not be sure they were even there. Casey was physically attracted to Kelly, but had felt more of a connection to the Tesla salesman, who'd taken her on a fun test drive. Still, that desire to touch Kelly remained strong. Would a touch be as charged as she expected? It was not the first time she'd been attracted to a woman, though she hadn't acted on it in years. Casey had no qualms about being attracted to Kelly—noticing attractive people was normal—but Kelly's pull had become alarmingly intense.

Casey stepped closer.

Kelly made eye contact, held it. She stretched out her hand. It was the promise of something. Casey took it.

The contact of skin was electric. Kelly pulled her in closer.

"I'm surprised . . ." Casey began, but Kelly leaned toward her. Their lips were so close now. Casey moved her hand to Kelly's bare arm, gliding over her skin. In her mind, she had already crossed that last inch, pressing Kelly's body to her own. She had imagined this. She felt flushed; her nipples were hardening.

Casey was fighting a desire to move toward Kelly and losing the battle. She licked her lips.

Kelly smirked.

Smirked? It was a full-blown smirk, worthy of the Hartley side gate. Now Casey felt out on a limb. She knew the desire for plausible deniability was common, but why did Kelly still want Casey off balance? She remembered that day she'd circled block after block fruitlessly while Kelly did her sun salutations. Casey was also reminded of her ex. He'd always held back on expressing his desires, even for simple things, so that Casey was put in the position of offering him options from which he could pick and choose. She had been so young, not thinking twice about expressing herself when she felt something nice about another person, so it had taken her a few years to realize what was happening.

She dropped Kelly's hand, stepped back and gave a deep

sigh. She was relieved to have noticed this dynamic so soon. She didn't trust Kelly, but she liked her. Kelly had been the sole mom at The Hartley to warm to her. Casey wanted to keep that going. She laughed.

"Look at us. Like we're in college or something. Hysterical!" Casey still felt attracted, but also dirty. Kelly's husband was downstairs, Kelly's children, her own children. Roger.

Kelly laughed too, but hollowly. Now it was Kelly who looked off balance.

"Remember LUGs? Lesbians until graduation? I kind of wanted to be one. It seemed fun." Casey was trying to sound nonchalant. She was anything but. She had fantasized about this but not expected to feel so much swirl through her physically. If Kelly made another move, Casey might not resist this time.

Kelly frowned, looking uncomfortable. Had Casey been too direct? Was the L word forbidden, even after Kelly's suggestive caress of the velvet drapes?

"Well . . ." Kelly began, but then nothing followed. Casey could feel it: Kelly would pause until the tension drove Casey to articulate what was going on.

No, Casey thought, I am not doing this. Casey did *not* want to start something more than friendship with Kelly. Or anyone, actually, apart from her husband, to whom she was genuinely attracted. No velvet would be tipped. She felt more thankful now for what she had in her increasingly dumpy, obliviously arrogant, too-fond-of-a-drink husband, who happened to also be funny, kind, and uncalculating. Obliviousness had as much of an upside as a downside.

She didn't share a shred of that inner dialog with Kelly, though. Casey was bi, big deal. This would be news to many, but it wasn't news to her. So she just said, "We're going to be great friends," meaning it, but also worried about how this would affect Abby's chances of getting into first-through-eighth.

Kelly, totally backfooted, now seemed to be looking at Casey with more appreciation, not less. "I . . ." she started.

Then they heard Demmy scream.

CHAPTER 21

Demmy did not understand what the fuss was about. First Dad, now Mom. Had they both forgotten she'd aced the practice test? OK, yes, she'd *screamed*, but did her mother have to clutch her so tightly? Still, the warmth felt good amidst the chilly air.

"Thanks, Mom," Demmy said.

Casey pulled back. "Mom?"

Demmy rolled her eyes. "Don't make a big deal of it," she said, despite knowing it was a big deal. "I've thought of you as 'Mom' for a while now."

Casey had her hand over her mouth. Oh no, her eyes were wet. Demmy did not want to dwell on this, especially with Kelly watching. The woman creeped her out. Casey was about to speak.

"Is our goose cooked?" Demmy asked. She had to get Casey, Jodee, and Kelly inside before slower members of the party came outside and made this into an even bigger deal. She ushered them inside and found her dad in the kitchen wiping up grease spattered over the brick-colored floor. He was now grumbling about no one having the sense to close the oven door as he reached for the meat thermometer and started stabbing.

"Our geese are cooked," he proclaimed.

"Ha," Demmy said.

He pulled the birds carefully from the oven and set them on the stove to rest.

Others sprang into action: Casey and Kelly pulled casseroles from the warming oven and set the dishes onto trivets on the sideboard, Abby sang more Lizzo, and Rich got in people's way as he served himself more glogg while his and Kelly's three children watched from the doorway like bored, abused waifs.

Settling down at the table seemed to take forever, with shouted commands but no commander, until Nana yelled for everyone to sit the fuck down.

"That's Nana," Demmy whispered to Jodee.

The taking of seats became a mini Rorschach of affinities: her parents sat side by side, Maude to her dad's right, Kelly to her mom's left. Abby and Jodee stuck close to Demmy, the other three children also fell in line, and, like driftwood on a far shore, Nana and Rich sat at the far end, somehow marooned in the outer reaches, despite being, in reality, no more separated from the others than any guest.

Food was passed and eaten; drinks were drunk.

Kelly pestered Demmy and Jodee with forgettable questions of the parental variety, while Roger did the same to Kelly and Rich's kids, dual interrogations incapable of sparking interest in any party. Demmy was irked by Kelly sitting so close to her mom. What *was* it with her? And with her dad and Maude? Equally annoying. Maude touched Roger's shoulder as she leaned for gravy, then his arm. Demmy realized how common that was. That and the kisses, the occasional shoulder rub. She dropped her fork. Like, literally. It clattered to the table.

People stared. Demmy grabbed it and continued eating.

Were Maude and her dad having an affair? Her dad laughed at something Maude said, relaxed and cheerful. Demmy also noticed that her mom and dad were sitting a bit farther apart than was normal, leaning away from each other. Were they not getting along? Was that why Kelly was coming over so often?

Oh. My. God. Her parents were both having affairs. Demmy motioned Jodee to follow her from the table.

"You're not leaving already, are you, Jodee?" Casey looked concerned. Guilty conscience for ignoring all her guests except Kelly?

Demmy shook her head, no. "Be right back." Demmy led a confused-looking Jodee up to her room and locked the door behind them.

"What is it? I'm still hungry," Jodee said.

"I think my Mom . . ." she didn't feel like going back to calling Casey her stepmother over this ". . . is having an affair with Kelly." She decided to not tell Jodee about her dad and Maude. Yet. "Let's go down there again. Watch them and give me your opinion."

"My lesbian opinion?" Jodee sounded miffed.

"Yes! I am invoking the best friend card. Thou shalt deploy thine gaydar to mine benefit."

"*Thy* gaydar." Jodee scoffingly muttered "seven-eighty in English" and followed Demmy back downstairs.

The whole room looked at them as they reentered, especially Rich, with that shaved head of his. Demmy could see from his scalp shadow that he actually would have a decent head of hair if he let it grow, just with a receding hairline. What was up with that? Hiding gray? He could just dye it, if he cared that much. He was maybe five years past the upper age for a hipster.

"Everything's fine!" Demmy sang. "Ready for dessert?" She began clearing plates from the table.

"Sit back down," Nana said. "I am nowhere near done and neither is anyone else." She served herself more goose.

Her dad, who had passed Demmy his mostly empty plate, took it back and served himself more sweet potatoes. He loosened his belt to make room for them. Demmy sat, huffing. Fine.

"It *is* about time to put the pies in the oven," Casey said, getting up.

"What's the rush, Casey? It's Thanksgiving. Sit down and tell us how your business is going," Nana said.

"Seriously? My business?"

"Yes," Nana said. "One entrepreneur to another."

Casey looked around the room at the state of everyone's plates, appraisingly, and sat down. "Honestly, not great," Casey said. "Prices are falling relentlessly. The state of New York is forcing me to switch to an LLC, or maybe a C corporation, which will cost either way, so I have to go to Delaware. And automation and foreign competition are going to put me out of a job, anyway, so I need a new business model if I don't want to take a full-time in-house position somewhere."

"What?" Abby, of all people, piped up, surprising Demmy.

Roger turned toward her. "Is it that bad?"

"I talk about this all the time," Casey said in a wounded tone.

"Sorry I asked," Nana said. The room in general looked uncomfortable with this news, Demmy thought, as though her mom had taken a dump on the dining room table. Nana was most likely worried about being hit up for cash, but Demmy found the whole thing more interesting than the usual art talk. A new business model to compete with automation? It sounded risky, and risky was exciting. She felt admiration for Casey. The whole question of how people found jobs fascinated her. It wasn't by studying ballet for two years.

"Those pies will take a while to warm," Casey said. This time Nana did not stop her. Kelly trundled after Casey.

Demmy nudged Jodee and motioned in their direction with their head.

Jodee shrugged, noncommittally.

Oh, come *on*. Jodee couldn't get a sapphic read from that? Seriously?

"I want a DNA test!" Abby announced, in a tone that suggested this was news to everyone. Please don't start singing Lizzo, Demmy thought. Although if you do, at least sing "bitch." It's about damn time.

"For God's sake, Roger, get the child her test already," Nana said.

Demmy got out her phone, brought up a DNA testing website, and filled out the information. "Credit card," she said, holding her open palm toward her dad. He handed the card over. Demmy entered the numbers and handed the card back.

"I got you one too, Dad," she said.

Abby squealed in delight. "Bitch!"

CHAPTER 22

R oger settled under the covers, enjoying his sleepiness. Casey was in the bathroom getting ready for bed. Downstairs, the dishwasher was churning, the big pans were drying on the rack by the sink, and the dining table was clean. He'd tackled the splattered goose grease from the kitchen tile again, with detergent, but it would stain permanently. He was grateful Abby hadn't wandered into the grease or the oven door while he was outside. That was one of the toughest things about being a parent: the need to keep part of his mind on one child while the other was in crisis. He'd fucked that up before, neglecting Demmy, just as he'd been neglected when his parents divorced, a shitty legacy.

He heard the bathroom tap running. Casey had left the bathroom door open. The bathroom sconces provided the only light in the bedroom other than Casey's tiny bedside light. Roger snuggled into the flannel sheets, enjoying the chill of the room on his face. Their bedroom was cool in winter, courtesy of single-pane streetside windows and a resolve to keep their fossil fuel consumption down.

Roger wasn't too taken with Casey's new friends. Rich had

been useless and bored, Kelly preening and self-satisfied, at least until something threw her off her game half-way through the evening. He supposed he should have kept Rich more entertained. He used to do that with colleagues but had fallen out of the habit. He might have enjoyed entertaining Rich, actually, but hadn't had the time. Somehow, he'd managed to make his one chore—cooking the geese—occupy more time and space and dishes and mess than all the myriad things Casey had done to make the party a success.

Now Roger felt warm and comfortable. He not only had his family and this house, he also had Maude's friendship and his mother—a challenge, but someone who added a lot to his life, both good and bad.

He remembered the fall he'd met Maude. He'd been twenty-two, was it? He'd been thinking about those days a lot lately, probably because of new Niamh, but had only remembered tonight how his growing infatuation with his mother's protégée Maude had erased the infatuation with previous Niamh that he'd brought back, like a deer tick, on his chastened return from England.

He'd met previous Niamh a few months into his Fulbright year at Oxbridge. Previous Niamh had had straight, jet-black hair and blue eyes, a combo Roger had found exotic. He still cringed with the memory of how they'd parted. He'd been so enraptured, first seeing her at the café where she'd been a server, then working up the nerve to talk to her, then going out, spending all their time together. It had been a summer idyll that lasted nine months, beginning in the dark of winter and self-immolating at the ass-end of summer, when days were long and the weather mild, despite another chilling autumn (British people didn't know what "fall" was) on its way. He remembered reading poetry to her on riverbanks, watching the boaters. Had tea been sipped and scones

slathered in Devon cream? They had. God, he'd been ignorant, thinking himself so cultured, and not like a dairy product, either. And to have it all culminate in a humiliating,
pitched, screaming argument on a flower-bedecked cobble-
stone street the week before he'd returned home. Gorgeous.
Brilliant. Fecking grand.

The bathroom door opened wider, lighting the bedroom
before Casey switched it off, clearly intending to tiptoe across
the dimly lit room.

"I'm still awake," Roger told her. He switched on his
bedside light. There was no need for her to stub a toe or trip
on a rug.

"Me, too," she said.

They both laughed. She slipped under the covers and
spooned her back into him.

CHAPTER 23

Casey wriggled against Roger, feeling the fur of his teddy-bear chest against her back. She would have been amenable to sex—Kelly had gotten her revved up—but soon heard gentle snores.

She was tired but couldn't sleep. She paid attention to her breathing in an attempt to clear her mind. Her mind did clear, but she was still awake.

The day's events played back in her mind. The events she would have expected to stand out—Kelly's face so close to hers, the SAT scores, the new children and husband to meet, the now-indelible grease stains on her beloved Saltillo tiles, hand-carried from Mexico with their animal paw prints—did not seem to have any more significance than making sure the pies and desserts had been the right temperature, that everyone found their coats when leaving. The one thing still tugging at her was that scream.

It had stabbed her like a knife, a girl's scream, like she'd heard it before, back in Memphis. But of course, she hadn't. There had been no scream then, only absence, cruelty, mystery.

She blamed herself, of course she did. She'd had no inkling of what was about to happen when she unthinkingly swallowed the headache pill Execrable offered and drank the glass of wine he'd handed her. Hours later, she'd opened her eyes, confused and alone. She'd struggled to wake. She'd searched the house and found no one. She'd been unaccountably groggy; the police could not even understand her slurred words the first time she called them. She searched again and found a vial of sedatives. She called the police a second time. They were skeptical but the next day they were calling her. Their pickup was in the river? It made no sense. Yes, she acknowledged, she and Execrable had been fighting in the months leading up to that day, but he hadn't seemed as devious or stupid as the police alternately intimated he was. How had she missed it? The events had left her feeling she had no ability to judge character. They had left her afraid of everyone, everything. To know that your life could be so swiftly torn apart, that your husband was a stranger, that your child was not safe.

She'd put it all behind her, as much as she could. She'd left town, after the weeks of vigils turned into months, half a year, a year, after her mama had returned home from Memphis to Missouri, after Casey could no longer stand to have people ask her how she was holding up. She wasn't holding up. She was imploding, a blob, no longer a person. She ceased to exist. She wandered around Memphis like a ghost from a fable, unable to remember who she was. They had expected her to stay in that shitty dump of a cottage forever, waiting for her baby to return, even as the police, the coroner, told her that she never would.

She made the choice to believe them. In the face of not knowing anything, she had to believe something. She chose not to construct a fantasy of hope but to believe the people who knew the most: the police who'd seen such situations, the coroner who knew what a body could survive in the Mississippi in January, the engineers who told her about currents, water speeds, human buoyancy within a flow.

She'd headed on the flimsiest of pretexts to UDLAP in Cholula, Mexico, where she knew no one. Five years there had given her a new language, two degrees, and a new direction, but those years hadn't made her a different person. She had needed to be a different person. So she tried the big city. Memphis had been plenty big-city, given her childhood in the Ozarks; so had Cholula. But New York had snow. She hoped for a completely different sort of anonymity, in which no one extended condolences.

And they didn't. They hadn't. When she'd drift off into space, staring at her Starbucks coffee as she grew later and later for her latest Midtown temp job, no one had asked, Are you all right? Naw, she was just another person going about a life, with worries, sure, but who didn't have worries? She wasn't bleeding. She wasn't shitting herself. She paid for her coffee—dark, no sugar, seriously, put the spoon down, NO SUGAR. No one offered politeness, and she rewarded them by not curling up into a screaming helpless ball.

Gradually, life returned. Not to normal, but to normal enough. She began to enjoy things. She began to blend in. She learned the lingo, the references, the complex parking holidays. (Rosh Hashanah, OK, but Purim? Really?) She changed her name. She moved a few times. She got help, therapy. She lost her old self, gained a new self. She reentered the world, stopped being late to work, dated, met Roger, conceived a child. She learned how to let that child grow up, normal, demanding Lizzo and pancakes, not burdened by the paranoia running deep within Casey that was not paranoia at all. Casey allowed this not-paranoia out to play only at night, when she alone in the house was awake, and only enough so that by morning she had put it away where it would hurt no one, least of all herself.

CHAPTER 24

Joshua shook his head angrily. "Yussef! Yussef is the one who shoots her."

"That's what I meant," Roger said. "You know that." Roger had indeed mixed up the two boy's names in the movie, despite rewatching *Babel* at home and hammering the three Arab names into his head—Yussef, Ahmed, and the father, Abdullah—so that he would *not* mix them up. And yet he had. Again.

He hit the remote button to send the screen sliding back up into the ceiling.

"Racist," he heard someone mutter, someone not Joshua, Niamh, or the skinny guy, who had become the only ones whose opinions, against his better judgment, he cared about.

"I'm not saying they are interchangeable. Obviously, Yussef is the one carrying the guilt, not just for shooting Susan but for Ahmed's death." He noticed a look from the skinny guy that Roger couldn't read. Roger would have expected him to be all over this, but the skinny guy said nothing. Did he not trust Roger enough after thirteen weeks of class to allow for an occasional honest mistake?

"We don't know Ahmed dies," Niamh said, crisply, acidly.

"Just like Yussef doesn't know that Susan *doesn't* die. Which is the point I am trying to make, as it relates to all our other films: the fractured narrative builds tension by withholding information from the characters and the audience in differing levels. When we don't know whether Susan has survived, that's one kind of tension. When Ahmed doesn't know that she's alive . . ."

"Yussef!" Joshua yelled, actually yelled.

This was getting out of control. But fuck! He'd done it again. Could he switch his point, cover his ass, make himself seem somewhat intelligent? After all, Ahmed doesn't know Susan is alive either. "When *Ahmed* doesn't know that she's alive, it doesn't matter, because the motivating factor is guilt, which is why the camera work stays close to Yussef. POV is established through close-up, highlighting the guilt that threads through each piece of the film."

Joshua frowned. "I'd say instead that the Richard-Susan story"—they'd collectively decided the rich-straight-white-couple narrative in multiple locales was a story on equal footing with the location-centered stories—"is characterized by a *lack* of guilt." Joshua looked smug, like he'd skewered Roger again.

"Which is my point: the centrality of guilt to all four narratives. When we see an utter lack of guilt on Richard's part for what he asks of Amelia—to take care of his children when she needs to take care of her own children—his refusal to treat her needs as being as important as his own, it is the guilt that we *long* for him to evidence that foregrounds the issues of race, gender, and class."

Roger stopped. Had he buzzworded currently enough to shut them up for a minute? They were quiet. Had he confused them enough to not get himself reported for racism? And *was* he guilty of racism for so thoroughly conflating two sort of brown boys? Probably. Fuck. He looked at the clock. They still had five minutes, maybe six. He could not bloviate that long, not on this topic. "Give me two pages next class on issues of racism and classicism, I mean classism, in *Babel* and *Kanchenjungha*, compared."

The class groaned. Extra assignments were never appreciated. It was his opening. "In exchange, you can go five minutes early." They laughed, and began packing up to leave. Now they were focused on him being an asshole, not a racist. Roger had wriggled out of it.

Or had he? The skinny guy appeared not to be leaving. He was saving whatever he had to say to deliver face to face. Shit. He was angry. Roger felt sad. And now his curly-haired kids were approaching him at the front of the lecture hall. Oh, joy. He imagined Joshua punching him to the floor, Niamh pissing on his face.

"Yes?" Roger chirped in their direction.

"What you said just now about withholding information," Niamh said. "I am writing a statement of purpose for a grant application, and I was focusing on when withholding is manipulative. You know, when it is organic as opposed to when it creates tension only because the audience expects a certain resolution?"

"Go on," Roger said.

Joshua slid a sheet of paper across the table toward him. It was a Fulbright application. Did they want a recommendation? After today's class? They had yelled at him.

"We both want to apply to be Geographic Digital Storytelling fellows."

"You mean the Fulbright–National Geographic Digital Storytelling Fellowships?"

They nodded.

"The deadline passed last month."

"For next year. We both want to apply for your spring semester screenwriting workshop."

So, not piss on his face, then. Was he flattered or scared? Or maybe *they* were scared; his workshop was pretty well thought of, and there were only twelve spots.

"We saw in your bio you did a Fulbright studying criticism in film at Oxbridge and thought you could take a look at our personal statements and our statements of grant purpose."

They both were smiling eagerly, curls bouncing with the energy of their bright futures.

"You are nearly a year ahead of time," he said.

"It's super competitive," Niamh said.

That meant they'd be revising and revising. So many drafts, he'd have to read. Neither, unfortunately, was a slacker.

And yet he couldn't afford to alienate them. Those two-page essays on racism would be coming back, and he'd need someone in his corner in case complaints were filed against him, preferably someone of color. These two were pretty damn white, but Joshua had a good set of lungs in him, if nothing else. "Uh, sure." Maybe they'd even win fellowships, boosting Roger's cred in the department. He could stand to rev up his profile; he hadn't so much as been to a conference in years.

"It's National Geographic, by the way," Roger said.

Niamh nodded. "The Geographic Digital Storytelling Fellowships."

"What I am trying to say is the word 'geographic' is there because one of the sponsors is National Geographic. The storytelling doesn't have to be geographic. Not like *Babel*."

She looked at him "But it's in the name of it."

Had she not heard of National Geographic? "It's an organization, the National Geographic Society. Like the Fulbright

Program." He picked up the application components sheet. "So this is a 'digital storytelling fellowship'"—he made quotation mark signs with his fingers—"that has two sponsors."

"That's the one! Geographic storytelling!"

Did she really not understand? My god, was she, in fact, a moron? Her written assignments had glimmers of promise but hadn't been anything to get excited about. Maybe the subtle way she looked down on him had misled him into thinking she was smart. He chided himself: remember how ignorant *you* were at that age. He glanced at her personal statement, tucked under the list of application components. Already it looked dreadful. It would be simplest to rewrite it. Then again, would his rewrite be that much better? He wanted the two to go away. Could he give them As and expel them? He'd rather be sketching out the new screenplay taking lumpen shape in his notebook.

He looked around for the skinny kid. He'd left without talking to Roger. Roger was disappointed. Was the look he'd flashed Roger something personal? Hurt, swiftly disguised? Might he be Arab? His name was Sam, so no help there. He could ask Sam where he was from, ha. Roger knew he was not supposed to have favorites, but realized Sam was his favorite. Roger would encourage him to apply for the fellowship. You get a fellowship, and you get a fellowship, and you get a fellowship.

Then karma would bring him one of his own. MacArthur, take me away!

CHAPTER 25

S herbeam passed the sheaf of notes she'd received from her collectors to Maude as they sat in Sherbeam's Morningside Heights coop. Sunlight streamed in through the tall wall of divided-light windows behind her. "Am I reading too much into this?"

Maude read the notes, one after the other. Each was accompanied by a signed agreement, on creamy 24-pound bond, bearing Pau's gallery's letterhead. She stirred oat milk into her coffee, recently poured from Sherbeam's avant-garde steel coffee pot into matching cups. The bundle was thicker than Maude would have expected so soon.

"They sound very willing to lend the works for the retrospective. What's the problem?"

"They are responding to the requests practically by return mail. We haven't even sent follow-up emails. It's like they want the paintings out of their hands."

"Sherbeam, it's quite a feather in a collector's cap to have a painting *that they own* included in a retrospective. Just being in a catalog increases the value."

Sherbeam flapped her hands angrily. "Yes, yes. But it's the

haste, the tone. They sound . . . *surprised!*" Sherbeam shuddered. "No one has asked about insurance, or shipping, or how long the paintings will be needed. Not one has asked about new work. Has my star dimmed *that* much?"

Maude understood about dimming stars. It still rankled that she'd gotten her audience with Elżbieta—drinks in the lobby of The Leary—and even gotten Roger's commitment to come without divulging the surprise to Roger. But then he'd stood them up. Maude sipped her coffee, already tepid. The factory-style, single-paned windows let in plenty of the mid-December cold. Their metal joints, white paint flaking, only expedited the seepage. "Do you have a throw or wrap or something?"

Sherbeam tossed her head, harrumphed, but got up. She returned from the other room with a quilted fleece thingie. Gray. She handed it to Maude. "Say something."

Maude winced at Sherbeam's tone but snuggled into the delightful warmth of the fleece. "You have a point, but it's nothing to worry about. This is exactly *why* you're having a retrospective. To get your name out there. Careers don't just happen."

"Yours being a case in point."

"Don't be mean."

"I'm not. It's just that you never cared."

"Of course I cared!"

"Not enough to make it your first priority! You don't even have a social media boy. Tell me I'm wrong."

Sherbeam wasn't wrong. Maude's family had been her top priority. She had put a respectable amount of effort into producing, promoting, showing up, but in the arts, respectable didn't cut it. You had to be psychopathic, sociopathic, telepathic. Or was that sentiment just disguised bitterness? "The coffee's gone cold."

"That's what microwaves are for. But decant it into a ceramic cup, first." Sherbeam finished her own cup of coffee and tilted the cup in her hand, examining the way the light bounced off its angular lines. "You wouldn't believe what these cost."

Wouldn't care, was more accurate. Maude was feeling maudlin. Even without Roger, she had spent a very enjoyable evening with Elż. But when she'd shown Elż her latest pieces, Elż's attention had visibly wandered. Elż had been a fan back in the day, but now Maude's work was no longer worthy of consideration. So that was the end of that.

Maude poured her coffee into a glass beaker, added a splash more, and put it in the microwave to heat. The machine whirred as the cup rotated behind the obscuring, protective glass. "How's your new work coming, then?"

Sherbeam shrugged. "So far so good. I'm putting in time, and liking the results. An idea of Casey's inspired me, actually. I'm just worried that Pau is going to slap bargain-basement prices on everything. He's demanding that I get a high-profile interview, preferably the *Times*, before he will agree to move up the show. Social media boy's already put together a launch that will top any *Times* article. Who even remembers newspapers exist? They're just headlines on a phone now, larded with a few vapid Twitter comments to give them enough length to hold an ad or two. Pau's never put conditions on me before, but apparently the time's booked and I have to make it worth his while to bump the other artists. Hurt feelings and such. Can you believe it? *I* have to make it worth *his* while!"

The microwave dinged. Maude returned the coffee to the expensive steel cup and took a sip. It was fine, but coffee was never the same reheated. Some part of it seemed to die.

"And look at these addresses. Not a one in Manhattan. Minnesota, Montana? Mississippi, for Christ's sake. Missisfucking-sippi! Did buying my paintings doom all my collectors to live in Outer Bumfuck? She tossed another one at Maude. "Wyoming!"

Maude looked at the envelope. It was from Jackson. She said that.

"And what's so special about Jackson?"

"You've heard of Jackson Hole? Jackson is the same thing. Lousy with money. Imagine skiers in shearling. And don't they have an art thing, too? Or was it film?"

"Honey, whatever it is, it's not Tribeca."

CHAPTER 26

Demmy's school was one of *those* schools, the kind that posted the scores of high-performing students on the bulletin board, and damn if they hadn't already been notified of hers and added them to those of the other five kids who'd logged an eight hundred (or in one case, Alix Sima, OFC, two eight hundreds).

Demmy stood standing in the hall, looking at the demure rectangle of white paper tacked to the announcements board, locked under glass. Lainie and Jodee were approaching. It was embarrassing. Neither Jodee nor Lainie had made the cut, though both had done well.

"An eight hundred in math! Slay! You realize that you are the second-highest scoring student in the school at this point, don't you?" Lainie said. "*Yatta yo!*" You did it.

"Ugh, don't remind me."

"Let's go celebrate, *o-iwai dokoka*, somewhere off-campus!" Lainie was always so generous.

"I feel self-conscious," Demmy said.

"Demmy, girl, you have never been shy."

Lainie was right. And it was also true that Alix's numbers

had been up for a while, so Demmy had known right away that she'd be second highest as soon as she'd seen the numbers. But now all the other students knew her score and would cheer when they beat it; she'd be a powerless spectator. There was a bit of ick to it.

"OK, fine, but I have something more important to talk to you about," Demmy said. Two things, actually. "Can we meet in No Woman's Land, after Delany-sensei's class?" They'd stopped referring to him as Martin at some point. He'd won that power struggle without even knowing about it.

Jodee nodded, but Lainie shrugged. "If you don't mind waiting fifteen minutes," she said. "I have something."

"Come on. *Kite yo.* It's important."

Lainie didn't say yes.

Demmy frowned. "It was your idea to go off campus *na no ni!* "

"*Dakara* I was going to meet you there, was the idea."

"Don't make her invoke the best-friend card," Jodee said.

"OK, OK," Lane said, looking irritated. "But five minutes late is the best I can manage."

"*Angatou,*" Demmy said. Thanks.

AND LAINIE WOULD HAVE ARRIVED five minutes after them, except that Demmy and Jodee, noticing Lainie not leaving after Delaney-sensei dismissed them, also hung back. They hovered outside the classroom door, watching through its eye-level portal, whose glass was wire reinforced, as though the administration expected someone to break in or out of *Intro to Kanbun.*

"She's talking to Delaney-sensei!"

"Her thing is with him? Can you hear anything?"

Jodee shook her head. Lainie had stepped closer to Delaney-sensei. She nodded.

"Crack the door open, quietly."

"They'll notice!"

Delaney-sensei was talking to her now, at greater length. He pushed a dark brown lock of hair back behind his ear.

Lainie was nodding now. What could be going on between them? If Lainie was genuinely hot for teacher, the two of them wouldn't be talking in the classroom like this. Neither had touched the other.

"Come on, Demmy. Let's give her space."

Demmy nodded. They went to their lockers. The things that were staying and the things that were going traded places in their backpacks.

"This better be good," Lainie said when she joined them breathless in No Woman's Land.

"My parents are both having affairs."

Jodee turned toward Demmy, shocked. "Both?"

"You have to be mistaken," Lainie said.

"She's not," Jodee said. "There is definitely some kind of drama going on between her mom and this woman . . ."

"Kelly."

"Woman?"

Jodee and Demmy nodded.

They all let that settle in for a moment.

"You're sure?"

Demmy shrugged. "Not a hundred percent, but something has been going on for a while, and the body language is off the charts." Demmy thought back to Lainie stepping toward Delaney-sensei. The way her mom and Kelly were around each other was *way* more intense, like they were feeding off each other's body heat.

"*Mita yo*. And there was definitely something to see. Although I have shitty gaydar," Jodee added.

"Is that a thing? Shitty gaydar?"

"I have, like, none. I keep waiting for it to kick in but . . ."

"Can we get back on topic?"

"*Gomen*."

"Sorry."

"So, your dad?"

"Yeah. Him and this woman Maude, who he's known for years. I'm not as sure about that, but they're a little *too* relaxed around each other. They touch *way* more than they should, especially her, which makes him seem like he feels guilty or something."

"That's terrible," Lainie said. "What are you going to do?"

"*Dakara* I'm asking your opinion, *ja nai*? I don't know what to do!"

"The smart thing is to do nothing," Jodee said.

"Why is that smart? It's my family! What if things haven't gone too far and now is my only chance to nip it in the bud? Or what if they secretly hate each other and are only staying together for my sake?"

"And Abby's."

Demmy glared at Jodee. The implicit accusation of narcissism felt unfair. Demmy was probably more worried for Abby than herself. Losing a parent at a young age was no picnic. "*Konchikusho!*" This couldn't be happening. Gain a mom, just to lose her? It was too painful to even tell Jodee and Lainie about.

Again, silence set it. Demmy hadn't expected Lainie and Jodee to have the perfect advice. But it did feel good to tell them, to have them listen, to not be alone with this.

"So, what's up with you and Delaney?" Demmy dropped the *sensei*.

"Yeah, *kakushiteru kakko mita yo.* You were keeping it secret. That window is small but not *that* small."

"It's nothing," Lainie said, but clearly she was embarrassed.

"Then why not tell us?"

"Because I knew it would be like this. He's arranging tutoring for me, OK?"

"In what?"

"In Japanese, OK? It's not as easy for me as for you two. You're a brain and you're a brain *and* a heritage speaker. Don't you know how hard it is to keep up? Half the class is heritage speakers. They'll snag all the fives on the AP test. I'll be lucky to get a three." Lainie's voice trailed off.

Demmy had had no idea Lainie worried. She thought Lainie's Japanese was pretty damn awesome. Her accent was better than Demmy's. But maybe tests were different. "Sorry," she mumbled. Jodee mumbled something similar.

"So is ice cream too boring a way to celebrate?" Lainie said.

Celebrate what? Demmy thought, but then remembered her scores posted on the board, that compulsory academic strip tease. "*Tondemonai,*" Demmy said. Not at all too boring. Ice cream sounded like a great idea, a throwback to younger, easier times, something they could all use a little of. Only . . . shit. How could Demmy have forgotten? "*Warui kedo sa. Ore,* I have my literacy tutoring today so we could only be there like fifteen minutes. I'm so sorry. Raincheck?"

Lainie nodded, but seemed raw, as though she'd revealed too much. Demmy wanted to explain why she'd forgotten, but all her rationalizations only revealed that Demmy in fact had *not* given Lainie's invitation the respect it deserved: Mark had asked Demmy to cover for him, Demmy was excited about Mark trusting her, she was too amped up over the posting of her scores. Me, me, me.

So Demmy hugged her. "*Ashita ne.* We are seriously going tomorrow." She nodded at Jodee. "*Ne?*"

"*Hai!*" Jodee shot back, emphatic. Whatever else happened, they were a unit. They had each other's backs. They had each other, and it wasn't just teenaged bullshit. It was forever.

CHAPTER 27

Casey sat in the Planetkiller trying not to watch for Abby with her usual psychotic vigilance as she typed a LinkedIn post into her laptop. Frannie and Kelly chatted at the gate with Paula, no doubt about the places they had already secured at The Hartley for their collective brood. How did Paula get away with her name? Frannie, Kelly, Casey. Demmy, Jodee, Lainie. What was this tyranny of sound? Casey resolved to start calling her younger daughter "Abigail." She'd tell Roger to call her "Case." She looked down at her screen. She'd tweeted today, but hadn't yet retweeted. She was becoming one of those annoying self-promoters whom others instinctively tune out. Early on, she'd received nibbles from colleagues at the NYC Translators Association about working together as a collective, but as her posts swelled in number and frenzied cheer, no other nibbles had followed.

She looked up from her screen. Abby—Abigail—was coming out of the building. How had Casey—Case—known to look up just then? That subconscious focus, like a heron tracking prey, would likely never shut off where her children were concerned. She unlocked the doors and got out to help Abby—Abigail—get situated, but by the time Casey got to the booster seat, Abby—dang, Abigail—had already strapped herself in.

"You are getting really good at things, Abigail."

"My teacher calls me Abigail."

"Do you not like it?"

She shook her head. "When kids call me Abigail, they are making fun of me." She looked near tears.

"You want me to call you Abby?"

Abby nodded.

"OK, Abby."

Her daughter's face brightened. Abby hit a few buttons and Lizzo began working her boas and telling the camera how good she was feeling.

CASEY TRIED to get in a little work while they waited at home for Abby's friend Edgar to be dropped off for a play date. The house was quiet, Abby in the kitchen with Constanza and a snack.

Casey's new post on LinkedIn had received just one like. Not good. She looked through her LinkedIn job suggestions, most of them radically inappropriate, but titillating in their way. Oh, the things LinkedIn thought her capable of. She should think of herself the same way. One looked for a PM— project manager. No reason she couldn't take a course and become the certified PM for this new collective she envisioned.

The original idea had been that having Constanza in the afternoons would free Casey up for work, but that had only made sense if Casey earned more than Constanza cost. At first she had, even earning enough for the Cayenne payments. But these last two years, job after job had gone to cheaper competitors who (industry rumor had it) unethically ran customer documents through online machine translators (powered by translations harvested without permission from people like Casey) and cleaned up the results for a pittance. This year, her clients were buying each other, becoming larger, diminishing her negotiating power and wiping out her connections as the acquiring companies laid off or reassigned personnel. Now what Casey made covered only what she paid Constanza. Plus a skinny latte.

That's where the collective came in. She could incorporate in Delaware, do that PM course, and take a cut for managing projects. That would cover the Cayenne payments, reducing her guilt at her dependence on Roger. Once Abby hit first grade, Casey could drop Abby off at school, go to a cheap rented office nearby and put in a solid six hours. Their living room would be roomy without her desk in it; she imagined how nice it would be not having to stash her work materials away every evening.

The doorbell rang.

It was Edgar and his nanny Stéphanie, a Haitian woman who spoke to Edgar exclusively in standard French. The futility of this had never been clearer to Casey. Teach Edgar the less global investor–seducing Haitian Kreyól, Casey warned Stéphanie, because every aspect of Parisian French was going to be handled by AI before the end of the decade, so what was the fucking point?

Casey packed up her laptop as Stéphanie hurried down the steps with a backward glance of concern. Whatever. Casey was just being honest. #Truthhurts. She skipped with the kids down the street to the park.

The park was chock-a-block with kids and nannies sitting or playing around a central fountain. In her pre-Abby days,

Casey had envied the groups of chatting nannies their
freedom to sit and socialize. She now knew they were a flock,
keeping their collective eyes out for perils and guarding the
children, all of whose names all of them knew.

Casey waved but sat apart from them so she could check in
with her online groups while her laptop still had charge. Her
psychotic vigilance now became a hypervigilant watchdog
that enabled her to monitor the two five-year-olds *and* work.
Paranoia was a job skill.

She searched Craigslist for cheap offices. There were none.
She posted a few answers to linguist questions on the query
board where her peers turned for help, zapping that particular
online presence with enough electricity to jiggle it like a worm
on a hook. Or was the electricity zapping her? Casey was tired.
Not just today-tired, long-term-tired.

She looked up. The nannies were watching her. She waved
again and closed her laptop. They waved back. One
approached. Mirlande, was her name, Casey remembered.
She made small talk with her. Mirlande had an accent similar
to Stéphanie's. They laughed and smiled. Then Mirlande
came the point: she could swing by Casey's house and bring
Abby and Edgar to the park, for a price, if Casey was interested. Casey was. That would give her time to take on enough
piecework to cover the car payments while Constanza cooked
dinner. Casey asked how much, calculated the total, and
weighed that against what five afternoons would bring in.

Casey felt her mouth hang open. Mirlande looked at her,
alarmed, but could not be as alarmed as Casey herself: the
value of watching Abby in the afternoon was more than a
Cayenne payment per month. All this flailing about had no
payoff whatsoever. The reality? She couldn't afford an office
and she needed Constanza for half a day at most. But
Constanza couldn't get by on only half a day's work, and if

they lost her, they'd never get her back. Unless Casey could change something, the only point to her business was to assuage her own paranoia. Something had to change, and Casey had only the ten Cayenne payments until first grade started to figure it all out.

CHAPTER 28

Roger texted Maude and prevailed on her to dump Sherbeam and meet him for serious day-drinking at the staid hotel bar with the Rockwell Hart Bentons. He wanted to know why she was mad at him.

Maude arrived looking wet. It was spitting rain outside, she said, taking off her scarf and 'tuque,' as she insisted on calling her knit cap. "Thanks for rescuing me. Your mother is hatching a nefarious scheme, and I am certain to be assigned the part that's actually illegal."

"Which you will refuse." He cleared his jacket off the bar chair he'd saved for her.

"Which I will *accept*. Have you learned nothing about me?" She raised her finger for the bartender. She looked Maude's way. Maude gestured at herself and Roger. The bartender nodded.

"It won't involve violence, will it?"

"I don't think either of us is bent that way."

"You mean 'inclined.'"

"P'raps. Still feeling like a fraud? Is that why you called?"

"No. I may be one, and others might not, but I'm the one in charge, so onward I go."

Maude nodded. "You've delivered, year in, year out." Two Negronis arrived. "Others with more talent—I know, I know, we're never supposed to say anyone has more talent—might have earned it, but then gotten into opioids and heroin and died in the gutter with a needle in their arm."

Roger nodded gravely. That exact thing had happened to one of his Yale dormmates a couple of years out from graduation. It had shocked and saddened Roger deeply. He'd cried. He'd looked up to the guy. Maude was giving him a puzzled look, her index finger twirling her cardboard coaster, spotted with icy droplets, atop the gleaming mahogany bar as she sucked her Negroni. Perhaps she didn't realize she wasn't exaggerating. She was probably imagining not publishing enough and being denied tenure rather than sudden death. Or maybe sleeping with a student and being denied tenure. Or being a lecturer so goddamned lousy you were denied tenure. None of which was statistically as likely as being driven to the brink in grad school by a PhD advisor and then, once you landed a poverty-wage adjunct position, getting a vindictive ass-kick from an insecure departmental chair that vaulted you over said brink, causing you to check yourself into a loony bin and *then* being denied tenure.

"Do you know one thing I've never done and would like to do?"

"What is that, Roger?"

"Make a film." The inkling of a new film sparked by his conversation with his dad was coalescing into an actual narrative.

"You made a film."

"No, I've had a screenplay produced. I want to . . . direct." Roger made a grand gesture on the word *direct*.

Maude chuckled. "Someone else's screenplay?"

Roger injected a burst of laughter. "I can't afford that. It would be like adopting when you're fertile enough to make your own kid. No, I'd write it. But I'd also direct. Me. Direct. Myself."

"Finally. So now are you ever going to ask me why I'm mad at you?"

"It's keeping me up nights!"

"Elżbieta was in town for a TED talk. I set up a meeting for us. And you didn't show!"

"Oh my God." He would love to see Elż. "Is she still in town?"

"Back to Wrocław."

"Fuck." He sipped his drink. "How did she look? How did she seem? How is she? God, I'd love to see her."

"Twenty years older, but good. I mean *really*. Still working with Bill on occasion."

"So *that* was what you were working on?"

Maude gave an affirmative shrug. "It was supposed to be a surprise."

"Did you tell them I want to direct? Crazy, huh?" Roger made a hand gesture of a plane going down and an explosion noise.

"Roger, I didn't know till literally five minutes ago. But don't expect *me* to discourage you. I don't see any reason for you not to do that."

"Not even if it's lousy and I am ridiculed? A lot would be expected of me. I teach people how to write screenplays."

"Let me enlighten you on a secret: each year that passes, such mockery becomes less likely. From my perspective, you're still young, but for most of those people who would, as you say, ridicule you, you are looking old. If you produce something tremendous, they will be shocked. If you flop, sadly, they won't notice. They won't even have the decency to feel schadenfreude."

"Well, you're a bundle of cheer, aren't you?"

"That *is* cheerful! Think about it. You can make a film, if you want. And you can *not* make a film, if you want that. Isn't that a good thing? I'm painting like a demon these days. People are buying my work. Not for your mother's six figures, but they're happy, I'm happy. Maybe they buy a piece because alizarin crimson looks good over the couch, but what do I care? I think it's, as the kids say, awesome."

"The kids don't say *awesome* anymore."

"What do they say?"

"It was *lit* for a while, but I think that's over. There's no point in trying to keep up. The kids want us not to keep up. That's the point."

"Now who's the bundle of cheer?"

"My students yell at me, then want me to write them recommendations. And I write those recommendations for those screaming students because I need them as much as they need me. What I'd really like to write is *Don't admit this one—he spends too much on hair product.*"

She raised her Negroni to toast the idea. He clinked glasses with her, delicately, not sloshing. "That does sound like fun," she said, "but don't."

"Fine," he said. "I'll rip it up."

CHAPTER 29

Asking Lainie for a "raincheck" on the ice cream had summoned angry rain gods, Demmy thought, because she had to run from the station and negotiate the slick library steps through a fierce, sleety downpour.

The hour for the lesson came and Marie did not show up. Had Mark told her Demmy was stepping in for him today? Demmy had felt honored—Mark must think she was doing well—but Marie, perhaps, had felt differently. Demmy wasn't sure she would like being tutored by someone thirty years her junior, which yes, would be someone negative thirteen.

But then Marie came through the door. "Hello, Demmy." Marie did not sound disappointed. She removed her clear plastic rain bonnet and blue raincoat, sprinkling droplets from its flower-patterned plastic onto the white laminated table that took up half the small room.

Marie pulled out a chair. She placed a hand on Demmy's arm. "Thank you for coming in," she said. "Mark just called to say his mother is feeling better."

Demmy was alarmed and relieved. Mark hadn't said anything about his mother to her, but since the crisis was resolved she took a deeper breath. She was glad she got to help out Mark by stepping in for him and relieved Marie considered her worth the trouble to come in for. Maybe Demmy was okay as a teacher after all.

"I struggled with this week's homework." Marie did not seem apologetic or bashful as she extracted sheets of hand-written text from her leather purse. Demmy noticed every so often an individual line was headed by an encircled number, written in a style Demmy was familiar with from vacations in France. The 1s had long hooked tops, looking like inverted Vs; the 2s sported cute little circles where the flat lines at the bottom started. "Could, would, should, must. It's all so different from my language."

Marie positioned her pages in front of Demmy, placing the assignment Mark had given her beside them. Mark had written out patterns for Marie to emulate and repeat. There were so many pages. She had repeated, all right. This was a woman on a mission.

Marie may have struggled, but she'd done so successfully. There were still things that Demmy could point out, though. And as they got into the nitty gritty, Demmy discovered that what Marie had written, though correct, was not always what she had meant. Which gave Demmy something to contribute. They talked about *must* versus *should* for a good fifteen minutes. By the time they were finished, Demmy was exhausted, as well as feeling the need to research grammar at home to confirm that what she was teaching Marie was correct.

"This was excellent work," Demmy told Marie, as the older woman packed up her books and the coming week's assign-ment, which Mark had left for her. "Most kids at my high school don't study this hard."

"But aren't they headed for college?" Marie sounded

shocked, eyes widening with a touch of outraged parent.

"They are," Demmy said, and they were, in fact, studying hard. Very hard. Why had Demmy lied? It was patronizing. She hated when people patronized her. "Actually, I should have said that you study *as hard* as the kids at my school. But that's pretty hard. Some kids crack under the strain. And you work a fulltime job, right?" Her mom didn't. Her dad did, though he hardly seemed like it.

"I do get tired," Marie said, "but I enjoy learning, and I need to set an example for my son. He is applying for college this year. He had dengue as a child. Such a severe case, and we had no hospital. I thought I would lose him. The doctors did, too. There's no cure, only treatment and hope. That's when I knew I had to come here. And look at him now. He studies so hard."

Demmy could see pride in her smile, her posture. She wondered if her parents were proud of her. Probably, she guessed. "Where is he applying?" Deadlines were coming up, so if he hadn't applied yet, he'd missed a few important schools, especially the state ones.

"Yale is his dream school," she said. "Close to home, right?"

"Maybe I'll see him there." Wait, did Demmy assume she'd get in? She did. And did she maybe assume she *wouldn't* see Marie's son there? She did. Whoa, racist much? But if he was anything like Marie, her son's chances might be pretty decent. Demmy's sense of the students out there she'd be competing against suddenly swelled beyond the kids at her school, and schools like it. Her classmate Alix Sima was just the beginning of the vast crowd of high-achieving students she'd be competing against. "What's his name?"

"Phillipe," Marie said. "But he goes by Philip. Or Phil. Which sounds like a girl, but it's fine." Demmy could hear conflict in Marie's voice about the not-quite-rightness of her adopted country.

"I hope I see him there." Demmy thought of Alix again, with her two eight-hundreds. Alix could write well, was on the field hockey team, had a profile filled with compassionate works and stunning accomplishments that seemed to defy time and space. And yet even Alix was no slam-dunk. Demmy remembered watching the seniors the year before, the outbreak of ulcers as they waited to hear from the Ivies. The heartbreak for those students who got in nowhere. After all the expectation, the shame was crushing. Demmy was doing well, but the odds were so slim, and there was a whole country, a whole *world* filled with hardworking people aiming for those same few slots. Realistically, neither she nor Phillipe— Phil—would get into Yale.

Now she felt scared. Did she secretly *want* to go?

Marie put her hand on Demmy's arm again. Demmy felt its warmth and weight comforting her. Had Demmy been that obvious? "You'll be fine, *cherie*. When Mark called this morning to cancel, I asked him if you could take his place. Just so you know."

"Really?" Demmy was thrilled.

Now Demmy pictured Marie getting the phone call from Mark at her job—cleaning houses, Demmy remembered her saying. She had probably consoled Mark in ways Demmy never could have. Demmy pictured Marie nursing Phillipe through dengue. What did that entail? She pictured Marie doing her homework at a kitchen table at night, elbow raised as she put pen to paper for the joy of learning. Also to get ahead, yes, and to set an example for her son, but, fundamentally, Marie wanted to learn the material. That showed in her homework, the careful, precise pages that only Mark and Demmy would see. Maybe the person with the most to learn here wasn't Marie.

CHAPTER 30

The morning was chilly. Casey pulled black jeans from her bedroom closet and shrugged them on. Their Christmas plans were in flux. Everyone was boosted, but Demmy had not yet committed to join them in Stowe (she had to finish her college applications), Roger was rumbling about a career change (what the hell?), Sherbeam was angling to get her retrospective rescheduled for earlier in the year (Pau was pushing back), and both Maude and Kelly were angling for invites. Casey would prefer a quiet week in the snow, but Frannie had let slip that Kelly was a schoolmate of The Hartley's principal and had leverage over whether Abby got in next year. Did everything have to be about The Hartley? Meanwhile Sherbeam was lobbying for Maude to come make phone calls to a final few recalcitrant collectors.

"Shoshana's planning something for Tu BiShvat," Roger called from the bathroom. These were his first words spoken after days burrowing gopherlike through the mounds of finals he had to grade for his three classes. Even with his TA doing the preliminary grading, it was intense. "We're expected!" he added.

Tu BiShvat? Wasn't that the one about the trees? Casey pulled a sweatshirt from her closet, the Middlebury College one. Tu BiShvat wasn't even a parking holiday. Was this a snub?

"When is it?"

He called out the date.

Casey checked her calendar. It was clear. "Fine." Casey wasn't sure what her problem was. An evening with Roger's dad, along with Shoshana and her friends and family, would be stress-free and enjoyable in a way that an evening with Sherbeam never was. Was her reluctance resentment? Roger's dad never did any of the heavy lifting of being a grandparent. Sherbeam was at least present in their lives.

"Thank you!" Roger called back.

Why *thank you*? Was it the lack of negotiating? Casey looked at herself in the mirror. Would she be too cold in jeans? Maybe. And the sweatshirt—Kelly had given it to her. She remembered Kelly tugging on it when Casey had tried it on. She'd been entirely too touchy for someone who was just a friend. Casey swapped the sweatshirt for a comfortable old Yale one of Roger's. That would set Demmy's nerves off, of course. She wished she had one for UDLAP, but that wouldn't sway Kelly into whispering into the principal's ear. Casey settled on a fluffy, black, lamb's wool/nylon pullover, warmer than any sweatshirt.

Roger came out of the bathroom, bare-chested but wearing trousers, socks and shoes. Shoes before shirt? "How'd the DNA thing come out?" he asked. "I need to find an ancestor in the New World pre-1650 to top Constanza."

Oh, God. She'd forgotten to send Roger and Abby's samples off. And Abby was expecting results for Christmas. Casey would need a cover story. "Those things take forever." She'd heard that. How long were those vials of spit good for?

And where had she left those envelopes? She kissed Roger goodbye. "Off to The Hartley!" She hurried downstairs and rooted around her desk. There were the envelopes. Constanza hadn't miraculously found them and mailed them, sadly.

"Abby, we're going to be late!" Casey had been trusting Abby to get herself ready, but this new idea of dressing after breakfast wasn't working. Though precocious, Abby was still just five. Very soon to be six, just as Demmy was soon to be eighteen.

Casey pawed again through her papers and found the DNA instructions. "Once it is mixed with the DNA stabilization buffer liquid, your saliva sample is stable at a wide range of temperatures (-4°F to 122°F)," she read.

She'd pop them in the mail today.

Casey heard footsteps. "Abby, come on!"

Demmy appeared instead. Wishful thinking that Abby might be ready. Demmy was smiling, but looked twenty-seven years old, not seventeen. "Got two more apps off. Looking good for Stowe."

"Which ones?" Roger had found a shirt. He had a stack of finals under his arm, which he'd grade at the kitchen table, getting in Constanza's way, not to mention Casey's. It was weird having him at home when she was trying to work, but his den was cold and his NYU office was too prone to interruption, he said, blissfully unaware that certain others might consider *him* the interruption.

"Providence."

"And?"

Demmy gave a meek little grin. "Yale."

Roger put up a hand for a high-five. Demmy indulged him, slapping her palm to his. "We had to send off thick envelopes of stuff in my day," Roger said. "None of this online stuff. Right, Case?"

Casey chuckled as she poured herself coffee. "It was all online in my day, baby."

Demmy made a sizzling hiss as she touched her dad's arm with a fingertip. "Ooh, burns."

"Yeah, ouch," Roger said. "Dad is oh el dee."

And then Abby was standing in the doorway, thin bangs hanging in her eyes, ready. Maybe they wouldn't be late after all. Casey did a spot check. Abby had everything she needed. She was growing up self-sufficient and confident, as Casey wanted. "You, my dear, are incredible," she said.

Kisses were dispensed. Casey grabbed Abby's hand and they made for the front door as Demmy, Roger, and Constanza compared the *21 Grams* storylines to those of *Babel*. Casey overheard Demmy telling Roger movies should have two hundred storylines, like TikTok, while Roger explained to her why that wouldn't work, sounding patronizing and horrified.

Casey fastened Abby into her booster seat. Abby hit play and in the backseat Lizzo began questioning why men had this need to be "great." Next would come the line about DNA. Casey hoped Abby didn't outgrow Lizzo, whom Casey had come to love. Realistically, Abby would move on and it would be another twelve years or so before she rediscovered her idol. Abby would then be shocked Casey had let her listen to Lizzo. Casey chuckled. She felt good as hell.

"I took um a DNA test," Abby sang out.

And soon she'd get her results. If not by Christmas, then by Tu BiShvat.

CHAPTER 31

Roger heard children's voices from the kitchen of the Stowe cabin as snow dusted the Vermont hills outside the window. Abby, her Hartley pal Joseph, and Joseph's seven-year-old sister were "helping" Casey and Kelly bake something. Abby had been pouting about her DNA test results not being among her Christmas gifts, but the prospect of poppy-seed cookies seemed to have restored her spirits.

Roger was happy, too. He was seated comfily in the den, grades turned in, twelve students selected for his spring screenwriting workshop (including Niamh, Joshua, and dark horse Sam). He faced the picture window overlooking the pine trees between their cabin and a ski run. He had been jokingly forbidden to touch the oven after the Thanksgiving splatter incident, allowing him to indulge in glogg, which he sipped as snow fell lightly on the just and the unjust alike.

"Pau has agreed to do April 1," his mother proclaimed in the adjoining living room as she ended a phone call.

"And you'll be ready?" Maude's voice competed with a crackling fire.

Casey had relented, inviting not only Maude, but Demmy's

friends Jodee and Lainie, who would join them to go skiing after Kelly and Rich went home with their brood in a few days. It felt to Roger like the way houses should always be—crazy, but fun.

"I've shipped two new oils, and they are large and showy. Another is virtually done, and two others sketched out."

"Describe them to me."

Sherbeam sighed dreamily. Through the open door Roger saw her stretch a languid limb along the rustic gnarled birch of the fireplace mantle. "That would spoil the surprise."

"I love a good surprise, but April Fools' Day? Really?"

"They don't have that in Catalunya." Sherbeam had lowered her voice, but Roger could still eavesdrop effortlessly. "The New Yorker interview convinced Pau. Though now you've got me worried. If 'April 1' is in the interview will people think it's all a prank? My agent pitched it as a comeback story, though they're not allowed to use that phrase. They are not even allowed to say that I've been away, which I haven't, if you think about it."

"No one does," Maude muttered audibly. Sherbeam had been asking more and more of Maude and the strain was showing.

Roger wanted to warn Maude she was skating on thin ice, but he'd noticed that was part of their dynamic: Sherbeam abused, Maude rebelled, Sherbeam placated: by dropping a word into a wealthy collector's ear, for example. Not Roger's cup of tea, but it seemed to work for them.

Sherbeam snarled, not yet feeling any need to placate, apparently. "You'd be shocked."

"I would."

Wow, was Maude angling for an early return to the city? After all these years being friends with his mother, she could get away with nearly anything, but his mother's limits could appear without warning, and the impact at running full speed into her brick walls could be brutal.

Roger crept into the kitchen to ladle himself a second serving of glogg. Rich had invited Roger to join him, Demmy, and his oldest son Fred or Frank or Will to do ice climbing, which sounded dangerous and probably was. Casey had wanted to forbid it for Demmy, but Rich really sounded experienced, so Roger had sided with Demmy, and Casey had relented.

It had to be tough for Demmy being in the cabin. That final Christmas he, Aline and Demmy had been together had been lovely, just the three of them snug amidst a very heavy snowfall. The girls had gone skiing while Roger had sat at that same window, in that same chair, and looked for his wife and daughter among the skiers shushing by. He did not see them till they returned after dusk. No glogg on that occasion. Hot spiced wine was a Swedish thing Casey had introduced them to. Holidays were easier when you were a little smashed.

Casey spied him stealthily moving in on the delicate glass punchbowl. "Roger, before you have more, can you go check on Demmy?" Kelly looked up. "And Wilf and Rich," Casey added.

"Sure, honey." Roger thought of the bitter cold out and shivered, but nodded, willing.

Truth was, he remained concerned about the ice climbing. He didn't have any personal knowledge of Rich's skills, and had largely trusted him on the strength of him taking his own son. That and pictures on Facebook of him boulder climbing in some desert in Utah, huge forearms working hard. His thumbs looked like they would punch holes through sheetrock like butter.

Roger added a scarf and a thick outer layer over his wool sweater and trekked in winter boots toward the frozen waterfall the trio had planned to scale. It was a cold, fifteen-minute hike, and his mustache and beard were chunked with crystals from his breath by the time he got to the waterfall, his alcohol buzz largely abated.

"Ahoy, mateys!" he called when he saw them.

Rich (or someone) had secured a big eyelet screw atop the frozen torrent, whose ice gleamed blue and translucent white. Through the eyelet, a rope had been threaded that Demmy was now using to climb. Rich called out pointers to her, while Wilf shouted encouragement. Rich nodded to Roger while keeping his eyes on Demmy.

Demmy looked down, smiled and waved at Roger, and continued her ascent. Roger felt nervous watching Demmy sway on that slender yellow rope. A wind was kicking up, grabbing at the tail of blond hair that emerged from the bottom lip at the back of her helmet. She had never done anything of the sort, to his knowledge, but seemed to be coping well.

"How secure is that hook at the top?" Roger quietly asked Rich.

"Very," Rich said. He called to Demmy. "You can use that crack to your left as a handhold."

Roger stepped back and let them focus. He stomped to warm his feet. Demmy used the handhold to pull herself up another couple feet, then repeated the move with another outcropping of gray rock, encrusted with panko-like greenish lichen. Two thick columns of ice rose on the rock face, former flows of water now immobilized by New England cold. She used some claw things attached to her boots to get leverage with her feet and boosted herself up to the top. She mounted the cornice (wasn't that what it was called) and threw up her arms in a screamed cry of victory.

Roger smiled, nervously wanting her to step back from the

edge, but she began clambering back down onto the ice face again, still linked to the hook, and belayed rapidly to the bottom.

"I can't believe you've never done this!" Wilf shouted to her. He was fourteen or fifteen, dark haired and big toothed, and seemed to shout most things he said.

"Dad, you have to try it," Demmy said.

"Oh, hell no." Roger didn't tell them about the glogg, but hoped his scholarly demeanor would persuade them to let him off the hook, so to speak.

But no.

"It's not a dangerous climb, Mr. White," Wilf shouted at him, robustly proffering a helmet.

Roger turned to Rich.

"Wilf is right," Rich said. "There's so much exposed rock we're not even using ice tools. You are basically just crawling up the surface. We've all tried it a couple times."

"Dad, you'll *love* it. Seriously."

Oh, sheesh. Maybe it was the glogg, but he found himself wanting to try it. They'd each done it a couple times. He could manage it, right?

"What have I got to lose," he said.

"All riiiight" Rich said, grinning. Roger felt manly approval from his fellow bearded dad. He was being inducted into this little cadre of adventurers. Rich removed his climbing claws, or whatever they were called, and fastened them onto Roger's boots, which he pronounced suitable. Rich's gloves were a little snug on Roger, but Rich insisted Roger swap his mittens for the gloves, for better grip and flexibility. Rich threaded rough nylon rope into a black harness they fastened onto Roger, snugger than it had seemed on Rich. Roger resolved to lose ten or twenty pounds. Or thirty.

Rich walked him through the process of belaying and had

him practice it, a couple feet off the packed ice and rock at the foot of the waterfall. Roger smiled. It was easy! Rich pointed out the handholds and footholds that they had been using and slapped him on the back. "And you're off."

The first few handholds were a snap, but Roger was glad to have swapped gloves, because even with the better grip, his assurance wavered with each inch he rose. He kicked the wicked-looking spikes into the ice. Wilf and Rich called out the handholds as he rose, Demmy, too, and hearing his daughter's voice spurred him upward.

He looked between his feet. Fuck! He was so high. When had that happened? It had not looked nearly that high watching Demmy from the ground. Now he envisioned himself falling, being injured, a tragic holiday tale of spinal fracture to blight the long history of happy family excursions to Vermont.

"You can do it, Dad!"

Had Demmy, too, felt her spirits quail at this point? He did not want to falter, not so much out of pride as fear of climbing down. The details of belaying, so simple a moment ago, now seemed hazy in his mind. And how high was he, anyway? Ten feet? Halfway there. He pushed himself up to the next handhold, then pulled, then pushed again from his new foothold, then repeated. He was sweating. This was work.

"You're doing great, Roger," Rich called. Demmy was silent now; Wilf, too. Maybe the height made them nervous, despite the bluster of their previous encouragement. Rich's approval kept him going.

He reached for a round knob of granite, only three or four feet from the top. It was slick. He could push off and make it to his goal in a lunge. Maybe. He applied pressure to his feet and realized, no, he couldn't.

"Easy does it," Rich called. "Just do what you've been doing."

In other words, don't panic. He felt the glogg rise within him, a burp flavored with bile. You're fine, Roger, fine, he told himself. He pushed his clawed boot toes into outcroppings, angled his feet to find something more to push against. A rock dislodged, skittered down the ice face. He pulled himself upward again, settled back into the rope, and felt a jerk downward. Just an inch, but still.

"Shit," he heard from below. Rich.

"Roger." Rich cleared his throat. "I don't mean to alarm you, but move cautiously. Try not to pull on the rope if you can. Support your own weight."

What?

He looked up. Surely the hook thingie had been pointed up before, not down. Terrific.

"All you have to do is grab the next handhold, to your left, then move your legs upward like a crab, like you've been doing, slowly."

Or come crashing down with limbs flailing. Crabs did that too, right? He pictured himself landing on his back in front of his daughter. Um, no. He was not going to do that to her.

"You're OK, Dad."

"I got it," he called. He grabbed the left handhold and moved his legs up, toeing in left and right. He raised his body. The eyelet was barely in the ice wall that had anchored it. If it had once been in the rock, it wasn't now. He reached for the right handhold.

"You're doing great," Rich called.

You could come up around and grab me, Roger thought. He knew from past seasons that there was a trail one could hike to the top. Then again, maybe Rich was planning to catch Roger. Splat.

Roger reached the right hand hold and crabbed up the next foot. His eyes were at the cornice. He'd have to google cornice, if he survived. He reached up with his left hand. The eyelet scuttled down the ice face. Roger was now entirely unsupported. He grabbed a solid dagger of rock, kicked his toes into the ice face, first left, then right.

His left foot slipped. There was no sound at all from below this time. His heart pounded. He tried again and got his toes into the ice. He pushed gently and flopped over the top of the surface. He hauled himself up and stood, victorious.

A cheer exploded from below. All three of them were jumping up and down, hugging. Had they written him off? He gave a cheer of his own, but it was not the scream of triumph Demmy had given them. It was a roar. Demmy and Abby were not to be left fatherless.

"Just stay there," Rich called up. "Don't try to belay. I'll come get you."

Did Rich think him unable to walk down on his own? Roger stood up. His legs were quivery. Fear was taking over. And gratitude.

"I'll wait right here."

CHAPTER 32

Had they been strong enough, Casey thought, the three of them—Demmy, Rich and Wilf—would have been carrying Roger home on their shoulders like a conquering hero when they all burst through the door.

"You should've seen him, Mom! He could've been killed! The piton had popped out so he had to make it to the top with no protection!"

Casey was appalled. She'd nearly lost her husband? But Roger was beaming like a fool, lapping up the attention.

"Handled it like a boss." Rich was sweating. She knew enough to recognize the energy of a near miss—disaster had been close, real.

"Rich, a word." Casey motioned for him to follow her into the next room.

"Casey, I know, I know," he said when they entered the small den off the living room.

"You do *not* know." She pointed her finger at him. "Do not ever, *ever* put my daughter or my husband in danger again." Not that she intended to ever give him a chance to.

He wet his lips. "I shouldn't have egged on Roger to climb. I know better. I got over-excited. We were having fun."

"God, you sound like a kid."

"I know, *I know*. Believe me, *I know*. You weren't there. It was heart-stopping." Another sheen of sweat seemed to race over his shaved head. He seemed sincere.

"That's supposed to make me feel better?"

He shook his head. "No, sorry. I'm still a little shook-up. Demmy was completely safe. That piton was secure. Wilf went up it too. So did I. Multiple times. It's just that Roger was last, and he weighs more than any of us."

"You're saying it's Roger's fault? Because he's fat?"

Rich made a face. "I wouldn't say *fat*, exactly."

"Fuck you." Casey stalked off, leaving him. Jackass. "Is something burning?" she yelled out as she entered the kitchen.

"No, all good!" Kelly sang back, pointing to a tray of cardamom cookies fresh from the oven. Like the poppyseed cookies, it was a recipe courtesy of Casey's Swedish forbears, who'd crossed the wide Mississippi from Quincy, Illinois, into Missouri. "The next tray just went in. What was all that about?"

"Nothing," Casey said, sweetly. She wondered how many techniques for lying she had amassed at this point in her life. The most important one was hiding just how much she worried about the safety of her children. Everyone thought she was a cool mom, letting her kids take risks, be independent. They had no idea how much it cost her.

"Hooooey!" Roger said, ladling himself the glogg she'd denied him earlier. He was still beaming. His skin looked dewy. The adrenaline, or whatever it was, seemed to have taken five years off him. Demmy was quizzing him on how it felt, standing atop the cliff.

Wilf joined in. "You were so cool up there, Mr. White. Keeping it together with Dad spraying beta!"

Roger took a sip of hot wine and acted like he understood what Wilf was saying. The shine on his face as he basked in the adulation of Wilf and his daughter almost made Casey think it had been worth it. Almost. She knew the risk had been far greater than this payoff, but she didn't have the heart to kill the party. She put her hand on Roger's back and leaned in to kiss him.

"Glad you had fun, honey," she said.

He raised his eyebrows at her. There was more to the story —he'd been through something—but she'd only hear it later, in bed. That was one of Casey's favorite times at the cabin, in bed with Roger when all was quiet, after sex, a little bit of calm and peace in a life that didn't have a lot of either. She raised her eyebrows back at him. He gulped his glogg and smiled.

"Isn't this fun," Kelly said.

"What did you say to Rich?" Kelly said later in the living room, when they were alone. "He seems sulky."

"Is that how he usually is with near-death experiences? Sulky?"

Kelly reared back. No caresses for velvet curtains this trip, Casey supposed. Not that she wanted any. They still went to yoga together, but that was mainly Casey grooming Kelly to get Abby accepted.

Kelly looked miffed.

Casey laughed. Ha ha ha. She'd play her dig at Rich as a joke.

Kelly laughed, too. So the "joke" strategy would work for Kelly. They still had a day to go before the Kelly-Riches returned to Park Slope. Sooo much easier to pretend they were friends.

"We should try rock climbing," Kelly said.

"Out there?" It was freezing outside.

"I mean at a gym! There's a great climbing wall in Prospect Park."

Prospect Park was a long drive for Casey, beyond Park Slope even, but this was what she wanted, right? To be friends with the other mothers? Was it worth another time-suck commute into the Promised Land to keep Kelly more friend than enemy? Casey had plenty else to do in her life. "I heard there's a great one in Linden Hill," Casey proposed. A good compromise, closer to Casey.

"Linden Hill?" Kelly sounded astonished. "But that's so far! Why don't you just come to Prospect Park?"

Casey forced a smile. Well bless your selfish little heart. She realized she had her first frenemy, the final stage in becoming a New Yorker. Her smile became genuine, if perhaps a tad predatory. Abby was so getting into The Hartley. "What a great idea. We'll rotate!" Casey said cheerily.

CHAPTER 33

Jodee was skeptical. "Your parents actually seem OK to me," she said to Demmy as the three tramped through the fresh, two-foot deep snow, headed for the scene of the recent excitement. "I mean, from what little I've seen."

Demmy's mouth gaped. This was a betrayal. "I thought you got it?" At Thanksgiving, Jodee had said she sensed the spark between her mom and Kelly. "Lainie?"

Lainie pulled off her glasses and began rubbing them with a cloth. "That Maude lady does seem awfully physical with your dad." Lainie put her glasses back on.

"Her dad? *Okaa-san desho?*" Jodee said. "It's her mom who's having the affair."

"It's both," Demmy said. "Or at least, that's what I am trying to figure out. I wish they would just be more open about things."

"But if they separate, won't you be separated from your sister?"

"Separate?" Was that what *being open* meant? "Wait, what? My sister?"

"Wouldn't Abby go with your stepmom and you with your dad?"

Demmy had not thought of this. They reached the base of the frozen waterfall. Demmy looked up the two pillars of ice, one on each side of a key boulder that in warmer days separated the stream into two halves. Watching her dad flirt with death up there had been terrifying, and yet, it now looked like halcyon days of yore.

"I don't want Abby to go away. I don't want anyone to go away."

"Maybe it's anxiety because we're all going away to college in less than a year," Lainie said. "I mean, this is the year we *graduate* high school!"

Demmy nodded ambivalently. "Maybe." It was as good a theory as any. Demmy herself was not so sure about this supposed romance between her mom and Kelly. There was something, but it was not like it had been, at Thanksgiving, and especially before that.

"You're sure your mom isn't into Kelly's husband?" Lainie and Jodee had overlapped the Kelly-Riches for a couple hours. "He was kinda sexy." Lainie dragged out *sexy*.

Demmy made a sour face. "She's into him like you're into Maaaaartiiiin." Demmy dragged her syllables out even longer.

"Peter," Lainie said.

"Peter what?"

"Maaaartin actually goes by Peter. It's his middle name."

Jodee grabbed Lainie's shoulder and spun her around to face Jodee. "OK, now you're scaring me."

"I'd been meaning to tell you."

"Tell us what?" Were they *dating*? Demmy's mind was kinda sorta spinning.

"He didn't want to tutor me, to avoid any appearance of anything, but no one else was working out, and it's technically not against any rules. My parents are paying him, like, nearly two hundred an hour."

Jodee said, "Listen to me carefully. You. Cannot. Date. Him."

"Stop shipping us all the time! God!"

"Seriously. You have not thought it through."

"I'm not dating him! God!"

"OK, let's say I believe you," Jodee said. "You still need to swear you've considered one thing."

"What?" Lainie said.

"Lainie . . . Delaney."

All three cracked up.

CHAPTER 34

His dad greeted Roger and his clan at the elevator door. They'd survived Stowe, Roger had launched his screenwriting workshop successfully, and it was already Tu BiShvat.

"Son," his dad said to Roger.

"I'm so glad you could all come." Shoshana hugged Demmy, Abby, and Casey in turn. "This won't be a traditional seder, more of a smorgasbord, let me warn you. Sadly, I can't handle fructose anymore, so I opted to mix things up."

"Sorry to hear that," Casey said.

Shoshana waved away Casey's concern. "I was diagnosed before Sukkot, so I saved each and every etrog. Joyous discovery: etrogim are good for more than just waving around for blessings. I candied their peel. In sucrose. So that's what *I'm* having. Also, nuts are fine, olives are fine. If I'm complaining about forgoing a few dates I should have my head examined."

She guided Roger into the living room, where he expected a large crowd to be mingling in front of the wall of windows with their view out over the Hudson to New Jersey, but he and his clan were supplemented only by two men his age (a couple?) and two older women (definitely not a couple). Shoshana's family continued to arrive over the next hour, filling the generous space.

"Happy eighteenth," his dad said to Demmy, who had celebrated her birthday two weeks before, although the real joy of the celebration had come from finishing the last of her applications. (Was she seriously thinking of going to Tulane?) "Don't leave without reminding me to give you your present." Abby had celebrated her sixth birthday two weeks before that, and his dad and Shoshana had attended in person.

"Thanks, Grandpa."

"Is Nana not here?" Demmy asked him.

Roger shook his head. "Nana? Are you kidding?"

"Roger, we invited your mother. She wanted to come but unfortunately couldn't make it," Nick said.

Had Roger been seated, he would have fallen off his chair, or at least clutched his brow like Obi-Wan Kenobi, staggering under the shockwaves of the Force after the destruction of Alderaan. "Say what?" He had not been in the same room with both his parents in years, and that last time they had sniped at each other till Roger thought they'd come to blows.

"Roger, your mother has been here a number of times. She and Shoshana get along great."

That was all thanks to Shoshana, Roger had no doubt.

"What's with the look? She's been here more than you."

"That's great, Dad."

"I know you don't like talking about this . . ." was his dad smothering an *either*? ". . . but the divorce was decades ago. How old were you? Fifteen?"

"Eight."

"We're friends now, Roger. She's told me all about the retrospective. We're thinking of going."

"Bad idea." Roger had seen a list of the paintings that were coming in from collectors. One was an early nude of his father that crystallized the arrogance his dad used to wear like a medal of honor. Roger couldn't stand it. *No nudes is good nudes*, had always been Roger's motto, but his mother kept painting them. She was famous for them, in fact, particularly for how they refused to flatter. He'd come home from school far too often to a naked person in the studio, men and women in equal proportion and every complexion. Fat ones, skinny ones. Old ones, young ones. Maude once. Aline once. So much posing.

"Tell him the truth, Nick." Shoshana appeared at his dad's side holding two bottles of wine, one red, one white.

His dad grimaced. Was being truthful to Roger that difficult? "We've already bought tickets to Barcelona."

Roger felt the impulse to swear, but reined it in. The impulse felt reflexive, ill considered. What was his objection? That he'd been subjected to too many dramas growing up? He was well past that with his mother, and it was time to detach from his adolescent anger at his father as well.

Roger took a breath. "OK, Dad. We'll set up a big dinner with everyone. Tapas. That smoked trout thing. Tortilla Española, cold with mayo. Do they have that in Catalunya?"

"That's the spirit," his dad said.

"Nicholas, can you give the blessing of the fruit? I'll start us on wine immediately after. People like things quick."

The couple proceeded to the table where all the fruits and nuts were arranged.

"Proud of you, Dad," Demmy said, to Roger.

For being willing to have dinner with his divorced parents together? Roger nodded. "You have to let people grow up, even your parents." He wasn't hating the idea.

Demmy smiled.

He liked this, being the hero, or at least not being an

embarrassment to his daughter, which might be the same thing.

Hands were washed. Food was arranged.

His dad gave the blessing of the wine, which shocked Roger. "*Baruch ata Adonai, Eloheinu Melech ha-olam, borei pri hagafen.*" Since when did his dad know Hebrew? Had he simply memorized the sounds? Not that Roger could tell, but it sounded right.

Shoshana gave a reading as white wine was poured, and soon his dad was giving the blessing of the first fruit. *Baruch ata Adonai, Eloheinu Melech ha-olam, borei pri ha-eitz.*

Maybe his dad had converted. There was so much he and Roger never talked about. Half the time they talked it was about money—accompanying Roger at twenty-one to meet with his lawyer about his trust fund (a small one from his grandparents, way less than a million), for example.

As folks finished their glasses, Shoshana moved on to the second wine, then the second fruit, as other relatives did readings and blessings. When the soft fruits came, Shoshana brought out her candied etrog. She'd always been on the rigid side where ritual was concerned, but now she was mixing things up, and not just white wines with red. The pace, the crowd, the options. Roger surveyed the gathered guests. Everyone was taking it in stride. Could he not do the same?

When they were done, his dad came over. Nick placed his hand on Roger's arm. "I want to apologize for last time you were here." His dad was apologizing? Becoming friendly with his ex-wife? Buying tickets to Barcelona? Maybe he had something terminal.

"What happened last time?" Roger did not remember anything deserving an apology. Then again, his mind had been wiped clean earlier that day when he'd read about a woman at Columbia getting a MacArthur. When did they announce them? He should look it up.

"To risk reoffending, I asked you about . . . you know."

Ah. Aline. Now he remembered, though not his own reaction. "No, Dad. No apology necessary."

His dad looked stricken, his eyes wider than usual under his surging mop of combed white hair, as though bringing this up had taken girding of loins, administration of iron to the spine. He remembered Maude's words at Thanksgiving, that Demmy was holding back on accepting Casey out of respect for *his* feelings. Did everyone find him that hard to deal with?

Roger took a deep breath. Demmy was calling Casey "Mom"; Shoshana was abandoning both traditional fruits and sit-down dinners; his dad and mom were socializing like normal people. He needed to move on as well.

"It's me who should be saying sorry. I should talk about her, Aline, more." His throat caught. Despite his best intentions, it was a struggle to say her name. "I've gotten into the bad habit of not talking about her."

His dad placed his hand on Roger's shoulder. "It's been eight years."

Roger nodded. He opened his mouth, closed it. He didn't want his dad—or anyone—to know how acute his awareness was. But hiding that was not moving on. Demmy was watching him. He needed to say it.

"Eight years and one month." He cleared his throat. "It was eight years, one month and two days ago that Aline died."

EIGHT YEARS, TWO MONTHS
AND THREE DAYS BEFORE

Casey had been coming to the group now gathered in the bleak Brooklyn church basement long enough to be a regular. It was a big step forward. She'd been in New York for five years. She'd achieved an income and an apartment. She'd survived. But being able to take care of herself was no longer enough. What she needed now was to heal.

Fluorescent bulbs buzzed above translucent panels inset into the acoustic panels over their heads. The people were more welcoming than the dingy space, but the courage to speak had so far eluded Casey. The point of the group was to work through trauma together, but her mouth went dry every time she'd tried. The best she'd done so far was to say I am Casey, I'm from outside New York, and I don't know if my husband is alive or dead.

"Can you have grief without loss?" a man asked the group.

Casey perked up in her chair immediately. She'd never seen the man before, but she had asked herself that same question. Many times. Of course the answer was yes. Or perhaps the answer was that the concept of loss was malleable enough that you could have grief without knowing you had the loss.

"I know that I will be single soon," the man went on, "but right now I still have a wife." He paused for breath. "Several of you have told me I belong here, but I haven't been through what you all have."

This guy seemed be reading her mind. She pegged him at early 40s. She liked his trimmed beard and his heavy New York accent, perhaps because it didn't remind her of anyone back home.

Like him, she didn't have a death certificate she could point to, no evidence to say "this is what happened to me." At that point, Casey could go around the room and recount the traumas of everyone there: The man whose wife had died of metastatic breast cancer, the woman whose girlfriend had OD'd on fentanyl on a bus stop bench, the mother whose son had OD'd on fentanyl in a park, the father whose son had been shot ten years ago in a drive-by but only died of the complications recently. She could go around the room: cancer, cancer, drugs, cancer, drugs, violence, dog lady.

Dog Lady was faunching as the bearded man spoke. Casey had seen her in action enough to know that Dog Lady had identified the segue she would soon use to take over.

The woman was "Dog Lady" because she always brought her emotional support animal—a small, white, fluffy thing locked up in a carrier made of breathable fabric. What had come to annoy Casey was that the woman always spoke far too long. They only had fifty minutes and Dog Lady always barreled through the five-minute limit, hitting ten, even fifteen minutes. If the moderator called on her gently to wind it up, the tears began flowing and the moderator did not seem to know how to cope.

Last week, Dog Lady's tearful, manipulative display had left exactly one minute for the woman whose girlfriend had died. Into those sixty seconds the woman had crammed her feelings about her years of crisis with her addict girlfriend reaching a fatal breaking point. Her girlfriend had turned cyanotic, alone on a dirty seat of molded red plastic, and the woman hadn't even known. Dog Lady's selfishness had angered Casey.

"I don't belong," the bearded guy now said.

Casey noticed that Dog Lady was now looking right at Casey. Her long gray hair was tangled and her sallow skin sweaty. She gave Casey a sour flip of the head.

The guy, name of Roger, had said he didn't belong here so the woman looked at Casey? The message was hard to miss: Dog Lady thought Casey didn't belong either. Casey lowered her gaze. She had no appetite to battle for turf. She wouldn't come back. There was no healing for her here.

Casey waited out the continuing shares, including a Dog Lady weep-fest, the closing mumbo-jumbo, and the shuffling of chairs out from the table. Some were pushed back in by those conscientious and clear-thinking enough to leave room for others to maneuver out of the crowded room. Dog Lady left her chair athwart the exit route as she wrestled with her tiny caged pooch, her sighs a performance of misery, even though none of her fellows in grief needed persuading.

Refreshments had been set out in a larger room. Casey noted the bearded man hovering over the cookies. Despite the late hour, Casey headed for the perennially lukewarm coffee. The bearded man joined her.

"I know what you mean about belonging," she said to him, in low tones so as not to attract a Dog Lady take-over.

He chuckled, which she appreciated. "I know, intellectu-

ally, that I am welcome here," he said in normal volume, "but
I've felt like a fraud my entire life."

Casey gave a snort of mirth. "It's a relief to hear somebody
else fess up to that."

Dog Lady reached the table and leaned in their direction.
"It's denial," she said. "It's a way to convince yourself you aren't
going to have a loss."

Casey recoiled. It felt like an attack, but surprisingly there
was also an implicit message that Roger belonged, that she
belonged. Casey struggled to reconcile that welcome with her
earlier desire to shake sense into Dog Lady as she gushed
tears.

Casey heard the dog breathing in its cage at her feet. Its
tiny claws poked at the holes in the carrier mesh. "You want to
get out of here?" she said to Roger.

"I know just the place." This time he whispered. He tossed
out his small Styrofoam cup.

They climbed the stairway out of the basement together
and walked a block to a brightly lit third-wave coffee place
with pricey pour-overs that took five minutes to prepare.

Roger pulled out a chair for Casey, then sat across from
her as they waited for their orders. "She's right, of course, but
in my opinion, denial's severely underrated."

Casey laughed. "Denial certainly has its uses." It had
allowed her to study in Cholula; it had allowed her to rebuild
in New York. She never forgot her losses, but some days she
needed to pack them away for safekeeping.

Their coffees were called out, retrieved.

"How about," Roger said, "if we just lay out all the gory
details this one time and then move onto something else?
Deal?"

"Deal," Casey said, and the words came pouring out of her,

and of him. But not quite everything for her, and she wondered if the same was true for him. Either way, the bargain was made and the word 'denial' never surfaced between them again.

PART II

CHAPTER 35

I hsan looked out the tenth-floor window at the Barcelona shore and wanted to move to Catalunya. He wasn't weary of Paris, but something about the sight of an ocean let him breathe.

"So, we'll let you know," the woman across the table said. In English.

Ihsan had just pitched a plan to partner his linguistic services firm with her Spanish localization company. He'd responded to her questions in Spanish throughout. He tried to convince himself that she was simply fond of using her English, which was excellent—albeit with an American accent, not the British accent typical in Spain—but coming from a fellow linguist, the comment on his language skills was clear.

Still, Ihsan wasn't ready to concede defeat. His uncle had advised him to build personal connections. He switched to English. "Have you seen the movie *Babel*?" González Iñárritu was a Spanish-speaking director; it must have been popular in Spain. "I was in it. As a child. Not Yussef or Ahmed. I was one of the kids in background."

Her face had been blank, but now grew irritated. "I'm not familiar with it." She picked up a stack of papers and stood.

OK, defeat, then. He had been dismissed. Maybe he needed to connect using a Spanish celebrity, not a Mexican one. He gave her a smile, thanked her for her time, and left.

So, there he was, dumped out on the Passeig de Josep Carner, trying to resuscitate his optimism. His phone buzzed to tell him his final appointment, the next day, had canceled. That owner, too, had decided he wasn't interested and didn't want to waste Ihsan's time. Perfect. So Ihsan had an entire day free in Barcelona that he hadn't counted on, hotel paid for, return ticket booked on the TGV for the next day.

He went back to his hotel room to stow his laptop and change into something unthreatening. Something to make him look less Arab. At home in Paris, he could lower his profile (ironically) by holding hands with his husband. Gay men were less threatening to French people, which made little sense. Had not enough horrid men of history been queer? Some respect, please.

With his husband not at hand, he settled for a pink, flowered-print shirt. Pink looked good on him. Maybe it would help people imagine him relaxing on a white-sand beach in Libya instead of toting a machine gun. It fit snugly, too. See, no explosives belt. (And check out these abs.)

He went back out to La Rambla, the tree-lined pedestrian street built on an old wadi running through the center of the city, and ambled—rambled—back toward the beach. He wore sunglasses, despite the menace they seemed to imbue him with, because damn it, the sun was bright!

The waiter at the café where he lunched was nice enough to him. He ordered in Spanish and the waiter responded in Spanish without hesitation. His language skills couldn't be *that* bad, then. Ihsan told himself three failed pitches was nothing much, but still, he was disappointed. He wanted his business to grow beyond the steady but familiar stream of jobs he got in Paris. Automation was the future, and he wanted to be part of it. And that meant partners abroad. He was devoting a lot of energy into building his firm, which had a splashy web presence he'd paid quite a few euros for, a real office, and an actual employee (Marta, a Spanish woman long resident in Paris whose German was also quite good). Ihsan had plunked down all the savings he'd accumulated during his previous career as a civil engineer (abandoned to the horror of his parents) into equipping the firm with all the latest software platforms. Their project management and multi-currency billing tools were especially robust.

But no. Not of interest to the worthy linguists of Catalunya.

Don't take it personally, he told himself. You're good at what you do. You may have to explain yourself all the time to everyone, but the reward is that you get to be you.

It was a good reward.

He walked down the arcade to the far end of the beach, near the breakwater. He entered a changing hut and slipped into the Club Monaco swim shorts he'd brought, his cossie (a word he suspected the Spanish woman wouldn't know). He checked his bag into a locker and stepped onto the sand. It was unnervingly warm for early April. He stretched, feeling fine under the sun in his trunks and sunglasses, and walked to the water's edge, into the sea. He swam carefully, keeping his sunglasses above water, which probably made him look vain and foolish, but he could hardly leave them with his towel on the beach. They were Oakleys. Someone would run off with them.

He was a good swimmer; he swam in his gym at home.

Now he swam parallel to the beach, heading a good distance up the coast, then back to the area where he'd entered the water, tracking the changing huts by their painted numbers.

When his arms and back felt like they'd done enough work, he made for the shore and stood, walking from the gentle surf onto the shore. He strode up onto the sand like Daniel Craig, feeling refreshed, glad to be in the sun, the warm water dripping from him. He shook the sand from his towel and began drying himself.

A pair of women whispered to each other from beach towels under a shading umbrella of lime-green canvas. Already he could sense the disguised attention: they didn't want him here. Now two men approached from the streetside promenade. One made eye contact. Was he going to hear the familiar "Is he bothering you?"

Ihsan felt a scowl forming. He hated scowling. He was just enjoying a swim. He wanted to relax at the beach after a tough three days of work. He tried to soften his expression into something neutral.

One of the women called to the men. Here it comes, Ihsan thought. But the men switched directions, heading back to the promenade vendors. Now he noticed the two empty towels stretched out beside the women. Ah, boyfriends. The men had been walking toward their girlfriends, not him.

He took a deep breath and began walking toward the changing hut serving as his landmark. It would take him close to the two women. But why should he change his direction? Honestly, there was nothing threatening about him.

He walked past them. The women angled themselves in his direction, both looking at him. He waited for harsh words, or a summoning call to the retreating boyfriends.

"Nice abs," one said. The other buried her face in her towel, laughing.

Ihsan broke into a grin. "You should see my husband's." He walked the rest of the way up to the changing rooms with, dare he say it, a bit of a strut.

CHAPTER 36

A thump on the runway and Casey and everyone on the airplane were pushed forward in their seats. Barcelona. Engines reversed thrust and flaps and spoilers slowed the plane. After months of preparation, the unveiling of Sherbeam's hush-hush new work was hours away.

The production of getting the four of them and their luggage into a taxi and checked in at a hotel was Casey's least favorite part of travel, but it had been accomplished and the four were settled in their adjoining rooms. Tucked in Casey's bag was a surprise. She flung open the curtains and called everyone over to take in the view of La Rambla and the beach. She was ready to unveil her surprise, but then Roger yelled something about absolutely needing to be on time for the opening that evening and collapsed onto the bed. Just jetlag, or nerves at the prospect of both his parents in the same room? Once Casey heard Abby's sleeping breaths through the cracked-open doors connecting their rooms, she closed the curtains and fell swiftly asleep herself.

She dreamed of mountain climbing with Kelly. High on a slippery granite massif, Casey took the lead. Kelly climbed after her through drizzle like a spandex-clad spider-creature from an alien planet. Casey kicked at Kelly as she drew close. Kelly slid off the granite face, saved from death only by her ropes, a human pendulum repeating "I thought we were friends," in the voice of that robot woman in *The Stepford Wives* who shorts out after Katherine Ross stabs her in the gut with a carving knife.

Casey sat up with her heart racing, but felt relieved.

She stepped to the window. They had two hours before they had to be at the gallery. Roger was still asleep, and from the other room she heard the gentle snoring of the girls.

She peeked between the drawn curtains. The setting sun cast a glow over La Rambla. Everyone else in town would be having a siesta so they could stay up half the night. A Spanish colleague back in New York, one of two who'd so far agreed to join Casey's collective, referred to 9 PM as 'nine in the afternoon.' So Casey luxuriated in a hot shower, catching a glimpse of the Barceloneta Beach promenade from a tiny, high-set window in the shower stall.

The shrieks that greeted Casey when she left the bathroom told her the girls were awake. Roger was too. Roger and Demmy were talking about movie structure and planning showers and wardrobe, but Casey was eager for her big reveal.

"Everybody, gather round."

Roger's face tensed. "We have to meet Mom in an hour." He was right to be antsy, but the rules were different in Spain and Casey was liking the idea of making Sherbeam cut *them* some slack for once.

"It will be worth it." Casey pulled out her laptop and opened up her browser. She typed in the appropriate codes. "Ta da!"

Roger leaned in. "It's your DNA test, Abby."

Demmy leaned in beside Abby. "Are you a hundred percent that . . . girl?"

Abby looked at Demmy. She seemed confused. Abby had drifted away from Lizzo the last few months—fickle youth—but surely she hadn't forgotten about the DNA.

Abby stared at the screen as Casey navigated to a colorful pie diagram. She pointed. "See all this English and Welsh? That's from Dad. And all this Irish and Scottish? That's from me. The Swedish is on both sides."

"Hey, you're three percent African, Abby," Roger said.

"That's from me, too." Casey turned to Roger. "My great-grandfather was fairly dark."

Roger looked at her, like, of course the African is you. (Roger's ancestry was entirely of Northwestern Europe. She'd already looked.)

"And one percent Native American, just like the president!" Demmy seemed thrilled; Roger surprised. Casey was surprised at their surprise: wasn't everyone in the US at least a percent or two indigenous?

"Cool," Abby said, and went to the window to watch the volleyball players, who'd been there since they arrived.

The other three looked at each other.

"Seriously?" Demmy said. "That's all we get from her? After all that?"

Casey felt shocked.

Roger laughed. "Passions that run deep are often quickly spent," he told Demmy.

"Who said that?" Casey asked. It didn't make any sense.

"Me," Roger said, proudly. "Should I write it down?"

"No," the other two chorused, but it went in his ever-present notebook anyway.

Someday, she thought, this will all be a movie.

CHAPTER 37

Maude had wondered if coming to this family affair was a good idea, but never, not once, for the reason that now stared at her through the brightly lit gallery window: nude portraits of herself and Roger, hanging side by side, aimed at the crowds of passersby traversing La Rambla, for the whole world to see. And Roger, beside her, sputtering, wordless. Sherbeam had gone too far.

He ran inside. "Mother!" he screamed, arm stretched behind him pointing toward the backs of the two canvasses suspended in the street-facing display window, the painting of Maude done decades ago, the one of Roger barely dry.

"It came out well, don't you think?" Sherbeam obliviously beamed. "Isn't it provocative the way my brushstrokes have become *more* structural over the decades?"

"That's not me," he fumed. He turned to Demmy. "That is not a naked picture of your father. That one, over there, that *is* a naked picture of your grandfather, but this one here? Not me. It's. Not. Me."

Sherbeam laughed airily and turned away, tossing her magenta scarf ends hither and yon. Maude would not have been shocked to see Roger inflict blunt force trauma on Sherbeam; instead he turned to Casey and Demmy. "I never, *ever* posed for her, nude or otherwise. She's my mother! My body doesn't even look like that."

Maude made a skeptical face, but said nothing. The new painting was not exactly the body of his twenty-three-year-old self, but Sherbeam had an artist's eye and visual memory and it was darned close. Despite the thick application of paint, the reduction of eyes to outlines and the trademark weird bendy fingers, the figure on the canvas was unmistakably Roger White.

"Well . . ." Casey stopped, silenced by a glare from Roger.

"Oh, God. Abby." Roger covered Abby's eyes.

"Huh," Maude said. Roger had never been prudish, but she understood he was caught off guard. She'd known for months that the nude of her would be in the show. Whereas Roger's was new, a fantasy, the one of her was old, familiar, and drawn from life. The image was a not-unwelcome reminder that she'd once been bold, unafraid, and a knockout. Unusually for Sherbeam, Roger was also rendered attractively. He wasn't vain enough, Maude suspected, for that to compensate for the invasion.

As Roger fumed furiously out front and Casey listened, Maude followed Sherbeam deeper into the gallery, past the older paintings loaned by collectors and even a museum or two. They entered the large room at the rear devoted to the rest of the new work. The opening night reception would not start for another hour, but the space was already prepped and decorated. Food was arranged on round, plastic-covered trays, waiting to be uncovered; crystal stemware sparkled; bottles stood lined up, ready to be opened and poured.

"Am I awful?" Sherbeam asked Maude.

Maude was about to reply both *Yes* and *No*, when she saw

the huge work, hanging between a portrait of Abby and Demmy seated (clothed) on a swing (the sentimentality of which made Maude wonder if Sherbeam had suffered a transient ischemic attack) and a rather unflattering self-portrait (but clothed this time, the coward).

Dominating the entire exhibition was a full-length portrait of Aline. She wore a white gown that was masterfully not painted in white at all, but spectrally fractured into a rainbow of color. It was as technically accomplished as anything Sherbeam had ever done. Given how pained Roger was by the mere mention of Aline's name, and the way her death had tossed a boulder across the roadway of his life, it was also cruel.

"Yes," Maude said, "you are unequivocally awful."

It was the largest piece in the show, larger even than the posturing, aggressive depiction of Sherbeam's ex-husband, painted back when the self-promoting pair had been lording it over the Greenwich Village art scene. Flanking the three new works were a pair of bronze sculptures, perfect size for bashing in maternal heads. "Roger cannot see this," Maude said.

"Of course he can. This is my family. He will love it. Eventually. He needs it."

Maude shook her head, slowly. Would he? Might he? Did he? He was so reticent to revisit Aline's death, Maude could not see how he could welcome such a callous appropriation of this most sensitive wound. And on a related note, where was the portrait of Casey? Did she not rate?

Maude went outside to head them off, cushion the blow.

Demmy was there; Abby was there. Roger and Casey were not.

CHAPTER 38

Chasing after an angry husband could not be anyone's idea of a good time, but Casey had to go after Roger.

She watched him stalk down the pavers of the pedestrian street. "Demmy, watch after your sister. Go inside where she can't see this . . . painting. I will bring him back."

"Mom . . ." Demmy looked shaken.

"I'll be back as soon as I can. Go inside! Wait!"

Casey sprinted down the wide street, weaving around throngs of tourists clad in colorful shirts and poorly fitting shorts with too many pockets. She made no pretense of walking; Roger could be headed anywhere. She spied him ahead, walking briskly, anger boiling off his shoulders.

"Roger!"

He turned. "I'm not talking about this in a crowd of tourists."

"The hotel is just ahead."

"Fine."

They went to the hotel and up to their room.

Roger spun around as soon as the door closed behind her. "Have you any idea what it's like to be someone's prop? All my life I have been a servant to her and her career. I can't pretend she's a normal person anymore. I can't!"

She reached for his hand, to tell him he had every right to be angry. He jerked his hand away, held both arms, both hands, up and out of reach, as though unable to bear being touched by her.

"Roger . . ."

"There's nothing to discuss. We're leaving. I am not *celebrating* this. I am not celebrating *her*." He sneered out the word "her."

"Can we think about . . ."

"There's nothing to think about."

Wasn't there? How about the fact that they had to come up with tuition not just for Abby's next year at The Hartley, if she was accepted (and Casey was optimistic), but for Demmy as well? How about the fact that they were living rent free in a house that Sherbeam owned? If she asked them to leave, it wouldn't be Park Slope they were going to.

"I understand that . . ." she started.

"Do you? Do you know what it's like to have your life paraded around by someone else, fodder for their ego and moneymaking schemes?"

"I don't," Casey said. Although, standing there, unable to finish a sentence, she was getting an inkling. She felt a sense of invasion for having her husband exposed.

"It's a lifetime of humiliation. Having her show up whenever and wherever she wants. But not show up if you want her to. Having the family you build be something that she can dip into whenever she's feeling lonely, but then treat as something she bears no obligation to, something she can ignore when you need her, when you ask her to . . ." His voice broke.

Casey moved to hug him.

He pushed her away. "Don't."

Casey steamed. None of this was her fault. It long predated her arrival on the scene.

Roger wiped his face. "I'll get the kids. You can pack and we'll leave tonight."

"Roger, we drained our bank account to buy these tickets."

"Well, the money isn't coming back if I humiliate myself before my mother."

Casey regretted mentioning money, but it could feel like the most important thing in the world. Not having quite enough of it, month after month, provoked its own brand of insanity. Always being that little bit short. Or worse. She was not used to being dependent. She'd supported herself, no help from anyone, no one able to, since her ex had disappeared into the Mississippi, but now she needed both Roger and Sherbeam to ensure Abby and Demmy never knew that financial terror. For Casey, too, there was more than a little humiliation in the bargain she'd struck, marrying Roger, raising a child in a city she could not afford.

But she loved him.

Now he was still crying, weeping even. Casey wanted him to stop hurting.

"She can't help herself, Roger." Casey had come to believe this was true. To think otherwise was too painful.

"I know," he mumbled. He stared out the corner window at the golden beach and city, heaving back turned toward her. "There's something wrong with her."

She could hear in his quiet voice that, on a deeper level, he'd long since made his peace with his mother's shortcomings and come to terms with her neglect, the way she treated people as objects. It was just that his equanimity had for the moment become unstuck.

He'd stopped crying.

She did not know what to say.

"As a kid I used to dream she wasn't my mother."

Roger turned away from the window. He sat at the table where Casey's laptop lay, and opened the screen. It started up at his touch. He clicked the open web page of the DNA site.

"Where are my results?"

She showed him.

"Doesn't it show health results, like genes for insanity. Let's see if she's really my mother."

"It won't show her. She hasn't taken the test. See? There's you. There's Abby."

He clicked Abby. Her page came up.

"All I want is to be a parent that my kids want. I don't care about my job, my career. I don't care where we live. I just don't want my children to ever wish I wasn't their father, you know?" He wiped his face again, the tears now stopped.

Casey nodded.

"Did Demmy take the test?" Roger pointed to a name.

Casey looked. Abby had a half-sibling, it looked like. Had Demmy taken the test, unknown to all of them? The user-name given was just the initials *S P*. Casey clicked on the link. No family names were given. Casey scanned *S P*'s ancestry breakdown. There was the African, the Native American, the Irish and Scottish, plus a grab bag of southern European countries. But none of Roger's English or Welsh. So it didn't match Roger. It matched her. It could not be Demmy. *S P* had given a location: Memphis.

Casey sat down hard on the carpeted floor.

"She's alive."

CHAPTER 39

N ow it was Roger's turn to race after Casey. He could not keep up. Casey was flat-out running to the gallery. She had to get the children, she said.

Roger had glanced at the website as Casey raced out the door, but had not seen an answer to his question—who's alive? —so he had followed. Did Casey have another daughter? He knew *he* didn't. Well, he *thought* he didn't. Could he have another child? He thought of past lovers who'd disappeared from his life. Niamh, from back in his Oxbridge days. Maude, same vintage. Aline. That was it.

Roger had completely lost sight of Casey, so he just got himself to the gallery—lungs straining against ribs, air scraping down his throat, as fast as he could.

The doors were open now, crowds gathered inside, more entering, milling. And there stood his mother's invasively imagined young Roger, strutting in the window. Roger had calmed down some, but it still pained him. He had to admit it was a good painting, and it made him look attractive, but he knew it was no accident she had given him an unearthly, curling smudge of a cock. Just like she'd given his dad a triumphantly realistic member, in that hated portrait she'd done back in the day. That and the strut was some agenda of hers. Revenge for his long-standing refusal to pose for her? It was counterproductive to try to decode her; that only fed her acting out. And inside the gallery, where he'd left it, the portrait of his dad, at least a decade younger than Roger was now. Smug, overdosed on personality, controlling. Not at all like the man who'd said the blessing at Tu BiShvat.

Roger entered the gallery, looking for Casey. Up ahead he heard what sounded like Casey arguing with someone. And, oh fuck, there was his dad and Shoshana. Not near his dad's portrait, mercifully, but just past the archway in a room labeled "New Work," hovering behind his mother's shoulder as she talked to a man with salt-and-pepper hair standing with Pau. The man was holding a recording device near his mother. So journalist, then, not boyfriend. An interview.

Roger rounded the corner into the room and stopped.

Aline.

And standing before the portrait, Demmy, looking as though the world around her no longer existed.

If Roger had been angry before, now he was enraged.

He had a vision of himself with a sharp blade, slashing the painting to ribbons. But of course he could not. Aline was in that painting. He could never harm her. Roger's world was contracting now, too, like Demmy's appeared to have done, taking him back in time, against his will. Extraneous people disappeared, irritating noise, smells, bright lights all faded away.

But only for a moment. Casey was yelling something. At Demmy. Demanding something.

"We have to leave now!" Casey had Abby by the hand. Abby was trying to shake her off.

"Casey," Roger said, quietly, his voice a fraction of Casey's as she tried to get through to Demmy.

"Come *on*, Demmy. Please."

Now it was Demmy shaking off Casey's hand.

"Casey, do you have another daughter?" Roger asked quietly.

Demmy spun, as though mounted on a pivot, her trance snapped. "What?"

Casey's face looked ashen. She said nothing.

"You have another daughter?" Demmy asked. "How?"

Casey shook her head, slowly, expressing emotion more than language.

"She was married before," Roger said to Demmy. He looked up at Aline. Casey had told him of the marriage the first time they'd met, but only in the vaguest of terms. She'd told him of the loss and its effect on her, but precious little about the man himself, and nothing about a child.

"I have to get to Memphis," she said, "and I am not leaving Demmy and Abby behind. I will not lose another daughter."

"You're not taking me with you," Demmy said. "I'm eighteen. I don't have to obey."

"Don't be such a child, Demmy. You *have to* come with us. To Memphis."

Demmy looked at Casey as though she were crazy. "Is that where Kelly is?"

"Who?" Roger said.

"Kelly is her Maude," Demmy said. "And frankly, if anyone needs to do some growing up here it's you two. You think no one sees?" Demmy turned to Roger, skewering him. "The little touches, the hand holds, the shared jokes? Shared from when? When did you lay down the shared experiences that you are trading your sly little glances about?"

Roger stepped back. "I don't know what you mean," he mumbled.

Casey laughed.

"Wait, *you* think there's something going on between me and Maude?"

"Demmy's right," Casey said, challenging. "That little dance between you and Maude, out on the street, looking at your nudes? Where is she, anyway?"

Roger looked around. Maude was not in the room. Roger knew what Casey was talking about, that intimate awareness he'd hoped she hadn't noticed. But that dated back decades!

Sherbeam and his dad watched him, as though their child was performance art the power couple had created and they were awed by themselves. The journalist held his phone toward them, its red light indicating it was recording. Sherbeam looked pleased with the spectacle, pupils dilated, nostrils flaring, face dancing with movement like a bull running Pamplona.

Roger wet his lips, brain in overdrive yet arriving nowhere.

"Yes, Roger, Demmy and I both picked up on it," Casey said. "Maude knows what your body looked like back then. So, you two slept together. It would have been nice to know, as your wife, as someone inviting Maude over for, well, everything. Is there still something going on between you?"

"No," Roger said. "No!" He felt color rise to his cheeks. This was worse than the painting, worse than actually being naked in front of the whole world. He'd been so raw when he'd come back from Oxbridge, his belief in himself shaken. He'd thought he was such hot shit when he'd gone there, the Yale student with his Fulbright. Everyone was jealous. And he'd floundered, been exposed, dumped, fallen short. Come home chastened to his mother's Brooklyn studio loft, to Maude, in all her glory, posing proudly for his mother, Maude a celebrated artist in her own right. How could he not have fallen for her?

"Who's Kelly?" he asked.

"The yoga lady, dad! Have you not noticed her preening? All those stretches, pretending to be athletic but actually just touching herself for Mom's benefit. I *cannot* believe this has gone by you."

That Kelly? Of course Roger had noticed. It was just that, well, the woman was ridiculous, running her hands over her spandex like she was in an infomercial. Her and her cartoon husband. Was he supposed to be paying attention to them?

"Casey, *that* Kelly?" Roger asked.

Now it was Casey's turn to blush. There was something to this? His wife had a hidden child and was also bi? "Do we even know each other?" Roger stated it more than asked.

"Well, we have a child together, so there's that."

"We can't have secrets like this!" Roger pleaded.

"You have nothing *but* secrets," Demmy said.

"Demmy, shut up," Roger said.

This seemed to incense Casey, somehow. She made a scoffing noise, which incensed Roger. "You should be on my side on this one, not Demmy's. I'm not the one with the secrets!" he said.

"Are you kidding?" Casey pointed at the huge portrait of Aline, which seemed to grow larger before his eyes. "The woman whose name cannot be spoken?" Casey looked ready to bite him, or someone. "Say it. Aline. Aline Aline Aline. Neither of you will ever talk about her. I thought at first it was some kind of guilt because she was still alive when you met me, but you're like that with everyone. You're stuck in the same world you were when we met. Frozen. Would you have even married me if I hadn't been pregnant? Did you even want a second child?"

"No," Roger said. "No." He wasn't saying *No* to anything specific beyond having his face shoved into the reality of it, like a puppy being punished for peeing in the wrong spot. He had just been ready to start talking about Aline, about those brutal years, when he'd met Casey. And then Aline had died, and the talking got derailed. And yes, he did sometimes feel that was unfortunate, that if they'd met a year later it would have been better. Because Casey was who he wanted to be with, his great stroke of fortune, but he hadn't been ready. What he *had* been was smart enough to know that things don't always come around at the right time; sometimes they even come at the exact wrong time. When something like him and Casey comes around, you have to grab it. If Aline's death had taught him anything, it was that.

"Where's Abby?" Shoshana said.

Roger looked around. Casey looked around. Demmy looked around.

"No, no, no, no, no." Casey raced around the room, looking under tablecloths, in closets, in corners. Demmy checked the back patio and behind the free-hanging picture of Aline, swaying in their frantic breeze.

"Anything?" Shoshana asked Demmy.

Demmy shook her head. "Abby's gone."

CHAPTER 40

Demmy ran out onto La Rambla and scanned north and south for her baby sister. This was all her parents' fault, both of them.

Did you even want a second child?

No.

If they had meant anything other than they wished Abby hadn't been born, Demmy didn't know what it could be. They were so wrapped up in their own heads they probably didn't even know that's what Abby would have heard. Abby was assertive, confident, strong willed. To find out you were unwanted, not the center of the universe, had to be a shock.

Her parents and the others followed Demmy out of the gallery. Casey called out instructions behind Demmy, telling everyone what to do as they milled frantically on the La Rambla pavers in front of the offending portraits.

Demmy wasn't listening; she was thinking. Heading back to the hotel was the natural choice, but Demmy remembered arriving at the gallery. Abby had wanted to keep going. She was enjoying the street and wanted to explore. And then when their parents had ditched them, Abby had wanted ice cream.

There had been a guy with a cart on wheels, like the heladeros back home. Demmy would have gladly pursued him for Abby's sake, but their parents had ordered them to stay and she had obeyed.

She hadn't wanted to stand outside, trying to keep her gaze off the naked pictures of her father and Maude, life-size behind them. When Abby had started pointing at "naked daddy," they'd gone inside.

Nana, Grandpa, and Shoshana had all been there, with Maude. What *was* it with old people, anyway? "Can't you just do normal paintings?" she'd asked Nana.

Nana said blah blah blah O'Keefe, Stieglitz, secrets, family, blah blah blah.

Art.

What did art matter when there were diseases out there like dengue, with no cure and heading for North America, along with other tropical diseases like chikungunya and Chagas? Demmy knew that everything had gone down the way Nana had wanted it. She'd wanted to set off her dad by broadcasting his affair to the world as he came in, so he'd have a fit. The gush of raw emotion would play as a testament to the power of her work. She'd probably filmed it, filtered it, and already posted it on TikTok. So 2019.

Now Demmy did not see Abby anywhere on the streets, whose lights were coming on amidst the April twilight glow. The heladero had been headed away from the beach, away from the gallery. That was where Abby would have gone.

"Demmy, wait," someone called.

But the words were fading, the speaker already unidentifiable and unimportant to her. Demmy was not waiting. She was not going home. She was not going to Memphis. Memphis? #WTF? What had her dad been on about? Another daughter? Another husband? That was crazy. Was he talking about Kelly and Rich? It made no sense whatsoever. She'd have to decipher all that later. Right now she had to find her sister.

Gently lit strings of bulbs climbed tree limbs upwards into the night; the harsh light of Galería Les Rambles, where secrets went to die, was now forgotten. Demmy looked for the ice cream man amidst the round, faux-marble tables and chairs of woven plastic cane that lined the pedestrian boulevard. Bicycles sat locked to racks; tourists checked their phones.

"Abby!" Demmy called out directionlessly.

People looked at her, but if anyone sought to help, they weren't fast enough to keep up with Demmy as she scanned the sides of the street for a tall, sturdy six-year-old who might feel like hiding right about now.

The crowds grew thicker, the night sky black between the trees. Demmy felt disconnected from her entire searching family. Hundreds, literal thousands of people now separated Demmy from all of them, and she was glad of it.

How could her parents each have been so clueless about what the other was doing? Did they not care what effect they were having on each other, let alone on Demmy and Abby? The one who made her the angriest was Maude. She had once been Demmy's confidante, making the betrayal sting all the more. She remembered Jodee and Lainie. Maude was her unt, she thought, Unt Maude. She wished her friends were with her now.

She also wished she had eaten more hors d'oeuvres. She was hungry. Was Abby also hungry? Demmy would feed her, if she found her; Demmy had money now, a credit card that drew on her trust fund, accessible since she'd turned eighteen before Tu BiShvat, but as yet untouched. Would the card work in Europe? She remembered the PIN code.

Demmy spotted the heladero and ran over to him. *"Buenas noches,"* she started, but she quickly saw he was not an ice cream vendor, not a vendor at all. He was a street cleaner, the bottles on his cart detergents, not syrups.

"Are there any ice cream vendors with carts?" she asked him, but he did not seem to understand. She asked again in French, and got a response she did not really understand, except for the most important part: No.

Demmy thanked him and resumed her scan of the crowded streets. She was being careful, thorough, but could easily miss Abby. She found a Japanese couple and asked them if they'd seen Abby: *Shitsurei desu ga. Rokusai no onnanoko wo mimashita ka . . . hitori de aruiteiru rokusai no onnanoko. Kami ga chairo de. Se ga takai, rokusai no wari ni. Kono gurai.* They hadn't seen her brunette sister, tall for six, this high.

Demmy absolutely *despised* her parents for being so self-indulgent. So many more important things had been said back there, but Demmy's mind kept coming back to that doofus tone of her dad's: *Who's Kelly?*

Forget Memphis; she did not even want to go back to Williamsburg with them.

And then there was Abby, twirling a fallen leaf, a big green thing the size of Demmy's hand that had been blown off the tree, despite being fresh and new.

"Abby!"

"Demmy!" Abby called back, with a smile, and ran to her.

CHAPTER 41

Casey ran toward the hotel. She could not lose her youngest daughter the same day she'd found out her oldest was still alive. Casey never should have accepted the word of the experts, those police, coroners, river experts who'd assured her repeatedly, relentlessly, frustratedly: after the pickup had entered the river, Execrable and her daughter had been swept to their deaths, because science.

Fuck water temperatures. Fuck river currents. Fuck science!

I have to find Abby, and I have to get to Memphis, Casey thought. And when she got there, Execrable had better be dead. If not, she'd kill him herself, skin him and tan his hide, just like she was ready to skin and gut Sherbeam, shit-disturber extraordinaire.

Casey banged through the hotel's front doors into the lobby and screamed at the concierges, pursers, night managers. No one had seen her daughter, any six-year-old girls, period. Their rooms were still, empty. Casey was ready to crawl out of her skin and shed it, this life and Roger with it. She'd take only Abby and Demmy, even though Demmy had refused to go with her and ignored Casey's calling after her on La Rambla.

Casey's laptop was sitting on the small round table in the hotel room, a link to her long-lost first daughter on the screen if she should tap it, but she had to focus on recently lost Abby now; whatever had happened to her eldest, to Elyse—how she'd avoided that name, and the memories that went with it —the priority right now was her youngest, wandering alone in this city because she and Roger could not conduct themselves like adults.

Casey called the police. They came rapidly, took Abby's description, and sent out radio calls and search parties. They told Casey to wait at the hotel in case Abby came back, but when Roger showed up, Casey made him wait and went searching on her own. The police tried to stop her (Roger's inability to speak Spanish concerned them), but she knew not to put another daughter's fate in their hands. The police could help, fine, but she would never ignore her gut again.

She went back to the gallery, saw Sherbeam and Nick inside with Shoshana, all three standing, arms crossed. Nick mad at Sherbeam? Sherbeam engaging in a little uncharacteristic introspection? Who cared? Abby clearly wasn't there.

Casey looked all around. She had to get into Abby's head. What would Lizzo do? #WWLD. Shampoo something, do her hair? Toss her hair? Something about her nails? Or was that Ariana Grande?

Casey was powerless. It was like that night watching the pickup dragged from the swirling gray river, the stabbing glare of searchlights turning an unknown pickup's unfamiliar black outline rising from the muddy flow into the dreaded familiar blue as it broke the water's surface. She felt anew that awful sense of not knowing what to hope. That Elyse wasn't dead in the cab, of course, but then what? She still had no real idea why Execrable had done it, even now. Yes, they'd fought a lot. Yes, their teenaged marriage was a disaster, yes, the idea of a divorce was a slam dunk. But what had he intended, drugging Casey, driving off with Elyse, a car seat and diaper bag? Him, a single dad? Had there been another woman? She'd seen no sign, had remembered no sign, had discovered no evidence of a sign.

#WWLD. Casey ran into the only nearby hair salon she saw. Asked about Abby—thank God her language was not something useless like Demmy's Japanese—found nothing, learned nothing. She went back out to La Rambla and stamped the pavers in frustration.

At least Roger hadn't taken Abby. Unless he'd had someone do it for him. Shit, *that* was truly paranoid. Be calm, she told herself. Don't trust anyone's word. Be focused. Find your daughter. Find Abby.

CHAPTER 42

Roger sat in the lobby, eyes pointed at the front door. He watched its two glass panels slide open as a pod of travelers triggered its electric eye, then creep closed behind them and their mounds of bags on rattling plastic wheels. His chest felt tight. Don't you dare have a heart attack, he told himself. This was like climbing the frozen waterfall: he could not do anything to leave his daughters unprotected. Tough as it was, he had to stay seated. The least satisfying job, but the most crucial one. Somebody had to be the center for everyone to come back to.

He got out his keys and asked the police officer stationed with him, a young woman, to go upstairs to his room to fetch Casey's laptop. She refused. Her orders were clear and he could not argue her out of them by promising to stay put.

He checked his phone instead, texted Demmy again. Texted Abby again. The police were initiating a trace on Abby's phone. In a few minutes, they will have her location, Roger told himself.

The policewoman's radio squawked. She turned to him. "Your daughter is here," she said in heavily accented English.

"Where?" Roger looked around.

"In the building. No es exact," she said.

"The room? Could she have gotten by us?"

"Try."

"I can't leave here."

"I will stay, sir. Please. Check the room."

Roger winced. He did not want to abandon his station. "You promise?"

The policewoman nodded.

Roger took the elevator up, cursing its slow rise, cursing that it had to go ten floors, but it did at last arrive. He went to the room. No Abby. He dialed her cell phone, heard its Lizzo ringtone.

He went over to the phone. She'd left it behind. She was only six. Roger's eyes watered. Keep it together, he told himself. He grabbed the laptop, went downstairs. The police woman was there.

Roger shook his head, showed her the phone. "You were here the whole time, right?"

The policewoman nodded, not taking offense. "Track my other daughter's phone. Maybe she found her." Demmy seemed the most likely to be able to locate Abby, being her sister; even if they sometimes fought, they loved each other.

The policewoman took Demmy's phone number and read it to the headquarters. Roger's Spanish was sufficient to know when numbers were being spoken. *Cinco de Mayo. Calle Ocho. Uno, dos.* One, two, *tres, cuatro!*

He sat down in the same chair as before. He faced the front doors, comforted by the availability of that particular chair, somehow, feeling like any mistake he made now could be crucial.

He thought of that larger-than-life oil of Aline. Larger than death, was that a thing? He remembered Demmy entranced, himself entranced. He remembered that final moment, when Aline had been home on hospice. He'd been with her, neither able to sleep. The nurse-practitioner dispatched each Monday by the hospice had said Aline had another few weeks, but the health worker who came to bathe Aline had noted something about Aline's feet and said it would be much sooner. He'd believed the health worker, not the nurse, so he'd stayed up with Aline, sitting beside the hospital bed in the living room, holding her hand. Eleven-year-old Demmy had begged him to wake her when "it was time." He'd consulted Demmy's therapist, who'd thought Demmy mature enough to cope, should she wish to do this, so he'd agreed. But how do you know when it is time? Around four A.M. he'd sensed something was up. Aline's breathing was worsening. He'd called the hospice line.

They'd said to give her more morphine, to aid her breathing.

He did that. Aline had been fully conscious, not demented or drugged or exhausted. She'd known she was struggling for breath.

"Help me," she'd said.

He'd adjusted the bed, raising the head. It helped her breathing. Then it didn't. He lowered it. It helped. Then it didn't. More morphine?

"Help me," she'd said. He raised the foot, the head, lowered both. He stood to get Demmy. "Roger, help me out here." Aline shifted and twisted in bed, as though terribly itchy.

Was that a plea for more morphine? Her breath was ragged. "Help me." Should he get Demmy? He should. Aline grabbed his hand.

He called the hospice line again. The new nurse recommended giving Aline a different medication. Roger remembered the nurse explaining it when Aline had first come home five months before, just after the rented hospital bed, before the hefty cardboard boxes of medical supplies.

"That's the one for the death rattle," the nurse had said. It wouldn't help Aline breathe, merely quiet her. It was to comfort Roger, not her.

"Give it to her," the hospice nurse said in his ear.

"Help me. Help me out here, Roger." He gave her the second drug.

Now Aline was panicking. She couldn't breathe. He could call 911, get her intubated, extend her life another few days. She'd said she didn't want that, but was she changing her mind?

"Should I give her more morphine?" he asked the nurse on the line.

"Yes," the man said.

Roger squirted morphine under her tongue. He wanted to save her. He didn't want to kill her. The morphine could kill her, but it also helped her breathe easier. She'd said not to save her. She had a DNR. "Help me," she said. Did she now want intervention? He wanted to call 911. He knew he shouldn't.

He clutched her hot dry hand, leaning his forearm on the cold rail of the bed. Her wet breathing grew worse, gurgling. The medications had not had time to take effect. Her breathing grew louder, louder. Stopped. Resumed. Stopped again.

"Are you there?" the deep male voice on the phone asked.

He was. Aline wasn't.

"I think she's gone," he told the nurse.

"I'll send someone."

Roger heard the phone shut off. There was no mechanical noise of ending in his ear, just an absence of presence. He hadn't woken Demmy. Was there any point in waking her now? It was too late for goodbye. He was sweating, nauseated, fearful of something, he wasn't sure what. What was there to fear now?

He held Aline's hand, not yet growing cold. It was too late for goodbye, but maybe Demmy wanted to hold her mother's hand before it felt dead. Roger knew Demmy would be furious with him. He went to wake her.

CHAPTER 43

Demmy looked back down La Rambla toward the hotel, the direction she'd seen her parents run in search of Abby. The wrong direction, as it had turned out. She looked down at Abby.

"Why'd you leave?"

"Am I an accident?"

Oh, shit. That *was* it. But no one tonight had said *accident*. "Did some kid say that at school?"

Abby shrugged. "I guess."

"Are you ready to go back?"

Abby shook her head.

Demmy wasn't either, not at all. Seeing her mother returned to life had been a shock. Over the past seven plus years, Demmy had come to feel safe, knowing that no one would ever mention her mother. That left Demmy in control of her emotions, able to summon her mother in her mind when she needed to. And then Nana blasts through that safety with all the subtlety of a subway train. Nothing would ever be the same.

"It'll be fine." Demmy took Abby's hand to guide her back to the gallery. People were worried.

Abby shook it off. "No! No!"

"Okay, okay." Demmy wasn't prepared for this. But she remembered being younger, no one thinking she had a brain, opinions, ideas. "Where to, then? The beach?" The beach meant passing by the gallery, the hotel, the known world. Demmy wished this had happened in Paris, where at least she knew where things were.

"The beach is the wrong way."

Demmy wouldn't sneak anything past Abby. "Okay, you lead."

Demmy pulled out her phone.

"Don't call them," Abby said.

"I just want to let them know you're all right."

Abby shook her head. She didn't, perhaps, have the words for it, but Demmy got it. As soon as parental contact was made, bargaining would ensue, angry tones designed to subdue, and that could only end one way: lockdown, followed by Memphis.

She looked at her phone. Eleven missed calls. Seven messages.

"How about if it's not Mom and Dad?"

Abby shook her head so vigorously Demmy worried for her spinal cord.

"Nana?"

Abby shook her head again.

"Pau?"

"*Who?*"

"Pau. The gallery guy."

"No!"

Maybe Demmy should drag Abby back by force. "They need to know."

"Maude," Abby said.

"You gotta be kidding." Maude was the one destroying the family. Compared to her, Kelly was nothing.

"Grandpa? Shoshana?"

"*Maude!*"

Demmy couldn't *not* do it, but she did not want to call. She texted instead:

> Found Abby. She's fine, but doesn't want to come back

She hit send.

The phone began ringing. Maude.

Demmy refused the call. She texted again.

> We'll walk around a bit, then I drag her back to the hotel. Tell Casey

MAUDE FRIENDLY

> K

K? Was Maude being cute?

The phone rang again. Did Maude not get that Demmy didn't want to talk? Demmy refused the call. Maude called again. Demmy powered down her phone. *Now* try calling me, she thought.

"How about some ice cream?" Demmy asked.

Abby's eyes widened. She nodded. What was with the mute nodding? Psychic shock? Abby was normally verbal, precocious. Demmy would make her order her own ice cream, to get her mouth moving. On a street like this, everyone in the shops would surely speak English.

They entered an ice cream shop. There were several to choose from. They went into one called an orxateria, whatever that was. Anyway, they had ice cream, and Demmy made

Abby order for both of them, which she did. They received cones of something brown that satisfied Abby. Demmy used her new credit card, which spouted trust-fund money like magic.

Demmy powered up her phone, texted Casey a photo of Abby seated on the curb eating her ice cream cone. Demmy powered the phone down immediately. She needed to think. They wandered further up La Rambla. It must be a good mile to the hotel, she thought. The evening was peaceful, the breeze cool. Demmy was not eager to plunge back into the heated accusations her parents had been hurling at one another. Her parents. Her father and Casey, really. Casey did not feel like "Mom" at the moment.

"They love you," Demmy said to Abby.

Abby shook her head. She was regressing.

Demmy thought back to her dad's cluelessness, Casey's accusations about Maude, and saying they'd married only because Casey had been pregnant. Who had said that? Casey? Demmy couldn't remember. Did it matter? Abby wasn't wrong: they'd said it.

They finished their ice cream, began walking again. Demmy got them a couple small toasted sandwiches for dinner, which they ate sitting on another curb. Wow, she was tired.

Demmy thought back to that portrait of her mother, her real mother. It was exactly how she'd looked maybe a year before she'd died. It felt to Demmy like Nana had stolen something from Demmy's memory. How did she do that? Demmy remembered her mother's last day. It was actually beyond the last day, because her mother had been dead when Demmy had been awakened by her father's hand on her shoulder. Earlier, they'd both been alive, Demmy and her mom, but Demmy had been asleep. Then, when she'd awoken, her mother was dead. Demmy had held her still-warm hand, the opportunity her dad had woken her for.

"If you want," he'd said.

She hadn't wanted to, but did, for him. And also because she'd been so vociferous before, demanding the right to be with *her mother* when she died, an insistence she'd regretted as her mother's hand had grown cold in hers. She'd wanted to run from the apartment screaming. How long do I have to sit here, holding this dead hand? she'd wondered. Is there a certain temperature? Should she ask for a thermometer? Demmy had been less assertive at eleven than Abby already was at six. In that, she was like her dad.

That was the first day of having no mother. Demmy had felt like she should be a different person that morning, but knew she wasn't. Whatever changing was going to happen had already happened. That new person had appeared over the previous three years, starting on the day she'd been told that her mother was dying and there was no cure.

Abby finished her sandwich and handed Demmy the greasy paper wrapper, red with tomato sauce, sticky with cheese. Demmy stuffed it into a curbside bin.

Demmy did not want to go back to their "parents" any more than Abby did. But where else could they go?

CHAPTER 44

The police officer looked excited. "We've got her," she said.

"Thank you, Jesus," Casey said in English. "Where are they?" She switched back to Spanish.

"It looks like an ice cream shop on Les Rambles," she said. "She must have turned her phone on. We have officers heading there now."

Casey's phone buzzed. She opened it to find a photo of Abby eating chocolate ice cream from a cone. Casey felt a sharp pain in her side, below her stomach. She needed to find Abby and fly to Memphis immediately, at that exact moment, and here was Demmy buying Abby ice cream? Demmy was making an adolescent point when Casey was at her most vulnerable. Casey dialed. The phone rang and rang. Went to voicemail. Casey called again. Again. Again. And then the call was picked up.

"Hello?" It was Demmy.

"Bring me my daughter, Demmy."

"Your daughter doesn't want to go back yet."

"Abby is six, Demmy. She doesn't get to decide." Raising

Abby to be self-confident and outspoken was biting Casey on the ass.

The connection was silent. "We're on our way. I just don't want to drag her screaming down La Rambla, you know?"

"You drag her screaming down La Rambla, young lady, right now!" Casey was chewing a hole in her cheek. She had to see her daughter. She had to hold her daughter. "Where are you? I'm coming to you."

Demmy went quiet again. The policeman, who had been listening, looked at his own phone screen and pointed in a direction. Casey set out walking up La Rambla, phone against her ear, the policeman walking by her side.

"Fine," Demmy said. "But she doesn't want to see you. She thinks you didn't want her."

"What!"

"You said it."

"I did no such thing."

"I heard it too. You said you and Dad wouldn't have gotten married if you hadn't been pregnant."

"Of course we would have. I did not say that. He did not say that."

"You don't even remember?"

The policeman made hand gestures that Casey interpreted as meaning she should keep talking.

"I *do* remember. I said no such thing. Why would I? It's not true! We were desperately in love."

Casey could hear Demmy breathing, even against the background of static and the noise of the bustling street on both ends of the connection. Why was she breathing so loudly? Was Demmy that upset?

"Like you . . . like there's nothing between you and Kelly?"

Casey shouldn't have said *were* desperately in love. "There's nothing between me and Kelly!" Casey screamed into the phone. Why was everything she said wrong? She was losing control. She had to have Abby back.

"You are such a liar." Demmy was going to hang up, Casey could feel it.

"Do not kidnap my daughter!"

"Maybe I'm not your daughter, but she's my sister," Demmy said. "I always take good care of her." She hung up.

The policeman listened to his earpiece. He turned to Casey. "She powered down. The signal's gone."

"That's not what I meant!" Casey screamed at the phone and took off running. She was going to strangle Demmy. "You're my daughter!" she screamed at the street. "You're my daughter too!"

CHAPTER 45

The policewoman shook her head at Roger. "She powered the phone down again. Who taught her to do this?"

Roger muttered, "TV." Or maybe Jodee and Lainie. Evading parental control was a teenager's core lifehack. "Next she'll be buying burners and dropping them in glasses of water after using them once."

The policewoman looked at him like he was crazy, but at least she didn't think Roger was joking.

His phone rang. Casey. "Any news?"

"I screwed up, Roger. I told Demmy not to kidnap 'my daughter.' She's back to calling me 'Casey' and said she'd 'take care' of Abby."

"So they're both mad at us."

"You knew Abby was mad at us?" Her surprise sounded genuine.

"We said we only got married because of her, while yelling at each other. Of course she's mad at us!"

"I do *not* remember that at all. This is bringing back such horrible memories." Her voice cracked. "I'm going crazy, Roger."

"I know. Why don't you come back here, tell me about it?"

"Okay," Casey said.

"I love you," he said.

"I love you, too." Casey hung up.

He blew out a loud breath, trying to calm himself. He believed Casey when she said she did not remember what she'd said, what they'd said. He'd been off-the-charts upset, too, and was not confident he remembered the scene in its entirety. That was probably a defense mechanism.

"We'll find them." The policewoman sounded confident, but Roger was far from it.

The phone rang again. Demmy. "Where are you?" he asked, trying not to sound demanding. She was enough like him she'd not obey when pushed, out of obstinance if nothing else.

"Abby and I are heading your way. Abby doesn't want to see you, though."

"Tell her I love her."

"I have. She yells 'no.' All caps. With about five exclamation points. She's going to take time to come down off this." Demmy's voice changed to a whisper. "You know how she gets."

"It's good to hear your voice, to know you're all right."

"It's good to not be yelled at." Demmy paused. Roger imagined Casey yelling. "You know Abby is in good hands with me, right?"

"Yes."

"You trust me, right?"

As much as anyone could trust an eighteen-year-old, he did, but that would be entirely the wrong thing to say. "Yes," he said.

"Is Casey there?"

"No. She's up near you."

"We are almost at the hotel."

"Okay, then she's nowhere near you. Last I heard she was the other side of the gallery."

"Is Maude with you?"

Jesus, she was still heated up about Maude? We're just friends, he wanted to yell. "No, Maude's at the gallery with your grandparents and Shoshana."

"Wow, all broken up about Abby's absence, are they?"

"Maude was out searching with Shoshana. They just got back to the gallery."

"I'm touched." The sarcasm was thick. Roger hadn't heard Demmy this angry in a long time, maybe ever. Something told him it had been a long time building. He had to get them back into the hotel.

"Listen," he said. "If Abby really doesn't want to see me, how would it be if I ducked out of sight, you two came in and Abby went to bed? You could close the door between the rooms. Your mom and I could leave you alone, let Abby calm down. She can't seriously think we don't love her, that we didn't want her. We adore her. We adore you. Casey adores you."

Demmy snorted. He'd pushed it too hard. Maybe he shouldn't have said 'your mom.' But she didn't hang up. Finally, she said, "okay."

He gave a loud sigh of relief. "Thank you."

"But get out of sight quick. Because we are walking up to the front door."

"Okay, okay," he said, but he realized she'd hung up.

"They're coming into the hotel," Roger said to the policewoman. "We have to get out of sight."

"What?"

"Weren't you listening to my phone call?"

"Listening, yes. Believing, no. Is this situation not an emergency?"

"Yes, it is, but she won't come otherwise. They are going to go upstairs and take a nap."

"¿De debò?" He didn't know what it meant, but "withering" was the word for the glance she gave him.

"I had to get her to come back," he said, not expecting her to understand. He felt like becoming one of those asshole parents who asked, *Do you have kids?* but refrained. He went into the gift shop off the lobby, motioning her to come with him.

She hesitated. "It's not me she is angry with," the police-woman sensibly said, but Roger still feared Demmy would be spooked. His churned his hands in a manic gesture that probably made little sense to her, but conveyed his desperation enough that she came with him.

They stood beside a stocky refrigerator of canned drinks, trying to look invisible. Roger wished for sunglasses and a large potted plant. Demmy walked by, dragging Abby. "Come on!" Demmy said, in that special, put-upon teenager way. Roger did not feel reassured about Demmy's maturity, hearing her tone, but stayed put as the girls walked to the elevator, pressed the button, got on.

The policewoman got on her walkie-talkie. "They are home," she said. "All clear."

Roger felt vaguely betrayed as the policewoman called off the search, nodded and left. It was far from "all clear," as far as he was concerned, but yes, the civic aspect of the crisis was over.

CHAPTER 46

After hearing from Roger that Abby was back at the hotel, that he had seen her and could now hear Abby's chattering voice in the neighboring room, Casey should have run to them. But Roger had also told Casey of his and Demmy's plan for a cool-down period, and after sprinting halfway to Andorra in fruitless pursuit of the girls, Casey was spent.

S P. The name on the DNA results.

She was alive.

Despite Casey's urgent need to tell Abby face to face that she had never felt anything other than gratitude for her existence, Casey trudged home, exhausted, trying to regain sanity as she pushed through the tourist throngs.

Casey walked past the Galería Les Rambles, glancing at the two nudes. Why had Sherbeam given Roger such a shapeless penis, twisty, as though trying to squirm away? Had she simply run out of time? And had Maude been that much of a knockout? Casey knew agendas were everywhere with Sherbeam, but a desire to grab the world's attention seemed top of the list. "Hope you're happy with the result," she muttered to herself.

She needed to go in two directions at once—the hotel room and Memphis—and was ready to burst through that door into the girls' room when she arrived at the hotel, but Roger was adamant. "I promised Demmy that we would let Abby cool down."

"And we have." Casey moved to the connecting door.

"Let them sleep. In the morning, Abby will be better. She knows we love her. She knows that."

"She doesn't know in the way that she will only know if I hold her."

Roger continued talking, rationalizing, sharing his own feelings, expecting her to care about tactics. She did care on some level, but in her mind she was also holding her other daughter. She had not held Elyse in nearly twenty years. Elyse had been seven months old when Execrable had spirited her away in the night. Seven months was not enough love to carry Elyse through a lifetime. Casey had banked six solid years of lavished affection with Abby. Much of it had been a flood of love diverted from Elyse, retained in Casey's body, an edema of yearning, before Abby was even conceived. Caught between two impulses, Casey restrained herself from opening the door.

"There's a lot I haven't told you," Casey said.

"You think?" Roger sounded angry.

"Really? Anger? At me?" She saw the open laptop on the table beside him. The DNA results. What had he gleaned from them?

His body posture softened, shoulders falling, but arms still crossed. "Just tell me."

"We were eighteen when we were married."

"What was his name?"

She gave him a silencing glance. "Voldemort."

"Sorry," he mumbled, sitting on the edge of the bed.

"I was in love, stupid love, not thinking beyond my desire to be with him. I lived and breathed him. I did not see any problems. How could I? He loved me."

"Your parents..."

Casey held a hand up. "Do you want me to tell you, or what?"

"Sorry," Roger mumbled again.

"I won't drag this out. It was like the Chicks' "White Trash Wedding" song—Mama not approving, Daddy convinced the guy is the best the town has to offer his daughter. We married in secret, moved across the river to Memphis, got me pregnant, had a beautiful little girl, Elyse."

Roger nodded now, silently. Good. Let him sit there in his white T-shirt, ready for bed when he should instead be standing guard with a machete outside the girls' bedroom. He had no idea what terrors life really held.

"So Mama was right. There was something off with the man. It hadn't been so apparent in our small town, where he knew everyone, but in the big city he was overwhelmed. He could not read strangers. He said the wrong thing constantly. Alienated everyone he met. Blamed me for it. Became jealous. I didn't understand it all, even then. I only put a picture together of all this afterwards. I wondered for a time if he was autistic, and I just never noticed, but he was different with me, back home, so it wasn't that. If it had just been a world of him, me and Elyse, maybe we would have been fine. Maybe if I hadn't pushed him to get used to city life, we could have worked things out. He wanted to go back, or at least move somewhere quieter. I didn't understand. If he hadn't done what he did, I could maybe even feel guilty, or sorry for him."

"What did he do?"

"Slipped me some sedative I thought was aspirin that I washed down with a glass of wine. Left me to wake up hours later to an empty house. I swear I heard Elyse crying, even though I know now that she had been gone from the house for hours at that point. I waited for them till I could not stand it, sitting up in the living room. I wandered the neighborhood. I called the police. They asked if I thought he had kidnapped her. I said no. Why would he? He had made no threats or anything like that. Big mistake."

Casey cleared her throat, rubbed her dry eyes. It felt like yesterday. The need to have her infant next to her buzzed in her skin. That infant was nearly twenty years old, now. That infant was a young woman, maybe going by another name, maybe with another family. Did she even know her own birthday?

"A day later the police took me seriously. They searched. His pickup was gone, after all. And that left me with no wheels. I called Mama, who came out with Daddy, and had the good sense not to say I-told-you-so.

"The pickup turned up a week later, in the Mississippi, under six feet of water. They dredged it up. There was no one inside. Six feet of water may not sound like a lot, but the experts said he wouldn't have been able to get the door open right away against the inflow of pressure. The window wasn't down either. "

She cleared her throat.

"The guard rail of the bridge was smashed off. They'd gone off the bridge. There was skin and hair stuck to the steering wheel. They tested it. It was his. So he'd been in there when they went over. They said you have to wait until the cab fills up, to equalize the pressure, before you can open the door.

But to survive, you have to take a deep breath at the last possible moment, leave your seat belt on for leverage, hold your breath till you can open the door . . . you have about thirty seconds. Babies lose that reflex to hold their breath after six months. Her car seat was still there . . ." She felt her voice crack.

Roger put his arms around her.

"They said she couldn't possibly have survived. Him neither."

He rubbed her back. It was comforting.

"They said opening the door only allowed them to be swept into the river and drown.' She gulped. "All this time . . . I should never have given up."

"I'm so sorry, Casey, so sorry."

"I should have told you, but letting go was such a hard-won victory. It took me years, you know?"

He nodded. "I do know."

"I have to go to her. She's been without me all this time. She must think I didn't want her. All these years, she must have thought her mother didn't want her."

Roger released her, walked to the connecting door. "We'll just take a look, shall we? Quietly?"

Casey nodded.

They opened the door, peeked inside. The girls were there, both asleep. Outside the night was now charcoal dark, a few stars shining. Casey crept over to them, ran a hand over Abby's hair, placed a hand lightly on Demmy's shoulder. How she wanted to wake them both, but there was only one flight that would get her to Memphis today—she'd checked—and she had to trust Roger. She kissed them both ever so gently and they returned to the other room.

"I have to go to Elyse, Roger. Now. I mean, really, right now."

"Abby knows we love her, Casey. She was just upset. She *knows*. Demmy does too. I can explain to them. You go. We'll follow in the morning. You can trust me."

Casey nodded. She did trust him; Demmy and Abby, too. She packed a bag, and caught a taxi to the airport.

CHAPTER 47

Ihsan left his hotel room to catch the early morning train to Gare de Lyon, phoning his husband Nabil from the taxi to Barcelona Sants. He told Nabil his final pitches had not gone well.

"Did you tell them about *Babel*?" Nabil asked.

"It didn't help."

"It always helps!"

Ihsan shook his head reflexively. "They didn't see a profit in it for them. Third-hand celebrity doesn't change that."

"Apparently," Nabil said in English, with a posh accent, their inside joke.

"Apparently," Ihsan replied. They both laughed.

Ihsan joined the mad dash to stow bags in the luggage rack. The train was about three-quarters full, but the seat beside him and two seats across the table from him were empty. After being on duty for two days in Spain—policing his body language to not seem too gay or too Arab in an environment whose dangers he was ignorant of—he welcomed the chance to relax in his reserved seat. The train was familiar territory. Being alone meant he could have a beer and watch the Catalan countryside furl by without judgment. Even easygoing Nabil sometimes looked at him askance when he had alcohol, although his parents, mercifully, did not. There was an upside to having communist parents.

A young blond woman arrived with a small child in tow, a girl of around six or seven whose dark brown hair fell below her collar. They sat in the two seats opposite Ihsan, on the other side of the table. Ihsan looked warily for a parent or two who might be following. Seats were reserved, but sometimes people asked others to trade so they could sit together. Especially him, it felt to Ihsan, but maybe he was oversensitive. Honestly, after the trip he'd had, he would say no. It wasn't his fault if a family of Americans couldn't plan ahead. But no such parents appeared.

The little girl seemed very excited to be on the train. Her eyes widened as the TGV eased into motion and the station began to drift past their window. Like Ihsan, she watched the Catalan countryside with interest. Which was good, because once they got into France, the train would traverse mostly built-up areas.

The older girl seemed less excited, morose even. She did not meet his eyes. She stared mainly at the floor or the table or tried to read a newspaper—in English, he noted—but concentration clearly eluded her. He wanted to ask what was on her mind. He was nosy by nature, wanting to know about other people. It was the key reason he had become a linguist instead of remaining an engineer.

Eventually, he could not stop himself. "Have you been to Paris before?" he asked in English. The train was nonstop, so there was no point asking where she was going.

"Yes," she said, in a small voice. "Many times," she added, with more vigor, a touch of pride. "*J'ai été plusieurs fois,*" she repeated hesitantly in French. Her accent was unexpected, like she was from Asia or somewhere. The pair had one modest backpack for luggage.

He was happy to speak French with her, if she wanted practice, to return the favor that had been done for him many times, in many languages. "*Vous rencontrez quelqu'un?*" Are you meeting anyone?

"Um, *non, nous sommes,* um, *en vacances.*" No, we are on vacation.

A French official entered the car as it gained serious speed. The official started asking for passports. Ihsan grew nervous. Document checks like this did not happen often. They always spent more time on him. It would take five or ten minutes before the official reached their seats, minutes for Ihsan to worry.

He turned to the girls.

"*Par vous même? Vraiment?*" By yourselves? Really? (Was that too nosy?)

The older girl gave him a blank look. She had not understood.

"Demmy, what are you saying?" the smaller girl asked.

So the older girl's name was Demmy.

"It's French," Demmy said.

"She just told me you are on vacation," Ihsan said to the younger one. "And I am on my way home to Paris, after working a bit in Barcelona."

"What's your name," the younger girl asked.

"Ethan," he said.

"You don't look like an Ethan," the older girl said. Young woman, really.

"And what do Ethans look like?"

She appeared to give this consideration. Going over Ethans in her mind? "Good point," she said.

He smiled. He turned back to the younger one. "And what is your name?"

"Abby," she said.

The French official arrived at their table. "*Passeports s'il vous plait.*"

Demmy handed the man two passports; Ihsan handed him one. The official looked them over and handed Ihsan his back promptly. He examined those of the girls more closely. Ihsan felt guilty enjoying the unexpected reversal.

"*Vous êtes sœurs?*"

"*Oui, nous sommes sœurs,*" Demmy said. She apparently had enough French to understand he was asking if they were sisters.

"*Avez-vous des documents indiquant que vos parents vous ont autorisé à voyager avec votre sœur mineure?*"

Ihsan was curious how well she'd handle that. She paused. Ihsan was about to explain that the official wanted documentation that Demmy was allowed to travel internationally with her minor sister, but Demmy pulled out a paper form.

The official read it, checked it against the two passports. "*Bon séjour en France.*" Enjoy your trip to France.

Ihsan smiled. "I'm impressed!"

Demmy gave him a half smile. "I was guessing with that last one, but I had the letter and I figured what else could it be?"

"They make me nervous," he confessed. "I'm always afraid they won't let me in, even though I am a French citizen by birth. You know, because of how I look."

"Handsome and fit?" Now the girl gave him a full-blown smile, clearly enjoying the winking pretense that there was no such thing as racism. "Think he's jealous?"

He laughed. "A flirt. You'll do fine in Paris." She wouldn't need much French there.

"I was more afraid they wouldn't let us out of Spain. Like when you visit someone on a locked ward," Demmy said. "I always see myself clutching the bars and screaming 'but I'm not crazy!'"

"When did you ever visit someone on a locked ward? And, oh, what are you trying to say about Spain?" Ihsan asked.

"A high school friend had to go for a while." She switched to a whisper and leaned close to his ear. "*Il a tenté de se suicider.* Did I say that right?"

Attempted suicide. "Yes, I'm sorry to hear that."

Demmy shrugged. "He's much better now."

Whatever happened to carefree childhoods? Ihsan wondered. His had been fairly carefree, considering. He attributed that to his parents; he'd been lucky on that score.

She looked out the window. Good! She shouldn't miss the lovely countryside. He made a mental note to make sure the train hadn't lulled them to sleep when they went through Béziers. They'd love that view.

"Well, the doorman has deemed us worthy of la belle France. How do you feel about that?"

The little girl sang a familiar Lizzo line. She tossed her hair and checked her nails.

The older girl sang the next line to the little sister, asking "baby" how she was doing.

"Gud as 'ell!" Ihsan answered, singing in a pitch-perfect falsetto so loud people turned. Abby's eyes went as wide as saucers.

"What?" he asked.

CHAPTER 48

Roger opened the door to the adjoining hotel room, no longer able to fight the need to confirm the girls were there. Home, safe, even if home was a hotel room. But to his horror the beds were empty.

He sat on the rumpled sheets, no warmth in them whatsoever, and bypassed *maybe they've gone for croissants* in favor of *they've been kidnapped*, touching base at *Casey is going to kill me*.

He looked at the hotel phone. He couldn't call the police: Can you track my daughters' phones again? I'm worried they may have gone for breakfast.

He opened the curtains to let in the sun. The room looked emptier than ever, though strangely pretty, with its baroque furniture and clean carpets. Demmy's phone went straight to voicemail. He left a message. Just "You promised."

Casey could not know about this, he thought. That this was his main concern was reassuring; at heart, he knew eighteen-year-old Demmy was perfectly capable of safely navigating Barcelona—she'd been on her own in Paris before, for weeks at a time—and he knew Abby was safe with Demmy.

Demmy was responsible. Maybe too responsible. And where could they go?

To Maude? They liked Maude. But then he remembered Demmy accusing him and Maude of an affair at the gallery. So not Maude.

His mom? Abby loved her nana in a way that baffled Roger. Not that he didn't love her. She was his mother, for all her faults, and even that gallery fiasco had likely been guided in part by a twisted impulse to do something she felt was right. In a self-aggrandizing way, sure, but still. She'd created a huge, gorgeous portrait of Roger's late wife and Demmy's late mother. Given the time and attention invested, it was a magnanimous gesture. It wasn't her fault Roger that had kept all their emotions static in an undigested, neurotic stew.

Roger knocked on his mother's door. He was about to give up on her when she cracked the door open, sleepy-eyed, white hair teased by the pillow into full bag-lady.

He didn't even need to ask, but still: "Are Demmy and Abby with you?"

She reared back. "You've lost them again?"

He nodded.

"Dear. Losing them once is tragic; twice is careless, *pace* Oscar Wilde."

"Only you would use the word *pace* when her grandchildren are missing."

"Which is why you love me. Good luck."

"You're not going to help me look for them?"

"Roger, it's not even six AM. They are just out having fun, enjoying being in a big city."

"They live in New York!"

"So they can handle measly Barcelona."

"Is Maude up?"

"She's out. Maybe with the girls." She closed the door.

He tried Maude's phone. It went to voicemail. He tried his dad's room.

Shoshana answered the door. Roger explained the situation, including the bargain he'd struck with Demmy, that he would let the girls sleep undisturbed and in the morning everything would be back to normal.

"Your dad's dead to the world," Shoshana said, eyes blinking with sleep. "The jet lag has hit him hard. But give me a minute to get dressed. I'll help you find them."

"Thank you so much." Roger was glad to have an ally.

Shoshana was good as her word, ready in about a minute, and Roger appreciated her taking this seriously. They struck out onto quiet La Rambla, searching the leafy pedestrian space as city workers mopped up after the previous day's hordes with sweeping machines. The greens of the machines' broom bristles were color-coordinated with the worker's outfits, a display of urban moxie Roger found alarming.

Shoshana scanned the street. "You wouldn't think a six-year-old would be upset for this long about her parents fighting." Shoshana had raised two kids. "I mean, sure, twenty years after the fact it will be six months of therapy over a stray word, but the next day they are usually fine."

"I know, right?"

"Demmy, now that's another story."

Roger blanched. "What do you mean?"

"She's been nursing those grievances a while."

Roger did not want to hear this. "About me and Maude? Casey and Kelly?"

Shoshana nodded. He mentally categorized Shoshana as his parents' generation, but she was a handful of years younger than them, and those years seemed enough to allow her to spring into action looking halfway decent, vigorous. Irrationally, this also made her seem wise.

"But there's nothing going on!"

"Are you sure?"

He thought about it. Maybe he wasn't.

"I've wondered myself. About you and Maude, that is. I don't know this Kelly person."

"Maude and I are friends."

Shoshana allowed the silence to speak for her.

"Okay," Roger said, as they finished inspecting another café. "Here's the deal: Maude and I had a short, torrid thing a million years ago, when she and her husband were separated. But they got back together, had Scott and Jared, and I met Aline. *So* much water under the bridge. Maude and I may be too touchy feely, but it's just familiarity. She's my oldest friend. That's all there is to it."

Shoshana nodded. "I believe you. It fits. Now you just need to get Demmy to believe you. And you'll need to talk this through with Casey as well, after that blow-up at the gallery."

"It wasn't that bad."

"Not that bad? Roger, it was worse. Shrieking accusations of cruelty, manipulation, and affairs. Hidden husbands and children. Penises! It's hard to think of what wasn't covered. And your mother is famous. Reporters were there. Do *not* check your Twitter feed."

"Oh God." Roger sat on a bench and covered his face in his hands. All his life it had been like this, only now everyone had cameras. No wonder he couldn't remember what had happened at the gallery: his mind couldn't face it.

The sun was well up, now. They'd canvassed the street. Almost all the nearby cafés. Were the girls perhaps at the beach? He and Shoshana walked back. When they got to the hotel, Shoshana said she'd go rouse Roger's parents and Maude, get more "geriatric" feet on the ground. They'd find the girls.

Roger went back upstairs, imagining he'd find his girls there, mocking his excessive worry. They were not there. He sat on the bed, hand on the mattress where his babies had been sleeping, and from there he saw the note. On paper. Written in block letters, like a kidnapper would use. It was from Demmy, who knew no cursive.

ABBY IS STILL HYSTERICAL. GUESS YOU CAN'T HEAR THE TANTRUMS. SHE WANTS TO SEE FRANCE

Oh, no, thought Roger. He read on.

I HAVE MY TRUST FUND, SO I'LL TAKE HER TO PARIS. SHE IS GOING TO MISS CASEY ANY MINUTE NOW. SHE'LL BE HOMESICK AND SCREAMING TO SEE YOU BOTH IN NO TIME, PROBABLY BEFORE WE GET THERE. NO, ARIANA! NO, LIZZO! ACK! SEE YOU SOON! XOXO

He remembered all those times over the years he'd praised Demmy's independence—for riding the subway alone to school, getting a job—all those times he'd encouraged her to get out there, have experiences. Roger remembered the just-in-case letter he'd written Demmy, giving her permission to travel with Abby, egged on by what Constanza had said about the stranded nanny and kids in *Babel* nearly dying in the desert.

"What have I done?"

CHAPTER 49

Casey stayed at Memphis International only long enough to top off her phone and laptop batteries as she checked the DNA testing site to see if *S P* had replied to the message Casey had sent from the airport in Barcelona. She had written a hundred or so wildly different messages before settling on the simple truth: *I believe I am your mother. Please reply.* She'd included the number of her phone, which she now checked again to make sure airplane mode was off and the ringer was on.

She found a motel not far from downtown to set up her base of operations. It was nothing special, but had a business nook for guests, where she printed out the relevant pages of Abby and Roger's DNA reports. She'd examined endless scenarios in her head on the flight over. How had Execrable escaped, that was her first question. Somehow, he'd defied the odds and swum with Elyse to safety. Or, he'd drowned but Elyse had made it to shore. That seemed impossible, but something unforeseen had occurred. And she would find out what.

She called her mother back in Eldon, deep in the Ozarks on the Missouri side, to let her and her father know that Elyse was alive and somewhere in Memphis. The shock in their voices reassured her: she had allowed herself to wonder if they had somehow been involved, though why ever would they have been? She would later make other phone calls, but before that she went to nearby Memphis Police Headquarters and walked in the door with her printouts.

It took some convincing, but she was shown into a room and told to wait. Within ten minutes, a tall officer entered, clean-shaven, in uniform. About her age, but his skin looked more weathered.

"Sergeant Dunne," he introduced himself. He carried a sheaf of papers in a folder.

"Is that Elyse's case report?" Casey asked, fearing it was random, unrelated paperwork. Please don't blow me off as a kook, she prayed.

"Yes, ma'am." He nodded. "Unfortunately, the officer in charge is no longer with us."

"Retired?"

"Deceased, I'm afraid. You have a DNA report, I'm told?"

"Two." Casey slid them across the table. "I printed out copies for you." She pointed to the key bits: Abby and *S P*'s results, pointing to the percentages. "It's over 26% in common, and there's no Y chromosome, so that means *S P* is Abby's aunt, niece, grandmother or half-sibling. My parents have reaffirmed I have no sister. My brother has no daughters. And my mother swears up and down she's never swabbed her cheeks or spit in a vial."

"Does your daughter's father have any sisters or nieces? Is *his* mother still alive?"

"You mean Abby? My daughter Abby is not related to *S P*'s

father. Her father is my second husband, and *S P* is not flagged as related to him."

The sergeant gave this some thought. "Of course. Got it." He looked embarrassed, which was a good sign.

"Two husbands, two daughters. It's tricky," Casey conceded. She showed him Roger's printout and its list of close relatives. No *S P*.

The sergeant went over the printed pages, following the text and diagrams with his index finger. Casey wanted to get off on the right foot with him, to let the man familiarize himself with the data without recrimination, but couldn't help blurting, "They told me there was no chance she had survived."

"Clearly they were wrong." Dunne reached the end of the two reports. "Now it's my job—the Department's job—to find out where they went astray. I've looked at the earlier report. Nothing jumped out at me, but we need to look at this from a different perspective. Knowing that Elyse survived, we need to work backwards to learn what happened. Have you tried to contact her?"

"I emailed through the site. Whether she responds is up to her." Casey shook her head. "I should never have stopped looking."

"Don't do that to yourself. I've skimmed the coroner's and river hydrologist's reports as well. As I said, nothing obviously haywire, but I will have professionals reexamine them. I will also run DMV searches to see if we can find this *S P*. And I will get a warrant to get her information from the DNA company. I need you to reach out to your family as well as your first husband's. If he is alive as well, he may be in contact with his family."

Casey's immediate thought was that his parents, if they were in on it, would alert Execrable and he'd flee with Elyse all over again. But Elyse was a grown woman now, with a life, so that would be harder than spiriting off a seven-month-old baby. Dunne was right. She'd have to risk it. But not by phone; she'd go in person. She needed to see their faces, read their expressions. Missouri, she thought, here I come.

CHAPTER 50

R oger forced laughter. "She's asleep in the other room," he told Casey when she asked to speak to Abby.

He ran his hands over the light-blocking drapes of the hotel room, now open to let in the noonday sun. Casey had more than enough to contend with, and Roger had everything handled. French immigration authorities had identified the train that his daughters were on. The police had located the girls' seat numbers. The immigration official on board had confirmed their presence. He had assured Roger he would escort the girls to the police when they reached Paris. Roger's flight was due to land shortly thereafter, whereupon he would escort his girls home. Once they were in his custody, safely back in Williamsburg, *then* Casey could know the full dimensions of his lapse.

He picked up his overnight bag and left for the airport.

"At this hour?" Casey was naturally skeptical. Abby was not a great napper.

Roger stopped at the elevator, hesitating to get on for fear of losing the call. "Jet lag plus emotional exhaustion," Roger said. All these fibs could come back to haunt him, but the girls traveled together regularly throughout New York City; he doubted they were in any more danger in Paris than at home.

"Is Demmy around?"

This might be his last chance to come clean, but Roger needed to take this responsibility off her hands. "Out with Maude."

"The woman she thinks you had an affair with?"

Oops. "That doesn't sound likely, does it?"

"No, it does not."

"Teenagers." He felt like adding, *am I right?*, but had enough sense not to overegg a gilded lily.

"I suppose." Casey's voice sounded tiny over the line, like it had to squeeze through a tube to make it to Spain, Catalunya, whatever this place was.

"Any luck out there?"

"I'm at Memphis police headquarters. They are taking me seriously, which is a miracle. The officer who is helping me is young, so maybe he wants to make a name for himself. Or maybe he's just a professional. I'm about to head out to Missouri to talk to my ex-in-laws. The police think there's a reasonable chance they are involved. If my ex is alive and has raised Elyse . . ."

Casey's voice trailed off. Roger could hear the hurt running through her voice like grain through wood.

". . . if he's alive, they may know. I'm confronting them face to face, so I will have a chance to tell if they are lying."

"Do you have anyone to go with you?"

"No," Casey said.

"I'm sorry," Roger said.

"Don't be sorry. I see now it's better this way. It would be too hard if Demmy and Abby were here. Though once this is over? I want us all to come here, for a vacation."

"A vacation? In Missouri!" He'd blurted it out.

"Roger." Reproach filled her voice. "There's some beautiful countryside here. We can hit Lake of the Ozarks, Branson, maybe even nip down to Eureka Springs. We'll do that float down the Sweet Oak I told you about."

He had no idea what she was talking about. The closest he'd ever gotten to that part of the country was listening to Terry Gross interview Jan Stites, the author of a book Casey had raved about.

"Absolutely." For Casey, he'd swap their usual Tuscany home-exchange for the jungle. Casey didn't need to know the idea of Missouri scared him. Hell, Pennsylvania made him wary, and that was even before Terry Gross had brought up a childhood encounter with chiggers, whatever they were.

"I'm flying up but driving back. I need to talk to everyone I can find who knew us, which means going to Eldon and Jeff City."

"Flying?" Roger had a hard time articulating his question. If you were driving one way, why not both? How long was the flight? Twenty minutes?

"Roger, it's 450 miles away?"

"Where exactly do these in-laws live?"

"Peculiar."

There was a town called Peculiar? Seriously? He remembered the warm, bantering tone in Stites' voice over the radio as she advised Terry to focus on fireflies, not chiggers, and the two had laughed like old friends. In all honesty, the whole thing had sounded lovely, and he'd idly imagined himself swimming in warm, gently flowing water. He now added fireflies to the idyllic picture and made a mental note to not look up *chiggers* on Wikipedia.

CHAPTER 51

Maude walked down La Rambla with Sherbeam toward Galería Les Rambles. Her phone screen was free of text flurries between estranged parents and children. The marital bickering and resulting drama of misplaced children had been sucking up her entire attention. Now that the girls were safe and sound, Maude found herself facing a new emotion: disgust for the woman walking alongside her.

"I hope I don't give the wrong impression by visiting the gallery again," Sherbeam said as they strolled through a flock of midday tourists, darting like finches gobbling up a scattering of seed. "People will think I have nothing to do besides haunt my past life in search of former glory."

Which was pretty much the case, as far as Maude could tell. With the rabid onslaught of the media over the past twelve hours, Sherbeam's star was shining brighter than ever. Sherbeam's new art provided scrumptious images for the media.

"You might want to think about living in the gallery. You could be an installation in the front window. Just shove my naked body and Roger's into the back room." Sherbeam was easy to needle.

Sherbeam rolled her eyes. "See, this is your problem: you ignore marketing. Two beautiful naked people will draw more attention than a ratty-haired broad wiping the sleep from her eyes in a gallery window. I'm better suited to evil Svengali bitch in this passion play. That's the angle I told social media boy to push."

They arrived at the gallery. Maude's former self loomed before her. she had to acknowledge Sherbeam's point. She and Roger were attractive in their youthful glory.

"How do you know Roger's adult naked body so well?"

"His torso looks rather like his father's. The rest I could make up."

The portrait showed Roger as a good-looking young man, but no more than he'd actually been, and "the rest" was not flattering. Sherbeam would rather die than flatter, Maude thought. If one was to remain friends with an influential egomaniac, chunks of the relationship were better invented than delved into. Maude had excelled at that over the years, but all roads eventually end.

"Is your evisceration of your son and your whole family due to artistic agenda, spite, or dogma?"

Sherbeam whipped her head around. She quickly plastered on a patronizing smile, but Maude saw she'd struck a vein.

"Artistic agenda—is that like you sucking off me? Spite—is that spite for Roger? *The Fix* is not enough of an accomplishment to inspire spite. And dogma? No one adapts to changing mores better than I do."

A bitter taste rose in Maude's throat. That certainly sounded like spite to Maude. "Go haunt your former glory."

"I'm here at the gallery to work," Sherbeam said.

"You're painting?"

Sherbeam nodded. "I've had an inspiration. Pau is letting me take over the back room. I have a new piece in mind. I see now it's crucial to the show. I have to get it done before we close. Even if it means making Pau extend the show."

"You can do that?"

"Honey, I can do anything," Sherbeam said.

Maude asked despite her revulsion. "Tell me about the new piece."

Sherbeam brought her index finger to her lips. "Secret," she whispered. She turned as she slipped into the gallery. "It's a shocking new direction you won't see coming. A repudiation of everything I ever stood for."

Maude knew this was supposed to draw her in; she refused to be drawn. Having belittled Maude's work, Sherbeam was now trying to tempt her with the chance to see how it was properly done. But Sherbeam had used this trick of withholding once too often. Ten times too often. Maude believed in her new work, even if Sherbeam didn't, even if Elż had been bored by it.

Maude stood at the front window, surveying Sherbeam's portrait of her. She'd already had her sons then, and her body showed that. Sherbeam had rendered her stretch marks as the emblem of accomplishment that they were; there was some respect between them. Something authentic had drawn them together: both were proud of the lives they'd led, every last bit of them.

"Is that you?" a woman beside Maude asked.

Maude turned to her. The woman was younger than her by ten years, Maude estimated, and of similar grand carriage. Though white was only beginning to streak through the woman's curly black hair, she gave an impression of strength that Maude approved of.

"More than a quarter-century ago," Maude said. "I was something, wasn't I?"

"You look very much the same, I'd say."

Maude felt a fillip of happiness. The woman did not look like she was softening her words to be kind. "Thank you."

"Does *he*?"

"He who? You mean Roger?"

The woman laughed. "Yes, Roger."

"He's changed more," Maude tactfully said. "You know him?" she asked, though from the woman's Scottish accent Maude already had an idea.

"I knew him in his Fulbright days."

Could Maude be standing beside *The Girl*? "How do you come to be here, in Barcelona?"

"I saw in *The New Yorker* that a retrospective was planned. I had plans to be in Bilbao, so I popped over." She held her hands clasped before her as she leaned back a bit, bouncing, as though pleased with herself, or enjoying the unlikelihood of an unexpected moment. "Is Roger in town?"

Maude looked at her phone. "Barely. He is boarding a flight to Paris momentarily. I'm afraid you've missed him."

"Oh, pity." She dug in her purse. "Would you tell him an old friend came by to see him?" She handed Maude a card. Professor of Econometrics at the London School of Economics. Niamh McNeese.

Well, well. Maude had guessed correctly. "I will make sure he gets it," she told The Girl, pocketing the card as the woman left.

And as fate would have it, Roger appeared minutes later, racing toward her bearing a shoulder bag. But before Maude could tell him about The Girl, he was already talking full tilt.

"Maude, I don't have much time. Can you do me a huge favor? The girls and I may leave from Paris, so can you make sure our bags get sent back home? They are packed but still in my and Casey's room." He handed her a cardkey.

Maude stared at it. It would be a lie to say she didn't mind. She stared at Roger, thinking *If you could shut up for ten seconds I could tell you something you'd want to know.*

"And don't tell Casey about the girls. Please."

Maude reminded herself Roger was not his mother. "I'm not the one you have to worry about." Maude shrugged toward the gallery. "The threat is in there."

"Thanks."

"Roger, do you need to see her?" She didn't want to see him debase himself to win anything from Sherbeam.

He stopped in the doorway to look back.

"She's never given you your due, Roger. Never will."

"I know that, Maude. But this is a necessary errand, for Casey."

Maude looked past him toward Sherbeam, whom she could see standing in the back facing a canvas similar in size to the ones of herself and Roger. Sherbeam had already made bold black marks on it. She must have a clear idea of what she wanted to do.

"Out! Out!" Maude heard Sherbeam yell at Roger as he entered.

"Mother, I'm off to Paris. Don't tell Casey about the girls. If you value your life."

"Out!" she yelled again.

"Mom, seriously!"

"Out!"

"You couldn't stop me leaving if you wanted to," Roger grumbled, exiting the room.

Maude stopped Roger at the gallery entrance and handed him the card, told him the story. *The Girl.* "You just missed her."

He looked at the card in shock.

Sherbeam's phone rang. She moved toward them, as though preferring to disturb them over disturbing her canvas. She answered it in the door, nodding, "yes, yes." Nodding some more. "That's wonderful news," she said loudly. "Thank you so much!"

She looked at Roger and Maude and screamed. "I've won a MacArthur!"

"Good for you." Maude turned and walked away.

CHAPTER 52

The train sped through the banlieues, Gare de Lyon fast approaching. Ihsan asked Demmy where they were planning to stay in Paris.

"Do they have Airbnbs here?" They used English exclusively now, Demmy having reached the limits of her French with *suicide attempt.*

"Only everywhere!" he said, Gallic pride rising. Paris had everything. Ten of everything. "My parents have one, even. Above their bakery. My ma decorated it."

And before he knew it, Demmy had found it on her phone. "Is this it?"

How she had located it without his parents' location or his last name? He sighed. She wasn't *that* much younger than Ihsan (he was just shy of thirty), but the difference was a couple of generations in digital terms.

His befuddlement must have shown, because she said, "I own Google."

Was her father a billionaire?

Her phone made a noise. "Booked it."

"You booked my parents Airbnb?" *Merde.* He was going to

have to take them there. Like that would look totally plausible: two American girls, chaperoned by him. If the police didn't stop them three times on the way it would be a miracle.

She was looking over the pictures of the flat. "Slay," she said.

He raised an eyebrow. Whatever did she mean? "It's not at all central," he warned her.

"We want to be where real people live, not the tourist areas."

It was not a tourist area, that was for sure. She would be pleased with the apartment—clean, comfy, en suite bathroom —and with the neighborhood, if she meant that about "real people." It was smack in the 21st arrondissement—near the banlieues that were home to his family's Benghazi village (as he thought of their circle of friends and relations) but within the bounds of Paris itself. It was a moderately prosperous area, quite pleasant to live in, with shopping streets, a few parks, a historic church or two, and a Metro station.

They pulled into Gare de Lyon. From the train carriage window, Abby pointed at the glass roof vaulting overhead while they waited with their meager bags in the crowded aisle for the doors to open. Outside, Ihsan spotted police hustling toward them, as though late for something. And damned if the immigration official wasn't entering the front end of their car, too. Ihsan felt paranoid, but for once he let himself indulge that feeling and flee. Why make a point asserting your right to exist every minute of the day when avoidance was so easy? He weaved with the girls through the passengers in the aisle —excusez-moi! excusez-moi!—to slip into the next carriage and exit there. He steered the three of them behind the screen of an immense pile of baggage being pushed on a cart and kept pace with the shelter of the slow-moving cart. No sense pressing one's luck.

"The room is quite remote," he told Demmy. "I can talk my parents out of the cancellation fee," he added as they exited the platform together.

Demmy shook her head.

Abby was taken with the station, pointing at the indoor palm trees, the arches, the clock tower, even the people, which felt rude to Ihsan, but was perhaps the American way.

Demmy kept Abby moving on their way to the Metro. Demmy seemed as eager to get settled somewhere as he was to get back to Nabil. He shepherded the two around another clot of police officers when the officers turned to look at a loud clang of some sort. The three trotted down into the Metro, which fortunately also captured the interest of the demanding younger girl, forestalling any demands to explore Gare de Lyon.

He explained the ticket machines, got them a Metro route map—paper could be nice to peruse in the quiet of one's own room—and once they were on the Metro he showed them on the map where they were and where they were headed.

They didn't need instructions on how to behave on the Metro. They were courteous, or at least not inconsiderate, although Abby wanted to talk to other passengers on the train, which Ihsan and the other passengers found odd. But he interpreted for them and no harm was done, beyond a few suspicious looks. He sent back a look of his own: No, he had not kidnapped the two girls.

It was with relief that he got the girls to his parents.

"Who are these two Americans? Where are their parents? You met them on the train? It looks like you kidnapped them!" his ma (Amal) said in a rush of Libyan Arabic that the girls would have no chance of understanding as they were escorted upstairs, given a key.

"They are very nice, just young," Ihsan said, once the door

closed on the girls settling into their room. "I made the mistake of mentioning the room and she reserved it herself." Ihsan was eager not to be blamed.

"The richer they are, the more trouble," his dad (Tareq) said. "This won't end well."

"It will be fine," his ma said. "The room wasn't booked. Who are we to turn them away?" His ma liked to have someone to disagree with and Ihsan was glad to have that role transferred to his father, putting his ma by default in Ihsan's corner. The ensuing debate gave Ihsan the chance to slip out and make his way around the block to his own apartment, where he let himself in and was greeted by Nabil, home early from his shift at the salon.

Ihsan told Nabil about the girls after his kiss of welcome subsided. (Their honeymoon phase had so far lasted five years.)

"You charmed them," Nabil said, in the French they used between themselves. "As always."

Ihsan smiled. Nothing beat the feeling of closing the world out when he was back in the apartment with Nabil. Not even his parent's house felt so safe. "You know what 'slay' means, in English?"

Nabil shook his head. "A cart for the snow?"

"Google says 'kill.'" Ihsan was going to have to go back and ask Demmy, even though he suspected the term, like so much of modern life, would be out of date by the time he understood it.

CHAPTER 53

Casey drove her rented Ford Fusion to Hank's house. A dusty beater was parked in the drive. Casey pulled up the short gravel driveway past a double-sized blue trash bin filled with wood planks from someone's scrapped project and parked between the beater and a makeshift work surface atop two oil drums. She walked up a brick pathway losing a battle with a burgeoning, bright green lawn. She rang the bell.

"Henrietta," Casey said when her ex-mother-in-law opened the door.

"Do I know you?" Hank looked at her through the screen door.

Casey stood, challenging the slender, older woman with her stance. Casey knew she had not changed *that* much. Did her in-laws have something to hide?

"Oh my lord," Hank said. "With my cataracts I didn't recognize you." She swung the screen door open. "Come in, Honey." She moved aside for Casey to enter, but Casey did not get too far before Hank enveloped her in her arms. "I've missed you so much."

Casey tried to return the hug, but her body rebelled. She

felt herself stiffen in Hank's embrace. This warmth, though welcome, was not a good sign. If Hank knew anything about Elyse, her reaction should have been guilt. Casey did not want her in-laws to be involved, but if they weren't, finding Elyse would be that much harder.

"Joe! Joe! Get in here!"

So her ex-father-in-law was home, too. Good.

Hank led Casey into the wide galley kitchen and sat her at the maple table, pushed against the far wall as it had been almost two decades ago. "Can I get you something?" She was already pulling a Tupperware pitcher of sweet tea from an ancient white fridge and setting it on the table, whose dark finish was marred by only a pair of white water rings and the carved initials *MTH*: Execrable.

Hank pulled three TEXAN tumblers from a dish drainer sitting on a Rubbermaid tray on the yellow tiled countertop. "Where have you been all this time? I've googled you many a time, but there's nothing." Hank ran a palm over her pulled-back gray hair. "Did you change your name?"

"I did," Casey said. "I'm Casey, now, Casey White."

"Casey. *All* the girls have boys' names now, don't they?"

"Like you?"

Hank laughed. "It suits you."

Joe came into the room, his gait still heavier on the left, the result of a minor birth defect, Execrable had told Casey. Joe grabbed the knotty pine doorframe for support when he saw who it was. It was a melodramatic gesture, but he was tearing up, and searching for words. Casey had expected a fight. Not this. Nothing like this.

"Oh, sweetheart." He barely got the words out. He sat at the chair beside her and took her hand.

Casey was now the one feeling guilty, leaving them alone

so long with their grief, for that's what this looked like. She felt no reproach.

"We heard you went to Mexico." Joe ran his hand over the few hairs remaining on his gleaming scalp, two shades lighter than the sweet tea.

Casey nodded. "I couldn't stay."

Hank poured her a drink, slid the cool tumbler of ice cubes and red-brown tea toward her. "We understand. Right, Joe?"

He nodded.

"Still, it's damn good to see you. I always thought the world of you. You know that, don't you? I'm sorry I didn't say that more."

"I would still have left." Casey wrapped her palm around the cool amber plastic of the tumbler. "But I wish now I hadn't."

"You needed to go. You had to," Hank said.

"No, it's not that. Or not just that. You see, I've had news."

"What news?" Casey could see in Hank's eyes, Joe's eyes, that they were expecting news of a body. Two bodies.

Casey pulled out the copies of Abby and Roger's results. She explained who Abby and Roger were, then brought her finger to the mysterious *S P*. "If there's another explanation, I haven't found anyone who could come up with it."

"Elyse is alive?" Joe got it faster than Detective Dunne had. Hank caught her breath.

"Looks like."

"But how?" Joe had been dogged in pushing the inquiry into the waterlogged pickup. He'd stayed with her in Memphis, studied up on the findings. He was a pipefitter by trade and able to explain a lot of it to Casey that she hadn't understood.

"I was hoping you could shed light on that," Casey said.

"The report was . . . wait, you think we . . ." Now Joe looked angry. Hank said nothing. Casey felt Hank had understood the implication as soon as the words left Casey's mouth, but her response had been milder. Joe sputtered. "You think we . . ."

"I'm asking. Did you have any role in this? Do you know anything?" Casey had no inclination to dance around the subject. Her daughter was out there.

"If I knew where she was, I'd take you there myself," Hank said. "Hell, I'd be there now. I lost a child, too, that day, as well as a granddaughter, and what you may not fully have cottoned onto yet is that something awful descended on this house when they found that truck. I raised that boy. I loved Mackie. And he does this? I wished I could go back in time and do something, but where would I go? There was something off in him from childhood. I should have talked to you about it. I can't wish he'd never been born; he was my baby, for all that. But sometimes I do."

Joe went into the other room and returned with a photograph of Casey, Mackie—ugh, that name—and Elyse, posing for a portrait.

"How could they be alive?" he asked.

"The detective in Memphis said the question is, knowing that she's alive, what did we get wrong?"

"You've been to the police?" He sounded oddly wounded.

"Of *course* I've been to the police," she snapped. Did they think she was useless?

"We've never had any indication that Mackie might be alive." Hank brought a little calm back. "No strange phone calls. No unexplained behavior from his brother and sister."

"There was one thing that made me think he was alive," Joe said.

"And you didn't tell me?"

"Now, hold your horses. I followed up on it. We figured it

out. We were so disappointed, believe me, like to die. We did *not* want to put you through that." Joe twisted his hands together.

"Well, tell me now."

"We received a warrant for his arrest, *after* he died. But it turned out to be for unpaid parking tickets, all from *before* he died."

He had certainly racked them up, had the whole time they'd lived in Memphis, but a week or two before his disappearance he'd finally got paid up, with money she gave him. Or so he'd said.

"We showed the police. They said it was nothing."

"They don't have the greatest record at this point."

Joe nodded. "I'll get it."

"You have it?" Casey asked.

Hank nodded. "We have everything." She held Casey's hand as they waited. Joe returned with a box, not much larger than a shoebox. "Everything" was not much.

Joe began pulling papers out, flipping through them. He located the warrant, showed her it was dated after Mackie's supposed death. Joe pointed to the citation numbers on the warrant. He explained the police codes. They had been explained to him, and he remembered. The paper looked worn, as though his fingers had worried the sheet many times. He found a parking ticket and showed Casey how the numbers corresponded. She checked the dates. He was right. This was nothing.

"Can I take these?" she asked.

They hesitated, both of them. Was this box of trash—that's what it was—so important to them? That, more than anything, convinced her they had not been involved. This box of nothing was what they had left of their youngest son.

"Please? I will return all of it."

"Sure, honey. Really, it's all yours, anyway. You're his wife."

Casey reached out, for the first time, and took their hands. She nodded. She didn't have any words that would remove the sadness. If she was successful, and she would be, she would return with something far more important than a handful of faded scraps of paper. She would return with their granddaughter.

CHAPTER 54

The flaxen-haired Paris police officer led Roger into a sofa lounge rather than the fraught pit he'd expected. He'd envisioned a decaying hell walled in those ubiquitous soundproofing tiles that Roger imagined muffled suspects' screams in police stations everywhere. He stared at the spiky blond coif spraying out from under the officer's black cap. He could tell she had bad news.

"What do you mean they weren't on the train?" The hesitant sense of security Roger had felt on the flight up was obliterated. His daughters could be anywhere, facing anything.

"I misspoke. They *were* on the train. The ticketing, passport records, and eyewitnesses all confirm it. But the officers did not see them disembark." She did not sound hostile, but neither did she sound apologetic. The police had the same basic outlook toward civilians as doctors: you were wrong and you were an idiot.

Roger wanted to yell at her, demand an explanation of the how of it, but he needed information more than satisfaction. "What eyewitnesses?"

"Other passengers. They saw two girls answering their

description in the company of an Arab man. They were making quite a ruckus."

Roger could not grasp this scene. "Ruckus?"

"It means lots of noise and activity."

"Yes, I know what *ruckus* means. Are you telling me they were kidnapped?" Roger's confidence in Demmy's maturity was now exposed as a fig leaf over massive anxiety.

The officer cocked her head. *Noncommittal*, Roger thought. Wasn't that, too, a Lizzo lyric? He pictured his sweet Abby listening to her idol.

"The security cameras do not seem to show them under duress."

"You have them on camera?"

"Yes, sir."

"And?"

"They went into the Metro with the Arab, whereupon it became much more difficult to track them. We may be able to find them, theoretically, on the video feeds of other stations, but it would take days and we do not have the personnel."

"I'll do it."

She laughed and shook her head. "We cannot allow that."

How dare she laugh. Don't let anything happen to my girls, he prayed. He'd been a fool to trust Demmy. God, Casey was going to kill him. "Here is my older daughter's cell phone number. She used the phone in Spain. Likely she will again here. I need something to go on."

"Go on?"

"I need someplace to start."

"Let me see if I can get someone with those skills." The officer directed him to an interview room. And now there they were, those beat-up asbestos wall and ceiling tiles, indeed the same worldwide, the world consisting, of course, of France, the United States, and possibly Spain.

He turned and she was gone. Better not be for long. He was in no mood to be stranded while his girls were missing. Again he thought of hospitals and doctors—the endless recapitulation of Aline's condition to each fresh professional determined to start from the very beginning, as their protocol demanded, until you thought you would scream. Until you did scream.

Roger sat, the minutes ticking by, calculating how counterproductive it would be to throw a good old American-style temper tantrum. He knew it would again be like doctors: any perceived lack of respect would be mercilessly punished. And he needed these people.

He instinctively reached for his wallet, as though some combination of credit and identity cards would bail him out. He found Niamh's card, pulled it out and stared at it, in his hand. He had not heard one word from her since that last, fateful Oxbridge screaming match—yes, more screaming—and now he'd missed her by ten minutes. Lucky or unlucky?

His phone rang. The number displayed was gibberish, only six digits, and those arranged oddly. It could be anyone. It could be salvation. "Hello?"

"It's Niamh."

"Niamh! I was just looking at your card." This was fucking unbelievable. She was European; could she have power, connections, advice? But it turned out to be the other Niamh. The redheaded student he'd forgotten existed. His heart sank.

"You have to check YouTube. I thought someone should give you the heads-up before you get back from spring break."

Oh, God. All this drama and they were still on spring break. "And what is it I am looking for on YouTube?"

"Yourself. And Barcelona."

"Barcelona?" As in Demmy and Abby? Since he couldn't do that and talk to her on the phone, he thanked her and ended the call. He did a search for himself, and there it was. So many Roger Whites in the world, and still he topped the list. He clicked and was rewarded with a gif of himself yelling *That's not me! That's not me! That's not me!* Etc. Then up flashed an image of the painting, or rather one key part of it: the snaking smudged member, stylized enough that the moderators hadn't vetoed it. Wonderful. Thanks, Mom.

But that was not the end of it.

It was a rapid-fire mashup horror set to a hip-hop beat. Roger saying *your grandfather* and *gratuitously realistic.* A surprising image of said gratuitous realism. Demmy saying, "You have another daughter?" Roger saying "Who is the father?" Casey screeching, "I am not leaving Demmy." Demmy screeching "I don't have to obey."

Roger wanted to shut it off, stop watching. But he didn't. Who had done this to them?

It kept going. The smudge came up again and again, the star of the show, really, the way every penis wants to be. Now Demmy was saying, "You think no one sees?" It went on. That reporter had filmed it all. Or someone had. Phrases were broken down and remixed into a graceless poem:

Little touches
hand holds, shared holds,
shared jokes, little jokes
Maude knows
bodybodybodybody
yoga lady, touching herself
bodybodybodybody.

A close-up of Demmy's horrified face now filled the screen. Then Casey's face, contorted in outrage.

Did you even want
a second child?

Roger saying, *No.*

Oh, God. No wonder Abby had fled. But he hadn't been saying no to that question. It had been no to the whole melt-down, no to doing this in public, in a gallery, in Barcelona, no to how his mother would find a way to benefit from this. No wonder Demmy had gone with Abby. She was punishing them in the guise of comforting Abby.

The realization made the YouTube less humiliating, almost salutary. His girls were not crazy, just hurt. Something in here would help him find them. And even at its worst, the mashup didn't match the humiliation of seeing that painting from the street, or the way his guts had been snatched from his body by Aline's portrait in the inner sanctum of the gallery. The way his mother had used him. That had felt like theft. Roger wondered if every painter's child felt that, at one time or another.

He knew that, professionally, he would have to deal with the video when he returned home. And how would he do that? Tell the world his actual body was nothing like that? Ha! Talk about digging yourself deeper. He'd have to accept that this would be his body in the popular imagination, that his cock would be in the popular imagination.

Was it too late to slap an eggplant emoji on there? He enlarged the smudge. Was that another curve? And the views. So many. He was a meme. Better learn some smudged penis jokes, because if he was going to have to roll with it, he'd better do so with grace. How many corkscrew cocks does it take to screw in a lightbulb?

He had tried to be a good father, a good teacher, to be a good guy, but he'd failed his daughters badly. And now Casey was halfway around the world, hunting through the Ozarks for yet another daughter, whose name, Roger was ashamed to realize, he did not even remember. Maybe hadn't even heard, even asked.

The police officer returned with a companion. They spread out pictures from the surveillance camera. The Arab wasn't sporting a bushy beard, wasn't dressed in thobe and gutra, or in a black leather jacket, or shouldering a machine gun. Nope. He was well dressed, clean shaven and carried himself with an easy manner; Demmy and Abby, too, seemed gleeful, relaxed. The Arab looked non-threatening, kind of gay (pink shirt, tight fade to his haircut, possibly threaded eyebrows). Roger felt easier. The guy oozed decency. Was there a chance this could work out?

The two officers rose to go track Demmy's phone. Roger warned them that Demmy powered her phone down frequently. They left him again, alone in the interview room.

Roger felt like a suspect: guilty, small. He felt anew the stunning blow of his mother's news. A MacArthur? He'd congratulated her, which had been hard, but he was a fool to feel jealous. After all, when the phone call came, she'd been working, as always, brush on canvas, while he had spent the morning trying to repair a crisis born of his own neuroses. Pretty much the same as ever, except this time he'd put his daughters at risk. He had not written a word of criticism since before midterms started. Or over the last year. Why would anyone in their right mind give Roger White a MacArthur?

He hadn't produced anything since Aline got sick, was the truth of it. He was crazy to think about any of this when his daughters were in peril. And yet he felt grief, not just for his losses and for his missing girls and for the inevitable hurt when Casey discovered he had lied to her, but also for the lives ended or upended, and everything that would never be. He ached. He wanted nothing more than to go home and sit in his kitchen with his girls and a cup of milky coffee waiting for Casey to come home as they listened to *Wait Wait . . . Don't Tell Me!* while pretending none of this had ever happened.

CHAPTER 55

Casey drove into the night, questions forming as her headlights illuminated the highway miles passing. Joe had insisted, before she left, on imparting every scrap of information and insight he had about the warrant. The three had sat at Hank and Joe's kitchen table and worked their way through the box. Casey photographed each scrap of paper. The traffic tickets in the box backed up what the police had said about the warrant. All were unpaid, despite money he'd wheedled from her, twenty, thirty, fifty bucks at a time. Way back when, Mackie had been squirreling away money to fund his crime. For months.

As Casey drove, a map of Memphis formed in her mind. One ticket was from their quiet street. More were in commercial areas. One address she remembered was near a movie theater. It was a diary of their life at the time.

With the aid of her phone's map app and Hank and Joe's memories, she had been able to account for all except one. It was over four hundred miles to Memphis, and had been pushing ten o'clock, but she was wide-eyed and had known she would not be able to sleep until she saw that address for herself.

Turning down Hank and Joe's repeated pleas to stay in the spare room, she hit the road. They waved goodbye from the stoop in their pajamas as Casey took their son from them in the shoebox of fading paper. She could read a long experience of defeat in their slack expressions, their raised inner brows, their pulled down lips. She resolved to change that.

She drove straight through the night, crossing over that bit of Lake of the Ozarks farthest from her parents, and arrived spent and gritty in Memphis just after dawn.

She drove to the address in question. It was a rundown block, not far from the river, near Mud Island. The location was home to an aging strip mall, half occupied. Not one store meant anything to her. A Chinese restaurant? A bail bond shop? A liquor store. Had she driven all night because Mackie had once bought a six pack of Country Club malt liquor?

Casey walked up and down the other side of the block, a row of brick houses in various states of repair, in the pre-dawn gloom. The block wasn't skid row, by any means, but its better days had long since passed. She checked the mailboxes of the houses for names. None was familiar. When it got a little later, she'd knock on doors.

She sat on the front steps of one of houses, a three-story job whose yellow-green lawn sported a *For Sale* sign home-printed from an online real-estate site. She imagined buying it. She looked up the price—a total bargain. What a relief it would be to live within their means.

The sun was still not up. She was hungry. Chinese food sounded appealing, but the restaurant didn't open until lunch. Maybe she would take the monorail over to Mud Island to seek out food. It was a bit of a tourist attraction. She remembered liking it.

She walked over to the stores again. One of the empty storefronts across the road had been an insurance agency. It was boarded up, but the front window still bore a company name painted in gold and black. The other empty stores had their signs reversed, the plastic flipped backwards so the innards of the electric signs would be protected without advertising a nonexistent store. She puzzled out the faded, inverted writing. A video shop. A dive shop.

In the morning quiet, Casey heard the front door of the for-sale house open across the street. A man stood on the magnificent front porch. Casey ran over to him.

"Excuse me sir?"

The man looked down at her. He was a middle-aged black man, a little overweight, his hairline dividing the dome of his head neatly into two halves, front and back.

"Have you lived here long?" Casey asked.

"Is eighteen years a long time?"

"It is to me," Casey said. "What was this neighborhood like when you first moved in?" Casey wasn't sure exactly what she was looking for.

"Better than now. These houses once had river views. Before my time, though." The man had his keys in hand, probably on his way to work. "Are you interested in the house?" he asked.

"I am, yes." It wasn't entirely a lie. Some part of the grand old structure called to her. It needed a lot of work, but it wasn't rotting away. The trim needed paint, some woodwork and gutters replacing. A new roof wouldn't be out of order. But it had once been lovely and some of that remained.

"I need to be off to work, but I could give you a five-minute tour."

"I would love that," Casey said.

The man took her inside and her fantasies took more

detailed shape. A grand staircase rose from just past the front door. There was original woodwork everywhere. The floors would look fine after a sanding and restaining. There was water damage in the ceiling, and the walls in one room needed attention, but the building screamed potential.

"Years ago, my husband at the time used to come to this neighborhood," Casey told him. "But I don't know why. I won't go into it, but anything you can share with me about those days would be helpful."

"You're not interested in the house?" He looked a bit grumpy now. She could understand that. She'd made him late for work.

"I'm interested, but more than that I need to find my ex-husband."

The man headed for the front door, and she followed him. "Folks were a little better off then, but not *that* much." His tone was grudging. "I inherited the house from my grand-mother, but never came here much growing up. It's quiet, and not in a good way. It wasn't even then, but now the neighbor-hood's dead."

They left the building.

"Well, thank you for your time." She handed the man her business card.

He looked at it, and said "New York?" in shocked surprise, as though that was the nail in the coffin.

No explanation she could give now would satisfy him. "If you think of anything . . ."

"Yeah, I'll be sure to let you know," he said sarcastically.

Casey watched him get in a car and drive off. She had fancied herself a detective there for a minute, but she clearly had no idea what to ask. What information had she thought she could gain? Should she show a photo of Mackey from twenty years ago and ask folks if they remembered this man getting a parking ticket here?

Weariness gripped her—not surprisingly, since she hadn't slept—and her body was demanding an extra meal in recompense for staying up all night. That was a familiar feeling from her initial search for Elyse.

Casey drove to a nearby café and ordered food. She barely glanced at the barista as she took her pastry and coffee to the counter. She chewed mouthfuls as she drew a map of the storefronts. She puzzled over them. Chinese restaurant, insurance, bail bonds, video, dive, unknown, liquor store (on the corner, of course).

She finished her coffee and ordered another. Finished that, too. Chinese, insurance, bail bonds, video, dive, unknown, liquor store. The video store seemed the most likely destination, but also the least consequential.

"What are you trying to figure out?"

"Excuse me?" Casey looked up at a young guy with cornrows on the other side of the counter, her barista for her last coffee.

"You've been working on that a good ninety minutes," he said.

"Sorry." Casey began to gather up her papers.

"Oh, you're no problem at all, ma'am. We're emptied out. Just curious."

Casey looked around the café. The breakfast crowd was indeed gone. Had she dozed off? "I'm trying to track down my husband."

"Cheatin' husband?"

"Near enough."

"Mind if I take a look?"

"You got expertise in cheating?"

He laughed. "Not so's you'd notice."

She turned the diagram towards him. "It's a strip mall down toward Mud Island. Half empty now, but it used to have more shops. Now it's got . . ." she looked down ". . . Chinese restaurant, insurance agent, bail bonds, video, dive shop, unknown, liquor store. Of those, only the restaurant, bail bonds, and liquor store are open."

"What, no nail salon?"

"Maybe that's what 'unknown' used to be."

"So your cheater might've had Chinese after bailing out his sidechick," the young man said.

Unless Casey was Mackey's sidechick. Casey was never going to share this conversation with Abby. "Then they got a bottle of Jack and headed out on a dive? Where?"

"I heard they got some nice caves out a ways in Arkansas."

Casey looked for them on her phone. She found caves you could dive in three hours away. "Nothing closer?"

The young man shrugged. Casey did another search. Nothing. "Why would there even be a dive shop in Memphis?"

The bell on the front door rang and a customer approached. "Beats me." The young man went back to his cash register.

The river was too muddy for diving, surely. Diving equipment would probably only be used in waterfront construction. She imagined divers welding steel underwater for a pier. She imagined them finishing, throwing the gear in the back up their pickup.

Bingo. She knew how he'd done it.

Casey drove back to the strip mall, took a close-up photo of the sign and raced to Memphis Police Headquarters. She found Dunne, who was just starting his day. She showed him the parking ticket, described the store, and her theory.

"Oh." He looked embarrassed again, as though the Memphis Police Department should have found this bit of intelligence. Thank you for believing me, she thought. "This is plausible," he said. "Let's call our river hydrologist."

They had to wait for the hydrologist to come in. The police station did not have need of a fulltime hydrologist, unsurprisingly. Dunne got them coffee.

"Your legwork puts us to shame, Mrs. White."

"Casey," she said. Her stomach was in knots. All those years ago, she should never have left Memphis.

At long last the hydrologist arrived, sleepy eyes beneath thick white eyebrows sharp against the contrast of dark skin. Detective Dunne filled him in, allowing Casey to share the final detail.

"What if he wanted to fake his death? He'd have to drive through the railing so we'd know where to look. Then he'd need a tank of air to give him time to escape." It sounded harebrained, but not if you knew Mackey.

"It's far-fetched," Dunne added, "but we know something out of the ordinary happened."

"I can't see him doing an escape artist routine with a baby in tow," the man said, rubbing his face, "but if your baby was elsewhere, he could have ditched the car and swum out. That would account for the open door, the angle against the mud. It would be one hell of a risk, not to mention a waste of a pick-up, but it is certainly doable. Could he swim?"

"Like a fish. Grew up on a river," Casey said. "I knew it!"

"Hold your horses. Even if he was a good swimmer and had a tank he could use to wait out the cab filling up, he still had to swim, with the tank, into the Mississippi, which is a powerful, powerful river. Before we assume he escaped alive, I suggest we drag a few particular spots downriver. We'd be looking in a completely different area. One of these anaerobic dead zones where water doesn't circulate. Let me run numbers with my team. This many years later, a lot could have happened, but I still think we should start there."

Dunne nodded. "I'll set it up."

"How soon?" Casey wanted this done twenty years ago, but failing that, she wanted it done now.

"We have clearly botched a number of things and we owe you," Dunne said. "I will see about getting started today." He made some calls. "Noon," he told Casey.

Casey got herself a room at the same motel she'd used before. She showered, set the alarm, and took an unavoidable nap.

A CALL from Dunne woke her before the alarm did. The team was starting early. Casey grabbed a sandwich from a convenience store, went down to the address Dunne gave her, and settled in to watch.

The hydrologist was on hand. He had mapped out a likely location and was confident: if they were to find anything, it would be here. It was farther than she'd expected from where the pickup had been found, and she was skeptical. A boat crew with sonar and radar swept the area. "We have better technology now," the hydrologist told her. There was even a dog on hand. The hydrologist and Dunne leaned on the waterfront railing, looking like father and son.

For a good hour, nothing happened. Casey thought of calling Roger, time zones be damned, but was too fidgety. She paced. Then there was gesturing on the boat deck, indistinct shouts. They had something. No way could it be this fast. Two divers went back down.

"Fingertip search," Dunne said.

Casey ground her teeth. She wanted answers, but they had to be the right answers. Time went by. A half hour. An hour.

Two. A diver surfaced, gave a thumbs up. Really? The second diver surfaced and tapped the side of the big rusty boat. Cables went down. The river slapped its small waves against the sides of the boat. Casey could hear the hydrologist chewing on something, sucking air through the side of his mouth, as though his hours-old coffee was hot. Then a winch was engaged, raising the cables from below. A net began to appear. A lumpy mass the right size emerged, coated in thick, black, river-bottom sludge that looked like it could hold a body together for centuries.

Dunne motioned to the boat. A zodiac was sent to ferry them out to the boat. The crew hosed down the mass on deck gently to keep it from disintegrating. Black mud fell off heavily in clumps. An oxygen tank, air hoses, and the angular gray of bones were slowly revealed: a body held together by clothing and clay emerged as rivulets carried muck away. The hydrologist had not been kidding when he called it a dead zone. All these years later most of him was still there, skeleton and tendons preserved in the mud, like a gnat in amber.

"Oh, Mackie."

He had not even geared up properly. He was wearing the same old jacket as ever: brown leather, fake Air Force stripes on the shoulders. He always thought his half-assed schemes would work out, and had come up short yet again.

The two divers approached, peeling back masks from pale faces.

"Anything else," Dunne asked, tactfully.

They shook their heads. "Just him," they said, but Casey already knew that. Because her daughter was alive. *S P* was alive and living in Memphis.

CHAPTER 56

I hsan answered his ma's call on the second ring. "I invited your friends to join us for dinner tonight," she said.

"What friends?"

"The two girls!"

"Them?"

"Yes, them! They're nice."

"Ma, everyone will be speaking Libyan Arabic. They won't understand a thing."

"That's why you must be sure to be there. Don't be late. Bring Nabil. No excuses."

"Of course I will bring Nabil, Ma." He appreciated how, even after years, his ma still let him know that Nabil was welcomed, not merely tolerated.

"Don't let him work late. I want you both here on time."

"Special occasion?"

"I need you to interpret. The girls are nice, but their French, sheesh!"

"We'll be there." He hung up. This was probably going to be a long night of eating, with his aunt, uncle, and cousins joining them. He hadn't seen his cousins in weeks and hoped all three would be there. He imagined the scene: him chatting away with his sisters and cousins, getting grilled by his uncle about the trip to Barcelona, maybe getting pointers. Nabil would meanwhile be in the kitchen trading neighborhood gossip with Ihsan's ma, while his dad would preside over the safe haven he and his wife had created, loaf by loaf, selling so many baguettes to the French that his progeny had become French themselves. And, oh yes, in the middle of it all, two girls from New York.

NABIL LOOKED HANDSOME, Ihsan thought, snug in his long, well-cut coat, with a light wool scarf in orange wrapped around his neck. They stood at the gateway to his parent's building, as Ihsan entered the door code. Nabil's dark, wavy hair looked fantastic, as always. Unlike a lot of hairdressers, Nabil opted for a more conventional look than the outlandish, unattractive styles that many professionals chose, a phenomenon Ihsan chalked up more to boredom than style.

They pushed through the gate and then through the open front door to the first-floor apartment above the bakery just as Ihsan's twin sisters, Fatima and Hoda, came down from the fourth-floor apartment where they lived. They all kissed cheeks amidst a traffic jam of coat and shoe removals.

"What, no blond girls?" Nabil asked Hoda. (Nabil had yet to meet them and assumed they were both blonde. Apparently.)

Fatima replied for her. (Twins!) "They will be down in a moment. We may have over-Arabbed them."

"Or over-twinned," Hoda added. "They've explored the neighborhood, but not gone any further. They hang out at home a lot."

"Can't be too over-Arabbed, then," Ihsan said.

"My babies!" their ma cried out, rushing toward the clot of them melodramatically, in a way that Ihsan enjoyed. It was nice to be fussed over, hugs and kisses galore for everyone, including son-in-law Nabil, at which point the twins squeezed into the living room.

"Hey, welcome back!" his uncle called to Ihsan, as though he had been gone for weeks, not days. They had become unexpectedly closer since Ihsan, the oldest of the yet-to-produce-grandchildren generation, had launched his own business. The status-drop from no longer being an engineer had been overcome by bonding over techniques for balancing accounts, flattering customers, and search engine optimization. "How was Barcelona?"

Ihsan made a minimizing gesture. He had been consoling himself the last few days that it hadn't been a total loss because now he knew he had to offer more to potential partners. He was educating himself. He was just about to ask for his uncle's opinions on this when the Americans arrived.

"Hey, you're here!" Hoda said to the girls in French, the warmth in her greeting exaggerated. Ihsan suspected she had wearied of playing host.

The two girls crept in like mice. "Ethan!" Demmy said as she spotted him. Abby rushed to him, arms outstretched, as though she'd been deprived of human contact. He crouched down and she hugged him so tightly and so long he began to worry. He'd seen Demmy's written permission from her father —which had satisfied the French official—but was Demmy keeping her here against her will?

"Are your parents joining you soon?" he asked Demmy in English.

She laughed and tossed her head. "Who knows? *Qui sait?* You know parents."

Not parents like that, he didn't. Ihsan's ma came over. "Are you liking the room? Are your parents joining you?" she asked in French. "We could put them on the third floor if they are."

Demmy looked to Ihsan. His ma spoke fast in North African–accented French, and Demmy appeared to have not understood any of it. He translated into English.

"*Nous aimons ça. Une telle vue incroyable! Étourdissant! Vous avez le trois?*" Demmy said.

It was an admirable attempt, but now *her* accent was so heavy that his ma didn't catch it, so again he interpreted: We love it. Such an incredible view! Stunning! Ihsan answered Demmy's question about the third floor rather than interpreting it: "They own the building," he told Demmy.

Demmy's face expressed surprise, which irked Ihsan. What was so surprising about that? They'd been putting in long days forever. There should be some reward.

The twins took advantage of Ihsan's presence to pepper their guests with an apparent backlog of questions about their plans and to instruct the two girls on the finer points of the etiquette of taking off and arranging their shoes. Ihsan interpreted, listening to Demmy's response as his ma simultaneously peppered him with additional demands. This was not what was meant by simultaneous interpreting. "Ask her again about the parents. If they are not joining them, we'll let the floor go to someone else."

He'd only got halfway through his sisters requests when his ma jumped in again. "And ask them if they eat eggplant. Tell them the baba is gluten-free."

He nodded, to give his ma something to tide her over, as he thought about how hungry he was while listening to and committing to memory Demmy's apologies over her and her sister's shoe faux-pas and passing that on in French to his sisters even as his ma barked out instructions on where to sit and who was to serve what to whom. And had Ihsan told them

he'd been in a famous movie? His ma asked. Demmy, meanwhile, seemed to be fascinated by Nabil, and wanted an intro-
duction. Yeah, I did good, didn't I? Ihsan thought, as he tried to
retain what Demmy was saying, what Nabil was saying, and
who understood what. This is your chosen profession, Ihsan
reminded himself, even as he thought about his uncle, and
wondered when—or if—he'd get a chance to pick his brain
about international cost-sharing strategy that night, let alone
have a moment to describe for his family his experiences in
Barcelona, generally.

That was the thing about interpreting: being so useful, you
ceased to be a person. Demmy and his sisters were still going
back and forth. They seemed to like each other, which was
great, but it probably also meant that Ihsan would not get a
chance to taste his mother's lamb till it was cold.

Abby hugged his leg and screeched with delight. Over the
brown-haired girl's shoulder, Demmy was laughing at a joke
of Nabil's she seemed pleased to have understood. Both girls
seemed happy, as though content to stay in the 21st arrondissement forever.

CHAPTER 57

S arah's favorite part of her job was that she could bring her foster dogs along on her shifts. She helped her latest —arthritic Xochi of the narrow waist and patchy, dry fur—up into the cab of her pickup, parked in front of her and Pell's house on a modest, leafy Memphis street.

"In you go." She raised the old brindle boxer's hindquarters, then hoisted her fifty-five pounds onto the seat. Xochi's part in this was to keep her front legs under her, first on the lip of the door and then on the seat cushion. She managed this well enough, though she was not a lot of help with actually pulling her body weight up. Once Sarah had Xochi settled on her pillow on the passenger seat and strapped in her harness, Sarah got in. She knew Xochi was not likely to be with them terribly long, which was sad, but there was something about a senior dog's gratitude for kindness that cut through the usual getting-acquainted period, going straight to friendship and love.

"No jacket?" Pell called out to her from up on their porch.

He was right. It was too cold for shirtsleeves. The wind off the Mississippi could still be biting this time of year. Her expression seemed to be enough of an answer, because he brought her red flannel jacket down and handed it to her through the open window of the sky-blue pickup, delivering it with a kiss.

"Bonus," Sarah said. She ran her fingers through his brown hair.

"What time do you get off today?"

"Depends on when Murdo gets in to relieve me."

"Ugh, Murdo."

"I know." The guy was never on time. He'd often come in an hour past the time his shift technically started. "Why, did you want to do something?"

"Yeah, but the framing's done, so I'm working a full day," he said. "I won't be home till seven thirty. It's more just curiosity."

Sarah liked that curiosity. Life was better when someone else was paying attention. Not that her life hadn't been like that before—her grandmother was never neglectful, always interested, in fact—but Sarah's life with Pell still struck her as something special.

Pell leaned forward for another kiss, which she gave him —lingering a bit longer than she should have, considering the time—before starting the truck and taking off for the highway.

The river looked a mite browner than it had the day before, and choppy, with that wind. The souvenir store where she worked was exposed. It needed to be visible to attract kids to play in the park. And they needed those kids. Business was down over the last year, as it was everywhere with inflation and the supply chain difficulties. Sarah suspected she'd need to find new work soon. She wasn't too broken up about that; she frequently thought of finding something better anyway.

She'd applied to the Memphis College of Art last year and not gotten in, despite the absence of a backup plan, which in a fair world should guarantee success, right? Though she missed her grandmother out in Wet Springs, Arkansas, she'd try University of Memphis, next time. Pell had too good a job to abandon (apprentice electrician, with a good boss), and she was not giving him up, that was for sure. How many twenty-one-year-old guys did you meet who were hard working, considerate, and willing to foster senior dogs?

She made the turn off Island Drive and trundled up the access road. She parked, put on the jacket Pell had so kindly brought, and helped Xochi ease herself down from the pickup. She leashed Xochi and they walked—Xochi teetering on her trembly hind legs but keeping up—past the Mississippi River Museum to the kiosk attached to the visitors center, where she worked.

Xochi watered a bush as Sarah unlocked the metal screen that protected the small store, rolling the aluminum up into its ceiling-mounted receptacle. Xochi settled into the back while Sarah turned on the space heater near Xochi's dog bed.

Customers—a white-haired couple in surgical masks—approached the store. Had they been waiting? Sarah opened two packages of ground coffee, poured them into the filter of the big urn, and put it on to brew. And wouldn't you know it, the customers wanted coffee. She told them it would be five minutes, so they browsed, picking out a pair of blue cloth-covered visors.

"Did you see the excitement up by the bridge?" the lady asked her.

Sarah shook her head. "The De Soto Bridge?" She hadn't seen a thing.

The man shook his head. "The Willis Avenue Bridge. They're dragging the Wolf River Harbor. They's divers and everything."

"Yes, and they found something. They were pulling up a big lump of something that looked like a body."

"You are so ghoulish," the man said. "It was probably an old tire."

"It weren't no old tire. It was long, big, like a growed man." The lenses of the lady's bifocals needed a good wipe-down.

"It was right by the base of the bridge. You didn't see it?" the man asked Sarah.

Sarah shook her head. "Must have been distracted." She'd been in a haze of satisfaction with her life all morning. She handed the couple their coffees and rang them up for those, plus two embroidered Mud Island visors.

CHAPTER 58

Roger was seated on a green wooden bench at the edge of a Parisian flower market, having made no progress in locating his daughters, when the phone rang. Casey. He answered and added another lie to his pile, telling Casey he was out buying breakfast pastries for the girls.

"I'm so glad I caught you," Casey said.

They'd been trading voicemails as Roger exploited the time difference to avoid difficult questions about Abby, whom Casey had not spoken to since Abby's flight from Galería Les Rambles.

"Big news," Casey continued. "We found him. We found Mackie."

Roger was still getting used to the idea of this previous husband having a name, or any identity at all. Casey's sketchiness about him allowed Roger the freedom to be sketchy about Aline. Before he hadn't wanted to lose that; now it didn't matter.

"Where is he? Does he have your daughter?"

"Elyse," Casey said.

Roger repeated the name to himself mentally—Elyse, Elyse, like the Beethoven.

"He's dead."

"Oh my god!"

"The police declared him 'presumed deceased' years ago, and I went to court to have him officially declared dead about a year before you and I met, but yeah, still a shock."

Roger leaned left as a hefty woman with a huge Rivera-esque bundle of calla lilies wedged herself in beside him on the flower-market bench. "What happened?"

She recounted the story. Mackie (was that a real name?) had been dead literally since the day he disappeared. Having to watch his body dragged from the river must have been horrifying, but Casey had a note of calm in her voice Roger hadn't heard since before Abby fled. She told him about her Barista-assisted discovery of the scuba shop and how that had led the police to drag a different area of the river.

"What are you, a detective?"

She laughed. "Seems like!"

It was good to hear her laughter. "Now what?"

"Indeed." Casey's voice broke off. "Where are you?" She sounded puzzled.

Roger's attention returned to his surroundings. Some guy was shouting something in French. "Nowhere we went."

"I'd forgotten how much Catalan can sound like French," Casey said.

Uh oh. He couldn't let Casey know he was not in Barcelona. He laughed nervously, then caught himself. Understanding neither language, why would he laugh at that? He walked away from the calla lily lady and the market, into a quiet side street where no flowermongers barking about begonias would give the game away.

"Now that the police believe you, they must have ideas on

how to find Elyse." Roger genuinely wanted to know, but he also wanted to turn Casey's attention away from questions about where Roger was.

"I hope so, because I am fresh out. I'm shocked they believed me from the start. I'm being helped by a great guy, Sergeant Dunne, a big young guy. It's nothing like what I expected. The police are focused, attentive, and everyone knows what they are doing. I should run my business so well."

Roger refrained from asking more about this wonderful Detective Dunne. "I'm guessing you're no longer searching in Missouri."

Casey gave a loud exhale. "I guess. I have no idea what Mackie had planned. He seems not to have told his family he was taking Elyse. *S P*'s profile on the DNA site says she is here in Memphis, so we are searching here, but public records have not turned up any likely matches, in terms of birthday. Which leaves a pretty wide net to cast."

Casey sounded glum now.

"Maybe she'll contact you."

"Maybe." She sounded uncertain. "I sent off for a DNA test of my own. When my result shows up on her report as her mother, that's bound to catch her attention. But they say they need nearly two months for results, even in these circumstances. What am I supposed to do in the meantime? It will take three or four days just to get the kit."

So he had at least three or four days to find the girls. "I'm sorry. The tension must be agonizing."

Casey sighed. "It's good, though. I now know Mackie is dead and Elyse is alive. You can't understand how important that is to me."

Roger had some idea, having a couple missing daughters of his own at the moment.

"Aren't you back yet? I have to speak to the girls."

"Oh, they're out already." He tried to sound casual.

"Why aren't you with them?"

"Wasn't up for ice cream," he said, instantly realizing he'd used the ice cream excuse before. Plus, he was supposedly buying pastries.

"At ten in the morning?"

"It's deep fried," he blurted. Good one, fried ice cream.

"Oh." She seemed to buy it. Deep-frying could sell anything. "Is that the sound of tires on cobblestones?" she asked.

A Citroen had just driven by. Was that rubbery rippling unusual?

"Where are you?" she asked.

"Out on La Rambla, waiting for them to come back."

"La Rambla is covered in pavers."

"Well, near La Rambla. In sight of La Rambla." She couldn't have memorized every side street in the area, although as he thought about it, he did not remember any cobblestoned streets anywhere in Barcelona.

"Can you call me back when they return? I haven't spoken to them in so long. I want to tell them about Elyse."

"Sure thing, Casey." He felt bad lying, and lying badly, but no way was he telling her that her children had gone to ground in Paris, last recorded slipping into the subway from the Gare de Lyon with an unknown man. She had enough to worry about. "Love you," he said. That, at least, was not a lie.

"Love you too," she said, and was gone.

CHAPTER 59

Demmy looked up at the evening lights of the Eiffel Tower. Dragging Abby around Paris was fun, Demmy thought, but college admissions boards would soon be posting their decisions. She imagined Jodee and Lainie celebrating and commiserating and wanted to be with them. She wasn't super concerned about the admissions decisions, she told herself, but she wouldn't mind being home, heading into school, and tutoring at the library. If Mark still wanted her, after this extended absence.

"Are you ready to go see Mom?" she asked Abby.

"No!" Abby shouted. It kind of sounded like *non*. How long could she keep this up, Demmy wondered. Demmy had expected this resistance to last four hours, not four days. Her little sister was kind of a brat.

"How 'bout Dad?"

"*Non!*" Abby was definitely going native.

"Okay, how about dinner?"

"*Non!*"

"At least be polite. *Non, merci!*"

"*Non merci je vais bien,*" Abby screeched. No, thanks, I'm fine.

Demmy winced at the noise. "Who taught you that?"

"Hoda."

Okay, let's see how you like no dinner then. Demmy would wait till Abby got hungry. She was tired of catering to a six-year-old's whims. Demmy bought tickets for the tower. If the cell reception was better she'd call Lainie and Jodee.

They went up the elevator. Demmy waited until they stepped out onto the enormous first platform before she powered up her phone. They were kinda captive up there. Maybe her mom and dad or the police would find them. That might be for the best. Let someone else take the rap for returning Abby to their parents. She called Jodee first.

A groggy voice answered.

"Jodee. 'sup?"

"No one says *sup*. It's four in the morning."

"Oh, shit. Sorry. I'll call later."

"Where are you?

"Eiffel Tower. The one in France." Demmy searched the twinkling cityscape for the 21st arrondissement.

"Yeah, call later. But check YouTube."

"For what?"

"Just google your dad's name."

She hung up and immediately searched her dad's name. It came up on YouTube, and the video thumbnail showed her and her dad yelling at each other. WTF? Over a million hits. #wtfuckingF?

She clicked. What followed was well edited, good filters, amusing, but grew less so as she realized how much of it was her. Mainly her yelling: *The little touches. Maude knows your body. Yoga lady, touching herself.* She cringed, but yep, she'd said all that. *I don't have to obey,* yelled out, the start of an ugly cry. *Now* who was the brat? And Nana's painting of her dad, *that* part of her dad. Was that considered weird? She did not trust the judgment of a popular culture flooded with unrealistic bodies, judgment manifested scathingly in the *Comments*, but she did not have enough experience to know. Somehow, knowing dick pics made up half the internet had always kept her from looking.

Demmy pressed the power-down buttons, swiped the *power off* icon. Now she did not want to go home. She did not want to tutor. She did not want to go to school. Over a million hits? She was mortified. And yet, she felt worse for her dad. He'd have to go to school and stand up *in front of* people. She imagined how ruthless she, Jodee, and Lainie would be if it were Delaney-sensei caught having that kind of meltdown.

And Casey. Her mom. In her mind, Casey was Mom again. That was all caught on camera too. Including Demmy's question: *You have another daughter?*

Was that true? She'd seen the video. She'd figured she had misheard, but that in fact had been what they were saying, her mom and dad. Her mom had another daughter. Demmy saw the image in her mind of Casey's face, torn with pain. And Demmy had made it all about herself.

"Come on, Abby!"

Demmy dragged her sister to the elevator.

"*Non merci je vais bien,*" Abby squealed.

"That's not even what you say in this situation," Demmy told her, overpowering Abby into the elevator.

"I want Hoda!"

But does Hoda want you, Demmy wondered. The elevator descended. Demmy no longer wanted to be caught. She needed time to think. She wanted to talk to Casey, her mom. But could she face her? Demmy blushed.

The elevator reached ground level; the doors opened;

disembarking tourists swept them out onto the off-white sand and pollarded trees of the park around the Tower. There were no police in sight. They rode a couple stops on the Metro, enough to avoid capture, and got off. Demmy bought frites and café au laits, one for Abby too. "Welcome to adulthood," she said, passing Abby the coffee.

Abby munched and sipped, docile. She hadn't been unruly or thrown a fit since getting on the elevator, a good forty-five minutes. Was it the forced march? Perhaps she'd been missing discipline, order.

Demmy took her into a department store. She and Abby had no clothes beyond what they were wearing and yesterday's Mona Lisa T-shirts from the Louvre, so Demmy picked out a couple of outfits each and charged them. How lovely to have a trust fund, darling.

The money was from her mother, of course, her real mother. Lots of her friends had to wait till they were twenty-five or something, but Demmy's mother had thought eighteen was the right age. Demmy wondered what the message had been there? Her mother had been diagnosed with terminal cancer when Demmy was seven and died when Demmy was eleven. The doctors had said she'd had it for at least a year before that first, fateful blood-test.

Her mother hadn't shown symptoms initially, but she had started chemo. She'd mainly been tired. It wasn't the type of chemo that knocks all your hair out, and Demmy hadn't developed a clear sense of what was normal-tired and what was sick-tired right away. For a while she'd thought everyone had cancer, which came and went; at the same time, she'd thought anyone around her could die without a lot of notice, not reconciling the two ideas. Her mom had set her straight.

She'd felt dumb, but her therapist had reassured her that her reactions were normal, and she'd been making sense of the information she had in a very rational way. That had helped. Yay, therapy!

Demmy's therapist and her mom had been full of wisdom —real, useful wisdom. Her dad had not. But he had been there, a constant presence. Goofy, warm, hers. This was probably the longest they'd been apart since the death. Was that normal? Didn't college professors normally travel? The others his dad knew all seemed to fly to conference after conference, where they "presented." He never did any of that.

She wanted to see him. She'd been such a brat, going on and on about Maude. How could she have thought that of him? He was never away from home long enough to have an affair, for one thing. He'd stayed close to home all these years for her, hadn't he? She could not bear to face him, but she wanted to see him more than anyone else in the world.

CHAPTER 60

S arah flopped onto the sofa. It was her night to cook. And she had no ideas. She heard Pell snoring in the living room, napping after a work day with a 5:30 start. Tomorrow afternoon, the positions would reverse. Sarah ruminated on how she'd enjoy that, but her musings didn't get her any closer to knowing what dinner would look like. She looked at Xochi, plastered across the floor beside the sofa, as close to Pell as she could get. Xochi's legs were twitching in a dream. Sarah wondered what scrumptious doggie meals she dreamed of. Would Pell go for a bowl of raw short ribs?

Her phone pinged in her pocket, the email sound. She wanted to ignore it in favor of a short nap of her own, but despite the growing number of pointless communications she received, email still felt like Christmas: what delights might a message reveal when opened?

It was a solitary email, from a testing company she'd sent her DNA to. When she'd moved to this new town, Memphis, she'd been surprised to not feel homesick. She came to realize it was because she'd arrived with a well-developed sense of loneliness already. Her grandmother, who'd raised her, was her only close blood relative, and her paltry few second and third cousins had always seemed foreign. She seemed to have no sense of family. Pell didn't suffer from anything of the sort, and Sarah wanted to know why.

Sarah, you have a new DNA match to explore, the email title read.

Another match. She was mildly interested, but she needed to get started on dinner. The names originally reported to her when she'd received her test were all distant relatives, with whom she shared at most 2% of her DNA. Most were anonymous, or used initials (as she herself had done). Of the few that had bonafide names, not a one did she recognize. The site let you send messages to your matches, and she'd done so, profusely. None had responded. Her initial enthusiastic visions of family had faded away.

This match, by contrast, bore a name, visible in the email preview. Abigail White. The name meant nothing, but she clicked the button: *Explore this match.*

A page opened up.

You and Abigail White. Predicted relationship: Grandchild, niece or half-sibling

Sarah sat bolt upright. "Whoa, Xochi. What have we here?"

Xochi's left ear perked up.

Sarah clicked a few links, but Abigail had entered no family tree, no personal information beyond her name, not even a location. Sarah had at least disclosed that much.

Sarah dialed her grandmother.

"Hi, hon." Her grandmother sounded happy to hear from her. Sarah felt guilty for not calling more.

Sarah jumped right in. "Do you know *nothing* about my father?" This had long been a source of friction. Her grand-

mother professed complete ignorance, but was also suspi-
ciously reticent to discuss the matter.

"You gnawing on that old bone again?"

"Listen, Granny, my DNA turned up a close relative:
Grandchild, niece or half-sibling, and I *know* I don't have any
grandchild. Did Mama have any siblings who might've birthed
a niece?"

"You know she didn't."

"Right? So that leaves half-siblings. Unless Mama had
another child, this person has to be through my father."

Granny cleared her throat, a phlegmy sound that was
becoming familiar of late. "She wouldn't have been able to
hide any other children from me. She wasn't out of sight long
enough but the one time. So that means it's your father."
Granny cleared her throat again, violently. "I'm happy for you,
honey. Maybe you can finally get those questions answered."

Sarah had not expected that response. "You *want* me to
find him?" Had her granny not been hiding the man all these
years?

"Why wouldn't I?"

"For starters, you always change the subject when I ask."
Sarah's voice came out quieter, more strained, than she
wanted.

Granny sighed a deliberate, decisive puff of air. "I suppose
we should talk about this. You're old enough." The phone
went quiet. "I know now people think nothing of it, but I felt
ashamed. My daughter came back with an out-of-wedlock
child that set the town to talking. And you *know* how people
are eager for something to talk about. Your mama refused to
talk about the daddy. And she was a girl who never dated.
Never. There weren't no stream of boys coming round the
house growing up, not before nor after your mama showed up
at the door with you. Those were a tough few years, when the

two of you came back to me, and once things settled down I didn't want to dredge it all up. Not for myself, and not for you neither."

Sarah could understand that. So little happened in Wet Springs that people would latch onto things and not let go. The circumstances of Sarah's birth had provided juicy gossip. She'd felt the after-effects her whole life. Likely, Granny had too.

"I'm curious myself, truth be told," Granny continued. "You let me know what you find out."

Sarah was eager to delve further and tell Granny what she found right that instant, but of course the links she needed were all on the phone she was talking on.

"Thanks, Granny. I'll do that."

"You take care now, hon. And bring that boy of yourn down here for a visit sometime. It's been months."

"I will. Pell would love to see you." Sarah hung up.

"Love to see who?" Pell said beside her.

Sarah looked up at him as he hovered over her phone screen scratching his brown hair. "Granny," she told him. "Here, Pell, look at this."

He read over the screen. "And you don't know who this Abigail is?"

"Granny thinks she's my half-sister on my dad's side."

He sucked in his breath. "The mysterious father."

"Right?" Sarah clicked on Abigail's information. Abigail's father had his DNA on the site, too.

"So your father is named Roger?"

"Hang on." Sarah looked again at the list of matches she and Abigail had in common. Abigail's father wasn't on it. She double checked. Nope. He was not there.

Pell had watched her click through the pages and lists. "So, you and Abigail *don't* have a father in common."

"But then who is she? All my life I've been searching for family." Those second and third cousins looked nothing like her. "All I had was my mother and grandmother, and I don't even remember my mother." A lifetime of watching her grandmother among the other kids' much younger mothers came back to her, as did the teasing at school. The throwaway girl, that's what they'd called her.

Sarah ran down the possibilities for Pell, describing how she and her grandmother had ruled them out, one by one. "So if she's not a niece, not a grandchild, and not a half-sibling, either the test is wrong, my grandmother is wrong, or my grandmother is lying."

"Sarah, look." Pell pointed at a tiny green icon on her phone screen. "You have a message."

Her first ever message through the site. Sarah clicked it. It was short, and made no sense. The woman writing her claimed to be Abigail White's mother. The woman had included her phone number and asked Sarah to call her. Because she was Sarah's mother.

Sarah's mother?

Sarah set her phone down on the table. She remembered being the throwaway girl, and how she'd fought back: I do *too* have a mother, she'd yelled at them. Her mother hadn't thrown Sarah away; her mother had *died*. So there! It was an odd thing to be proud of. But it was what she had.

Sarah picked up the phone and entered the digits. But she did not press the *Call* button. If her mother was not her mother, her granny was not her granny. Sarah felt her world crumble. She was indeed the throwaway girl. "I'm well and truly nobody."

"Sarah, you got the test because you wanted answers," Pell said. "Call her." He showed Sarah his phone. He'd looked up the area code. "Brooklyn." He took her hand in both of his. "You're not a nobody, Sarah."

But it made no sense. How could she have a mother in Brooklyn, of all the damned places? It made absolutely no sense. Sarah put the phone back down on the table. She had been searching for answers, but this was not one she wanted. Xochi lay her head on Sarah's thigh and looked up at her with rheumy brown eyes. Sarah stared at the phone. I'm not a nobody, she told herself. Xochi thinks I'm somebody; Pell thinks I'm somebody. And yet she was afraid; the throwaway girl was afraid.

CHAPTER 61

Maude was packing a small bag for a stroll down to La Barceloneta beach for a swim. Her quest to book a return flight to New York was in shambles as airlines left and right canceled flights due to Covid-related flight crew shortages. Barcelona hotels were all booked up, too, meaning Maude was still captive. Last night, Sherbeam had told Maude everything that Roger had told her that Casey had told him, and what Maude had come away with was an earworm: Elvis Costello singing in her head about the woman filing her nails as she watches the police drag the lake.

Entirely inappropriate for the tragic circumstance—the second wife of a man she'd had a fling with thirty years ago (almost) had witnessed the beaching of the corpse of her dead first husband after a submersion of similar vintage (did she have that right?)—but the song persisted in her head as the woman persisted in watching the detectives and lusting after the cute one.

Maude slipped a light skirt and blouse over her one-piece swimsuit, hung a slight bag of beach stuff over her shoulder and set out. Hadn't she been twenty just the other day, when that album came out? It was forty years ago, more. She'd thought it a masterpiece, but did anyone remember it? Did anyone remember anything? Apparently young people could no longer read or write cursive. No reason they should, but still, her world was disappearing before her eyes.

Her phone buzzed on her hip. She pulled it out, stopping her beachward march. Demmy? Demmy!

It was a text.

DEMMY WHITE

> We're still in Paris. All's fine. Returning soon.
> Abby wants to see you

Attached was a photo, the two girls in a selfie in front of Sacré-Cœur.

Maude replied.

> Come back. Everyone is worried sick
> about you

She typed a period at the end, then deleted it. Someone had told her young people did not take you seriously if you ended a text with a period. She did not know why.

Demmy did not respond.

Maude texted Roger, rapidly, so she could respond immediately to Demmy in the event she texted.

> Heard form the grils. They say their fine,
> retrning soon.

Roger did not respond either, possibly the professor in him offended by her poor typing. Or the final period. She forwarded the photo.

Maude texted Sherbeam. Roger had sworn Maude to secrecy vis-à-vis Casey, but Sherbeam was considered by Roger to be safe to include (unwisely, Maude thought) in the mystery of the missing daughters, European edition. Stockholm Syndrome, she figured.

> Girls safe in Paris. Promise to return soon.
> Secrecy still applies

SHERBEAM

> Working

Maude considered herself lucky to get that.

Maude wondered if Demmy knew that Roger was in Paris, looking for her. She texted again.

> Your dad in Paris. Call him

Again, no reply. Demmy likely had immediately powered her phone down, but she'd see the message next time she came online, or whatever the equivalent term was for phones.

Maude continued walking toward the Mediterranean, crossing the big oceanfront boulevard. The air was not the clearest today. It was odd how much one could communicate and still be alone. Maude was feeling old; this drama was not hers. She was hanging about as though she was family—first Sherbeam and now Abby had demanded that she stay—but she wasn't family. She had her own kids, her own life. Maybe she *wouldn't* actually charge into a burning building for Demmy or Abby, if it came to that. She was tired, maybe permanently, of Sherbeam's ego.

Roger was different. All those decades ago, they had labored under Sherbeam together. Allied, they each achieved their independence from her. And they had both been through the loss of a spouse, although they had reacted to that very differently.

She and Roger had never stopped being friends, and thinking now about how important his friendship had been for her since her husband's death, she now wondered if she had played the same role for him. But with different outcomes.

Perhaps because her husband was so much older when he died than Aline had been, Maude's refuge took the form of activity. Her painting wasn't obsessive, but it was active. Frank had always supported that, so she felt connected to him when she painted. The discipline of work and the immersion in the flow of painting had been helpful in keeping her grounded. She remained engaged with the world, her children, and with Frank's presence.

Roger had clearly gone the other direction. He had retreated into his home with his daughter. And then the advent of Casey had meant his family was complete again, and everything else vital in his life dropped away. He no longer wrote criticism, he no longer spoke at conferences, and he didn't work on screenplays like he had. Roger seemed to be embracing writing again, but if he were going to reengage with the world, he'd have to change the shape of his life. If he didn't want to do that—and Maude had herself had many a year where her domestic life mattered more to her—that was his privilege.

But Maude would change her life. She'd distance herself from this clan. That was her privilege.

Her phone buzzed. Perhaps Demmy was pondering whether or not to contact a parent. Maude wasn't needed as a conduit, and frankly, she didn't want to be one. The girls were safe. But Maude looked anyway.

I've been thinking so much about your new paintings.

Was this a message for Sherbeam? It had a period. A second message came in.

ELŻ

> Saw on YouTube you are in Europe. Any time to swing by Paris?

Now she noticed the name. After those few distracted glances at the images of Maude's work, Elż was now thinking about Maude's paintings? If that wasn't a lesson that needed reinforcing—that the minds of others will always be unknown —Maude didn't know what was.

Her phone buzzed a third time.

> Would love to meet. We didn't get enough time in NY. Bill's in Paris now, you see.

Elż was not only contacting her, she wanted to meet. And she hadn't even mentioned Roger. So what the fuck are you doing here, Maude asked herself, when trains to Paris are still running?

> Nothing would please me more. Text me the time and place.

Maude proudly typed in a final period and smiled.

CHAPTER 62

Casey stood outside the café with the helpful cornrowed barista. "What do you mean the girls are out again?" she asked Roger, incredulous.

"They, um, just . . ."

"Went to get fried ice cream?"

"Oh boy."

"You did find them, didn't you? Did you make that up?"

"No, no. I found them. You saw them sleeping in the hotel room."

He had not seen them since her final night in Barcelona? She knew it! She had trusted him and Demmy to act like sane adults while she went in search of her older daughter and ex-husband. Silence stretched between them.

"Shit," he finally said.

"You're such a bad liar, Roger." Casey burned with anger. She felt heat boil up from the sidewalk, the first taste of the muggy death of a Memphis summer and it was only April.

"I'm sorry."

"Are you telling me our six-year-old has been wandering the streets of Barcelona on her own for four days?"

"Not at all. She's, uh, with Demmy."

Casey was shocked. He'd honest-to-god lost them both again. Someone honked at her. She was somehow in the street. She leapt back onto the sidewalk.

"And they are in Paris, not Barcelona."

"What?!"

"I'm on it. I'm in Paris too."

"Those cobblestones. You were in Paris last time, too. You lied to me!"

He chuckled.

"You think this is funny?"

"I am so close, Case. We are tracking them. They've been in touch with Maude. The lawyers are on the verge of getting the bank to give us access to Demmy's trust credit card information."

Unbelievable. Maude? Lawyers? Banks? Without his connections to back him up, Roger was useless. Had he ever done a day's worth of real work in his life? And none of the rest of them had seen fit to keep her informed? Casey felt the danger of her deep dependence on Sherbeam, underscored by the absence of her likeness from the walls of the Galería. Selling the Cayenne would allow her to easily cover mortgage payments on that grand old house near the strip mall. Aging Southern beauties were available for a song. She could fix it up real nice. Without The Hartley to worry about, her income would be ample. Life would be a breeze, which she and her daughters would savor on that grand front porch.

"Trust me. Please," Roger implored her.

"That's the last thing I intend to do."

CASEY SQUIRMED in her aisle seat as her plane descended toward Wilmington, Delaware. Leaving Memphis to secure her financial future had seemed sensible when she'd bought the ticket but now seemed delusional. She was in danger of falling back into that familiar fog. She'd received no response from Elyse. She should be in Memphis, but she'd been task-less in Tennessee, unable to sit still. Detective Dunne's document searches would take days and it would be at least that long before her DNA kit arrived in Memphis. Her mind returned repeatedly to her endless struggle against poverty: as a teenager in Eldon, as a twenty-year-old alone in Memphis, as a student in Cholula, pushing thirty in Brooklyn. She would not let poverty hamper her search for Elyse, the way it had done, before. She'd need a functioning business and a place to live and work. In Memphis.

Her plane dropped, slowed, and touched down in Wilmington. That bedraggled old manse had rooms for each of her girls and an office for her business. She envisioned her company sign planted on its front lawn.

An hour later, Casey was in the office of a Delaware Registered Agent. His full-Bernie hairstyle had reassured her, irrationally, that he wasn't a scam artist. An additional hour later, she was walking out the door with paperwork for her shiny new C corporation. Now, none of her potential localization clients could reject her for being a measly freelancer. She could operate on an equal footing with every other business, nationally and internationally. With hours to go before her return flight, she got in her rental and drove.

A horn blared. She hit the brakes. The car slowed.

She was in Rehoboth Beach. How had that happened? Her eyelids were heavy. She had to park before she crashed the car or ran someone over.

A space was free in a parking lot beside an ale house clad in weathered gray shingles. She locked the car, stepped onto a shop-lined boardwalk and walked till she hit sand. She abandoned her shoes under the weathered gray planks of the boardwalk and strode across grass-crowned dunes of white sand down to the surf.

Chilly water curled over her toes. She checked her phone. Her test kit didn't even have tracking info yet. No messages on the DNA site, of course. No messages from Detective Dunne. No messages from her other daughters, gone rogue on the other shore of the same Atlantic now wetting her feet.

Casey felt like chucking the device into the ocean, for all the good it did her. Instead, she pocketed it and began to run. Away from her idiot husband. Away from C corporations. Away from her bratty daughters. Away from her nonresponsive kidnapped child.

She settled into a sustainable pace as the town disappeared behind her to the south. Her breathing steadied. Her body warmed. She ran and ran, breathing in salt air and the musky scent of creosote bushes.

The gently lapping waves lulled her. Images and sounds came: her ex-in-laws' house in Peculiar, the catching in their breath over the phone as she'd told them of their son's death, the same gasp from her parents in Eldon, the drip of Mississippi sludge from Mackie's body as the divers hauled his carcass from the mud that had entombed it so long. She, too, had gasped, when it had arisen from the depths, a decaying monster. Her breath, too, had caught.

Now she stopped, bent over, breathing, gasping. Her calves ached. She felt she could vomit, but nothing came.

"Are you all right?"

Casey looked up. A woman more or less Casey's age, with short, dykey salt-and-pepper hair—upright, yet soft looking—stared at her with concern. A flock of wild geese honked overhead.

Casey shook her head. "I'm really not."

The woman approached, put her arm around Casey as she straightened. She pulled Casey into a warm embrace, rocked her as Casey gave in to sobs.

"It'll be all right," the woman said.

Casey's sobs continued, lessened, abated. She stepped out of the hug. "Sorry about that."

"No need to apologize."

Casey wiped her eyes. "I'm going through a rough time."

"You want to talk about it?"

"No," Casey said.

"Enough said. You staying around here?"

Casey shook her head. She thought of the long drive to her airport hotel, her early morning flight to Memphis. "I have to get back to my car at the boardwalk."

"I was just walking back to my room at North Shores. Shall we walk together?"

Casey nodded. She liked the look of the woman: a little older than herself, fit and capable-seeming. They walked in silence over the cool evening sand. The woman was rather attractive, Casey decided, and she was grateful for her presence. The feel of the woman's body stayed with her. After a time, Casey began talking. She told the woman—Yvette was her name—pretty much everything. Yvette didn't act like she disbelieved her, which Casey might have, had the situations been reversed. Perhaps Yvette had dramas of her own, in her past. Being a human being and all.

It was comforting to have someone hold her hand, hear her story, to hear Yvette's inhaled shock, murmured sympathies, and outrage at Casey's (not entirely fair, but earned) description of Roger's intolerable conduct.

"What should I do?" Casey finally asked Yvette, as the lights of the north end of the boardwalk came into sight.

Yvette, unfortunately, did not have any stunning new

insights. "I wish I had something to offer, but I have as little experience with children and husbands as I do with C corporations."

In lieu of advice, Yvette closed the distance between them, took Casey's other hand, and leaned in slowly to kiss her. Casey returned the kiss, with a passion that drew Yvette in closer. This was something Casey had long secretly wanted. It confirmed her sexual pull toward women was no passing thing. Which, of course, she'd long known but never acknowledged. It was this stifled energy that had leaked out with Kelly —someone Casey had no desire to be with—which Demmy had picked up on, resulting in drama. Casey needed to be honest with her family if she was going to not have that happen again.

Casey leaned back.

"You could join me in my room tonight," Yvette offered. "For as much or as little as you're up for."

Casey shook her head. Some part of her that had never been given the opportunity to mature now had the idea that, having accepted the depth of her attraction to women, she could make a hard break for a same-sex relationship. But that was not how she wanted to change her life. She looked at Yvette's kind eyes. "There's just too much going on. Plus, I have a husband. As much as I am drawn to you, my marriage is not a sham. I could kill Roger, but I love that useless asshole, for all his faults." She ran her hand over Yvette's gorgeous hair. She sighed. "I'm bi," she said, as much to herself as to Yvette. "I'm not a closeted lesbian yearning to breathe free, but it *is* time I acknowledge who I am. To say it out loud. I've needed to be honest for a while. I've just never had the breathing room."

Yvette nodded her understanding.

"But thanks for, well, being there."

Yvette pressed a piece of paper into Casey's palm as they climbed up the stairs to the boardwalk. A phone number was written on it. "In case you ever need to talk. People need friendship as much as romance."

"Thanks," Casey said, knowing she'd never use it.

"Hey, I do have one idea for you," Yvette said.

"What?"

"Crowdsourcing. With your work, you must have connections in Paris. Why not enlist them to find your daughters?"

"That's brilliant." Casey should have thought of it herself. "Thank you." As they approached Casey's rental car, they kissed goodbye, a sweet, friendly kiss. Casey retrieved her shoes and drove to Wilmington, at a nearly legal speed, free of foggy blackouts. She checked herself into her hotel and booted up her laptop. She went on all her translator group websites and listservs and sent out calls for help in Paris: Could anyone help Casey find her two daughters, one blond, one brunette, one eighteen, one six?

Casey felt a glimmer of optimism. She'd find them. And when she was done crushing them in bear hugs, she'd apologize to Demmy in particular. The thing between Casey and Kelly hadn't been Demmy's imagination. Casey would tell Demmy, tell them all, the complete truth.

Casey logged into the DNA site, one more time. Still no tracking info on her test kit. But she did have a message. From *S P.*

Hi. I need to think about this. I have your number

That was all. Casey covered her mouth with her hand. Elyse had contacted her. And tomorrow they would be in the same town.

CHAPTER 63

Maude heard Sherbeam call to her in the murky dawn light of their shared hotel room. She looked up from the suitcase she was packing. She'd told Sherbeam she was going to Rome, but her real destination was Paris. The blue glow of Sherbeam's airbook illuminated her face.

"I found them."

Maude blinked. "Demmy? Abby?" She clicked on the bedside lamp.

Sherbeam nodded. "Look at this comment on the TikTok version of the YouTube mashup from the Galería opening." Sherbeam looked as though the opening had been a triumph, not a debacle. "Read it. *How would you feel if it was your family*, yada yada yada. So I followed that handle to its IG account, and guess who has a secret second IG account with a public profile!"

Sherbeam turned the screen toward Maude as she approached the desk. The TikTok comment Maude was supposed to read was already gone. Instead, there were Demmy and Abby: mugging in front of the Arc de Triomphe, half-smiling in front of the Mona Lisa, stuffing croissants into their maws at Les Trois Magots. Maude was genuinely impressed, even though Sherbeam made the process sound like child's play. "But we already knew they were in Paris."

"Keep going! Have I ever steered you wrong?"

Only all the time, Maude thought, but she sat and worked her way through the feed. Iconic scenes gave way to a neighborhood Maude did not recognize, a pair of twin young women with long, glossy black hair. They were older than Demmy, laughing with her and Abby in an apartment. One picture included a view from a window. Sherbeam had found where they were staying. "Well done, you!"

Sherbeam arose from her chair—she always *arose* rather than *rose*, or, heaven forbid, *got up*—and began dressing. "I have to get back to my easel—it's going phenomenally well—but alert Roger, will you?"

Maude kept scrolling. Demmy had taken a lovely selfie of herself amidst a large family of people laughing and gesticulating over a feast. Abby was in the middle of them, next to a thirty-something guy who appeared, in the series of pics, to be interpreting for her. He was nice looking, but the guy next to him, wow! They all seemed to be having a great time. Maude felt guilty about breaking up the party, which is what she'd be doing when she contacted Roger, which she did, nonetheless.

"You found them?" Roger sounded incredulous, and sleepy.

"Your mother did. She's quite amazing."

"Don't keep me in suspense."

Maude looked at the photos. "I just sent you the IG handle."

Roger was silent.

"Instagram?"

"I know what IG is!"

"Don't yell at me, Roger."

"This is important."

Maude frowned. "You better not be blaming me for this"

"Do you have to keep touching me in public? What's up with that?"

"I am the same in public as I am in private. I'm a very touchy person. I touch everyone."

"Well, stop."

"I won't. If you want it to stop, stay away from me. I've done nothing wrong." She'd planned to tell Roger about her trip to Paris but now did not.

The phone went silent again. Could he not acknowledge what she'd said? Did he have the gall to disagree?

Maude grew angry. She wanted to tell him about Elż and Bill, but she did not deserve this anger and resented the implication that she did. "If you're trying to avoid pissing me off because you need my help, I swear to God . . ."

"It's just too much, Maude. It's *all* too much. Us, Mom, Casey, Abby."

"The MacArthur?"

"Don't even."

"Not everyone gets a MacArthur, Roger. Your mom works at her profile. She posts video on TikTok. She knows what IG is."

"I know all about Insta."

"Okay, boomer."

Silence again. She felt for him. He *didn't* know, not in the way that mattered. Sherbeam probably spent an hour a day, every day, working with social media boy.

"Go find them, Roger. Leave me out of it."

CHAPTER 64

Roger stared at the phone. Maude was the boomer; he was Gen X. And, yes, Maude, I know what IG is, he thought snippily. The reason he hadn't got a MacArthur *wasn't* because he wasn't on social media. He was on Instagram. Hell, he had accounts on Snapchat, Discord, Vimeo, Venmo, Vine, Line, Twist, and Mixi, even Myspace, and he Hootsuited on all of them, for all the good it did. He signed into TikTok, checked in on "his" penis (a gazillion views), replied to Demmy (***This is Dad. Call me***), and went back to the IG account Maude had sent him.

The girls were having a blast, safe and sound, which was a relief, but where exactly were they? Nothing looked familiar. Roger took his laptop downstairs to the concierge for help.

"Hmm," the young Frenchman said. "This is not a neighborhood I know."

Roger made a sour face. "But it's Paris, right?" He pointed to the view from the apartment window.

The Frenchman made a face of his own. "Maybe a banlieue."

"Which is what?"

"A suburb, I think you say." He turned away, as though suburbs were beneath him, and should be beneath Roger, if he knew what was good for him.

"Please, I need to find them." Roger slid the laptop screen back in front of him. "They're my daughters."

"Why are they hanging out with a bunch of gay Arabs?"

Gay Arabs? Roger perused the photos. They just looked French to Roger. "Please . . ." But the guy was gone. "Fuck you!" Roger yelled after him. How did you say that in French? "*Mierda!*" he yelled after the prick. No, that was Spanish. The front desk woman looked up from the guests she was checking in, confused. Whatever. It was the best he could manage.

A guy with a broom sidled over, turned the laptop toward himself. Now this guy looked more like the folks in the photos, though Roger couldn't put his finger on how. The haircuts? But was that a gay thing or an Arab thing or just a young thing?

"21st arrondissement," the guy said. "A few stops from Gare de Lyon."

Roger knew where that was.

The broom guy pointed at a seated man in the picture with dark wavy hair, sitting next to the talking guy next to Abby. "That's a handsome fellow." He was. Kind of a supermodel type.

"Are *you* gay?" Roger asked the guy.

The guy snorted contemptuously and left, gesturing violently with his hands at Roger. All rightie, then.

Roger closed his laptop and left for the Gare de Lyon. If the police were making any progress they were keeping it a secret from him. He found a subway stop and looked at the map. There was only one likely line. He boarded, got off two stops later at Nation. A local told him he was not yet in the 21st.

He boarded again, got off at Port de Montreal. No, wait, Porte de Montreuil. These French people couldn't spell for shit.

Roger looked around. He could tell he was getting close. And yet. He opened up his laptop to show the photo in cafés, grocery stores, to random young-gay-Arab-looking people on the street—it was something about the jawline, Roger decided —but had no luck. Yes, the view from the window looked similar, they said, but was a little too far south, a little too far north, maybe too low, maybe too high. Roger walked and talked for hours. He felt so close to finding them, and yet his prowling seemed to be taking him away from his prize as often as it took him toward it. His laptop battery was at three percent. He was lost.

"*Merde!*" he yelled again. And from the looks he got, this time he'd chosen the right language.

CHAPTER 65

The female voice on the phone sounded small to Casey. "My mother died," it said.

Casey felt a stab of joy, despite the mention of death. Her daughter! But Elyse's timidity kept Casey's excitement in check. "I'm so glad you called me."

"Where are you?" the voice said, growing in strength a bit.

"In Memphis. Just outside the post office on B.B. King." She'd mailed in her DNA sample, which would normally seem coincidental, but every moment of her life involved Elyse right now. "I'd love to see you."

"Your story doesn't add up, I have to tell you." Elyse sounded more confident now, though the traffic growling down B.B. King made it hard to hear.

"You have the DNA report. I can prove everything I said. Please. Just a coffee."

Casey heard breathing. Not good. Of course Elyse had to think about it, but then she had to say yes. She *had to* say yes; she *had to*.

"I need more time," Elyse said.

"If I could just . . ."

But Casey could tell the connection was gone. Elyse had hung up.

CASEY CALMED down on the walk back to her hotel—this was not over—but still felt bereft. Elyse had blocked her phone number. What could Casey do now? She had to wait for a call that might never come. Casey called her parents, then Hank and Joe, and told them all she'd talked to Elyse amidst much joyful sobbing and repeated thank-yous. Casey ended the call and felt unspeakably lonely. Who did she know in town? Detective Dunne. She called him and told Dunne that she'd heard from Elyse. Dunne's voice relaxed a notch.

"That's a relief." He sighed. He asked for details. He became chatty.

Casey began to realize he now thought it was over. He'd unearthed a death, and Mackie's family had been informed. He'd needed to track down his missing person, and now Elyse had appeared.

"You're not done with this, are you? I haven't seen her," Casey mewled. "I lost my child. It can't end here."

"Listen. I'll talk to my captain. See where we stand." Dunne went quiet. She trusted that he was giving what she'd said careful consideration, as usual. He wasn't thinking what he'd say when he brushed the case aside. He better not be. "Hang tight," he said.

Casey went to a café near the National Civil Rights Museum, the Bluff City Coffee & Bakery. She ordered a black coffee and something that looked like a cross between a cinnamon twist and a pie. She sat at a black metal table on the sidewalk, outside where she wouldn't need a mask, under a red umbrella that felt surprisingly necessary in the muggy air. She bit into the gooey pastry. She heard Kelly's voice all the way from Park Slope: "The calories!" She scoffed at it, but the Kelly in Casey's head won: she pushed aside the rest of the delicious pastry.

The sun was strong for early April. It beat down on her bare arm where it lay outside the umbrella's protection. She placed her phone on the table and opened up her laptop to check if her pleas on the linguist listservs had paid off with intel on her two other daughters.

No, no, and no. She went through the lists one by one. She wasn't sure what she'd expected these people to do for her, but if someone had asked her for help regarding Williamsburg, she'd have done what she could. She found good wishes and blatantly obvious advice, but nothing actionable.

She opened up her email. It was all dross and dreck: this season's round of going-out-of-business sales at venerable department stores, deals on colorful new N95s, plus one tastefully eager missive from Porsche encouraging her to trade the Planetkiller for their new, even more expensive, electric vehicle.

An email popped its head up in the sea of garbage. Looked like France. It *was* France. Paris. An interpreter was asking for more details, coyly suggesting he might have relevant information to share. Fearing this was a scam, she checked the guy's website. It was professional. He had a small localization company. And a blog. Oh my god. According to his blog, he'd been to Barcelona the weekend before.

Casey dialed his office number. It rang.

"Way?" he said.

Ah, of course, the French often said 'way' for 'yes' rather than 'wee,' unless they felt certainty. "*Mon français n'est pas si bon,*" she said. My French is not so good.

"English is perfectly fine," he said, in a British accent.

"Are you Ethan? You sent me an email."

"Are you Ms. White, with the localization firm?"

"Casey. And please don't tell me you want to sell me something. Please tell me you know something about my daughters."

"I believe so, but I do not feel entirely comfortable divulging children's details over the phone to someone I haven't met. I have to know they are your children."

"Wait a sec." Casey emailed him a photo of the two girls, smiling beside Casey and Roger. She also sent a link to her site, which had her photo, her name and the phone number she was calling on. "Check your email."

She heard plasticky clicks. "Nothing so far."

"My husband told me they were with him in Barcelona. I never would have left if I'd known they'd taken off."

"They didn't have your permission?"

"No!"

"But the letter . . ."

"My idiot husband."

"Ah." Casey heard a chime and more clicking keys. "Got it," he said. "That's them!"

"Oh thank god. But how do I know *you* are legit?"

"Legit?"

"Above board. Legitimate. On the up and up."

Her phone chimed. She checked the message. It was a selfie of Ethan with Demmy and Abby and another handsome guy, all four smiling, on a tree-lined street in Paris.

"Their names are Demmy . . ."

". . . and Abby. Can I talk to them?"

"Let me check. I am at the office, myself. Hang on." He went away.

Casey looked at her phone screen. She had not missed any calls from Elyse. Ethan came back. "I'm afraid they are out."

"Don't tell me. For ice cream."

"How did you know?"

"You expect me to believe that!" Casey started swearing, in French. That was maybe most of the French she knew, but she knew it well.

"Wait, wait. I'm not lying! They were just there. With one of my sisters. I met them on the train from Barcelona. They've been staying at my parents' Airbnb. I swear. They are here. They are fine. Please don't worry. It's really just ice cream."

Casey calmed herself. Maybe sometimes an ice cream was just an ice cream. Ethan gave Casey his sisters' landline number. She gave him Roger's. Idiot or not, Roger was still her husband, the girls' father. "I will call him. Maybe you can call him, too."

"I will," Ethan said. "Nice website, by the way."

"Yours, too. I'm a C corporation now."

"I know what that is!" He sounded excited. "Nice."

Casey felt like she was melting. "I haven't thanked you, but I am deeply grateful, more than you could know. I will come to Paris as soon as I can."

He began talking, but her phone began buzzing. She had another call. A blocked number. Elyse. Casey did not want to give Ethan the impression her daughters were anything less than top priority, but Elyse was also her daughter.

"I'll call again," she said, hurriedly swapping calls. "Can we meet?" she now asked Elyse.

The pause on the other end did not last long. "My grandmother swears six ways from Sunday her daughter is my natural mother," Elyse said.

"No," Casey said, launching into her life's story, Elyse's life story.

"Hold on, hold on," Elyse said. "I didn't say I entirely believed her. Truth is, I've long had my doubts. I still do. I'm thinking we could take a little drive, to Arkansas. To ask her. What say you?"

"Yes!" Casey screamed it.

CHAPTER 66

Amal gathered weepy Abby into her arms. The little girl's pugilistic façade of self-sufficiency had finally crumbled. "I want Mommy," she wailed. Now *this*, Amal understood.

The little girl's older sister stood behind her, bags packed. Their final payment had registered moments ago on Amal's Airbnb app. The older girl looked ready to drug her sister senseless and drag her onto a flight to New York—school awaited them both, Amal deduced from the older girl's hesitant French—but seemed to have decided a train ride to Barcelona with a conscious child was easier.

"Where's Ihsan," the younger sister asked, sniffling. Amal's English was enough to understand that.

"We want to say goodbye," the older sister explained.

"Ihsan and Nabil don't live here," Amal tried to explain, working extra hard to flatten her accent into more standard French. "They live and work elsewhere." Was *elsewhere* too complex a word for her? "At another place." Amal glanced up at Demmy, who had understood enough to relay the disappointing news to Abby, who began wailing again, demanding

Ihsan. Amal was thinking drugging her might be a good idea, but instead kissed her. Abby quieted.

Demmy had reserved two tickets, she said in passable French, and they needed to get to Gare de Lyon, so she asked Amal to relay their deep gratitude to Ihsan, Nabil, Hoda, and Fatima and shoved off. Amal pressed a couple chocolatines on them for the road.

Not long after, Ihsan arrived at the bakery and was shocked to learn he'd missed them. "Barcelona? But I just spoke to their mother. She is flying to Paris!"

"Then you'd better hurry to Gare de Lyon, because they have a 10:14 train," Amal said.

Ihsan called Nabil, whose salon was closer to the station. Amal could hear Nabil's tiny tinny voice as he agreed to find the girls and let them know their mother was flying to Paris. Ihsan hung up, kissed his ma, and raced for the Metro to join his husband.

Not ten minutes later, a disheveled American man arrived at the bakery and opened up a laptop to show Amal a photo of himself with Demmy and Abby. He claimed to be their father. He had a police report. She believed him. She told the man in clumsy English that she knew the girls—they'd been staying there—but that the girls had left.

"Gare de Lyon. Garls. Barcelona. On *le Te Ge Ve*." Would he know the train? "Quick train." Ah, her English was dreadful. If it weren't for the Airbnb app, she wouldn't have the nerve to rent to foreign tourists at all.

"Barcelona?!" he cried out.

"*Oui*. Son stop them. Garls' mama *arrivée* to Paris today." Or sometime soon, anyway.

"Paris?!"

"*Oui*. It is story," she said.

"*Merde*." He said it well, for an American. Then he too left.

Tareq came down from their apartment. The bakery was empty. "Slow morning?" he asked.

She shrugged. "The usual."

IHSAN'S PHONE rang as he exited his Metro car. Nabil was upset. "I'm with the girls on the TGV, but I can't make them understand. I think the older girl said her mother is dead and now the little one is crying. We need you."

Dead? Then who had Ihsan given the girls' information to? "I'm just coming up the stairs from the Metro now." Ihsan raced to the platform number Nabil had given him and looked for the car number. He located it, got on board and looked up and down the aisle, spotting Nabil. He reached them.

"Ihsan!" Abby threw her arms up to him and stopped crying.

He leaned over and she hugged his neck, hanging off him even after he straightened up. He turned to Demmy. "Your mother is dead?"

"Yes, but no. Abby's mother is my stepmother."

"Oh, that's who I talked to then." Ihsan felt relieved.

"You talked to Mom?"

"Yes, she's coming to Paris."

"How did you find her?"

"She found me. She's been looking for you."

"She has?" Demmy sounded gleeful. Had she not expected her stepmother to look for her? "They're both looking for us?" Demmy sounded surprised, relieved, grateful. Had she thought her parents didn't care enough to turn the world upside down to find her?

"Ihsan, the train is about to leave," Nabil said, anxiously. "We don't have tickets. The bell already sounded. We should have gotten off five minutes ago."

Ihsan nodded. "Demmy, we have to get off the train now."

"You sure? That she's coming to Paris? I don't think I can get a refund."

"Ihsan, there." Nabil pointed at a group of policemen headed their way. "I don't want to get caught with these girls onboard the TGV without a ticket," he added in Libyan Arabic.

Ihsan turned back to Demmy. "Look, we have to hide from the police, but let's all get off and figure this out on the platform."

"Why hide?"

"It's just simpler, trust me. It's a gay Arab thing."

"A gay . . . ?"

But Demmy was interrupted by a screech.

"Daddy!" Abby was pointing out the window.

They all looked. The man Abby was pointing at, apparently her father, was standing with the policeman. Sweat beaded on his forehead. He was gesticulating, every bit as much as the policemen: toward each other, the train, and the clock hanging overhead. Or maybe he was invoking Allah, the merciful and compassionate. *Bismillah,* no, I will not let them go.

Ihsan watched, transfixed, with Nabil, Abby, and Demmy as the girls' father looked toward the train.

Abby slapped her hands forcefully onto the window. The father squinted. She slapped her hands on the window again. The father looked straight at them.

"Abby!" he cried out.

"Daddy!" Abby kept her hands pressed to the glass, and only then did Ihsan realize the train was in motion.

CHAPTER 67

C asey tried not to cry when she pulled her rental sedan into the riverside parking lot and saw Elyse standing beside the red pickup. She was about Casey's height, had Casey's dark brown curls and her father's pale brown skin tone. She looked athletic. A grizzled old boxer sat on its haunches beside her. Casey parked, got out. Her legs shook.

Casey walked the few steps to her daughter. Her daughter's face was Casey's at twenty. Elyse may have inherited the tan complexion and sturdy build of her father and grandfather, but her face was pure Casey. As much as she wanted to, Casey didn't dare hug her for fear she'd run away.

Elyse saw the resemblance, too. At least, that was how Casey read her silence. They stood, three feet apart. A young man came up bearing three cups in a cardboard tray, took a look at Casey, said, "Oh my God," and proceeded to fumble his tray, dropping one of the cups on the asphalt. Hot black coffee spilled between their feet.

"I'm . . . Casey." She didn't dare say "mother." Casey thought of Demmy, who had just begun calling her "Mom," or more accurately, had just stopped. Casey wanted to hold

Demmy, tell her it was all okay. And tell Abby she had always been wanted.

"I'm Sarah," the girl said.

Casey nodded. "*S P.*"

"Sarah Pellistrini. This is my husband, Pell."

Pell reached his free hand forward, shaking Casey's while keeping a firm grip on the remaining two coffees. "Pell is short for Pellistrini, obvi. Oh my god, I said obvi. My given name's David, but no one uses it. Are you both blown away by the . . ." He motioned his hand back and forth between their faces.

"We haven't really spoken," Elyse said. No, Casey corrected herself: Sarah. Her daughter's name was Sarah; she had to get that right immediately. She was Sarah. Sarah, Sarah, Sarah. Such a beautiful name.

"I'll shut up," Pell said. "Here's coffees. Hope you like it black." He handed them each one. "I'll get Xochi. Come 'ere, old girl. Come 'ere, good girl." Clearly, shutting up was not his strong suit. He opened up the rear door of the extended cab and lifted the decrepit dog into the rear seat. "How 'bout I drive, so's you two can talk?"

Sarah nodded, as did Casey, who climbed into the rear seat with the weirdly named dog—short for Xochimilco?—who was clearly not long for this world.

Sarah got into the front passenger seat and Pell started up the engine as they buckled in. "So y'all get to talking, 'cause I can't abide awkward silence and it's a near hunnert miles to the informatively named Wet Springs." He turned to Casey and grinned. "Arkansas here we come. Yee ha!"

If he hated silence, the miles must have been torture for Pell, because Sarah hardly responded to Casey, though she did turn to look at her from time to time. It was torture for Casey, too, being penned up in the cramped backseat and unable to hold a conversation with her daughter.

Casey tried easing into things, but when she referred to Mackie's parents up in Peculiar as Sarah's grandparents, Sarah turned away. She looked out the window for the most part after that, giving little sign she heard Casey's chatter. Miles rolled by as countryside drifted past the small tinted windows in the rear of the cab, occasional drops of moisture scrolling across the smoky glass as the day thought about whether it wanted to rain.

One small town after another went by, lost in a sea of green trees all the same height, the highway exits marked by round Gulf station signs here and there. Casey tried telling Sarah things about her life in New York, about Eldon where she'd grown up, about the FFA where she'd met Sarah's father, about her other daughters. The most she got was a furtive glance from Sarah through the rearview mirror, until Sarah responded, "My mother died." Pell was manfully silent.

Casey sipped the coffee and petted the dog, whose ribs were pronounced, fur dry. "Do you want me to keep talking?" she finally asked.

Sarah turned toward her, but did not speak.

"I know you're not convinced by me, Sarah, but I have a lot to say. Should I add *alleged* before everything I say? Would that help?"

Pell laughed.

Sarah shot him a wrinkled brow, the first sign of discord Casey had observed between them. He wisely said nothing.

"Nothing you say makes any sense with what I know about myself," Sarah said at last, "so let's just wait till we arrive."

"Does your grandmother . . ." whoever the woman was ". . . know to expect us?"

Pell laughed again. "Oh, no. We are coming in hot, on stealth mode."

Sarah crossed her arms and Casey took that as a sign. She

resumed petting the dog, calmer now, as they turned off 64 and onto 16, along the Little Red River. Before too long they were driving north into a leafy town of tall old trees and low brick buildings, a white water tower painted with the town name, and damp flags hanging limp in the breezeless gray day.

Pell drove the pickup through a series of turns with dispatch; clearly this was a place he knew well. He pulled up on the gravel verge of a road in front of a white bungalow with a glassed-in porch. A moth-eaten lawn still bore the fallen leaves of the previous winter. It wasn't much to look at, but the lot was large and the roof appeared sound. It was closer into town than what you might call the outskirts, but wasn't central, since they'd gone through what passed for a down-town—the "business district," a sign had proclaimed—a few minutes before.

They got out to a pulsing drone of unseasonably early cicadas, raucous in their thousands. A severe, white-haired woman in a faded house dress was visible standing in the glassed-in porch, watching them walk up the front path.

"Did you grow up here?" Casey ventured.

"She did," Pell answered for Sarah after a minute. "I grew up yonder." He pointed back toward the business district.

Up ahead the front door was opening, the woman stone-faced as she held it for them. Pell grabbed the screen door from her and Sarah walked in with a hug, but not any words that Casey could hear. Pell held the door for Casey and Xochi to follow.

The older woman's eyes widened in alarm when she saw Casey. "This is her?" she asked Sarah. Not much on social graces, was she? Casey bit back her urge to speak. The older woman's DNA test might well come back a hundred percent that you-know-what.

Sarah nodded. At least the woman had been informed of Casey's existence. They traded vaccination histories. All had received the latest Z.5-specific booster.

Casey extended her hand. "Casey." Her hand went unmet. "Lovely to meet you." Casey's sarcasm was as disguised as she could manage, but she'd likely be seen through. What went down smoothly undetected in Williamsburg would light up the snark detectors in any who grew up here.

"Let's sit in the parlor," the woman said.

Pell gave Casey an apologetic shrug of the shoulders. At least he was on her side. As was newfound friend Xochi, who curled up next to the chair Casey chose when Sarah disappeared into another room.

Pell drummed his fingers on the wooden arm of his maple chair as the absence of Sarah and her "grandmother" stretched out. Casey made a quick trip to the bathroom, returning to the room as Sarah and the "grandmother" carried in a stack of china cups, a pot of coffee and, under the grandmother's arm, an unopened pack of Nutter Butters. Casey was glad to see hospitality, brusque though it was.

"If you'd told me you were coming I'd'a had something presentable for you," the older woman complained.

"Would you, Grandma?" Sarah's tone was skeptical.

Grandma softened a bit. "Maybe," she conceded. "This is a shock," she added at length, as Sarah poured coffee into delicate cups with hand-painted yellow flowers, ancient things but unchipped.

Casey noted family photos on the nearby mantle. None of the other people had the touch of dark to their skin that Sarah did. Casey remembered the comments she'd received when Sarah was a baby—is she yours?—even though their difference in complexion was slight. She wondered how that had been for Sarah and what stories they had made up about the father. Maybe they didn't bother the way people used to. Most people Casey knew growing up had some degree of mixed background—mostly this but a little that, a little the other— and usually stories to go with it, folklore passed down like recipes and anecdotes of who killed who in The War.

"When did your 'mother' die, then?" Casey asked Sarah, her voice saying "mother" as though touching a dead thing with a stick.

"Violet died when Sarah was a month shy of five," Grandma supplied. "It's been the two of us since then."

"And you need to explain, Grandma, why me and this total stranger, whose daughter is my half-sister, appear to be near twins."

Casey felt as if she'd been zapped by a live wire. Sarah believed her. What feelings Sarah must be going through. She'd been lied to her entire life.

"Well, what if her brother . . ." Grandma trailed off. Casey wasn't sure how the woman had been intending to finish the sentence, and neither, it appeared, did she. No one else volunteered to help out.

Grandma turned to Casey now. "Is this true? Are you really Sarah's mother?"

Casey's eyes widened at the unexpected question. She nodded. Casey had no doubt whatsoever.

The old woman shook her head. Now *she* was tearing up. She brought her hand to her mouth. Her head continued to shake. Casey looked up at the mantel photo of a very young, very fair-skinned woman holding a tan-complexioned baby with thick dark hair and a button nose unlike her own. Violet and Sarah.

"I swear I did not know," Grandma said.

The room was quiet.

"Violet had been gone for quite some time. She was into

the drugs, you see. She'd used to go off for a week at a time, two, and swing home when she ran out of money or needed to hide out or something. Every time, she swore she'd get off the drugs, and every time I was taken in. But she never did, bless her heart. Just disappeared on me. The weeks would turn to months, sometimes a year. Just when I'd given up all hope of seeing my child again, she came home with an infant in her arms." Grandma nodded at Sarah. "Said you were hers. Why shouldn't I believe her?"

Pell mouthed 'whoa.' Sarah sat motionless. Casey got the sense this was news to them both.

"Things seemed to pick up for Violet after that. Maybe you focused her, Sarah. She lived here with you, honey, for a solid year." Grandma placed her hand on Sarah's hand. "But the drugs called her, and one day she was gone again, leaving you with me." Grandma stroked Sarah's arm. The older woman now seemed a world apart from the hostile creature who had opened the door, and Casey felt grateful. Perhaps growing up in that house had not been as grim as it had first seemed.

"Is she alive?" Sarah asked.

Oh, God. That had not even occurred to Casey, who only now realized she'd felt hard-to-acknowledge relief when Sarah had first said her mother was dead.

Grandma shook her head. "No, sadly, that part of it is all true. She came back when you were four, of course." Grandma cleared her throat and looked at Sarah, got nothing back. Grandma looked at the carpet. "Overdose, here in town. You must remember the funeral."

But Sarah shook her head. Her eyes were big, moist.

"I see," Grandma said.

Pell put his hand on Sarah's shoulder now, standing behind her. Sarah brought her hand up to his.

"She did try to be a good mother. That last year was a

better one. I thought her troubles were behind her, to be honest. But it's never that easy, is it?"

Sarah leaned forward. "But I have a birth certificate from when I got my passport. It says she was my mother."

"Violet had told me you were born at home. So that's what I told ole Edgar over at the county clerk's. Violet never put a name to your father, but she had quite the story of giving birth to you in a falling-down house. I felt I'd been there. If you'd seen her when she arrived . . ." Grandma's voice trailed off. "She'd had a baby, I could see that. The milk was still coming. She was nursing you. Why would I question that? But I can't deny what I see here before my own eyes, the connection between the two of you. Is there any other explanation?"

Casey shook her head.

Pell said, "No, ma'am." And that seemed to seal it for Grandma, because now she reached out to Casey.

"I'm so sorry," she said. "What you have been through! I honestly had no idea."

Sarah scoffed. "You had suspicions. I could tell. I always knew you were holding something back."

"No, honey. No. Not that. It was the drugs. I couldn't bear to tell you what happened to your mother."

"But everyone knew that," Sarah said.

Grandma reared back. "Of *course* they didn't," she snapped. The implacable woman who'd greeted them resurfaced. Clearly this was not an easy woman.

"Whoa, whoa," Pell said. The kid seemed to gravitate toward the peacemaker role. "Water under the bridge."

Casey shuddered violently at the phrase.

"What is it?" Pell asked.

"You haven't heard my story yet, any of you."

"Are you ready, baby?" Pell asked Sarah.

Sarah nodded. So Casey told them about Mackie, leaving

out nothing. If Casey had wondered whether Sarah still disbelieved her, the look of grief and horror when Sarah realized that the body hauled from the river, the body the whole town had read about, was her father, removed that doubt. Sarah had accepted her, Casey, this stranger, as her biological mother.

"Violet did tell me you were born in Memphis," Grandma said, amidst the general exhaustion that seemed to sweep the room when Casey finished.

No one moved. Were they all imagining the possibilities, as Casey was? Drug addict Violet has a baby and loses it. She stumbles across Elyse wrapped in a blanket on the Willis Avenue Bridge, waiting for a father who will never come. Violet simply walks off with her, crazy with longing. It wasn't a scenario the police had come up with, that was for sure.

"Why would he do that?" Sarah asked Casey, meaning her biological father, but it was her grandma who answered.

"Sometimes things happen to folks, sometimes people are born a little off, sometimes they are born a lot off," she said. The echoes of what Hank had said were strong. Grandma continued. "But mostly, people are born good. Like you, Sarah; like your man Pell, here. So let's just thank our stars for that."

Indeed. Now Casey swallowed. "I have to ask, do you think Violet could have been my husband Mackie's . . ." she spit the word out ". . . girlfriend?"

"Oh, Lord no." Grandma chuckled. "That girl never could abide a penis, or anything attached to one." She passed the package of Nutter Butters to Casey, ignoring the question of how Violet then had become pregnant. "So have you some of these and you two have a proper talk while I fix us something more substantial to eat. Lord knows I'm not perfect, but I can do better than I've done here this morning."

The woman stood and placed a palm to Sarah's cheek as Sarah and Casey looked at each other for what felt like the first time. Grandma kissed the top of Sarah's head, and hovered beside her, apparently unwilling yet to leave the room.

"I want you to come with me to Paris, to meet your sisters," Casey said to Sarah. "And for you to come too," she said to Pell.

Pell's eyes widened, but he seemed willing. Sarah, on the other hand, folded her arms across her chest. She took a deep breath. "Do you have any pictures?" Sarah asked.

Casey whipped out her phone and scrolled through her photos folder. Abby and Demmy beamed out at Sarah. Casey flipped from photo to photo till she saw Sarah getting bleary-eyed. Casey slowed down.

"Do you have any of my father?"

Casey shook her head. Casey had burned all of them privately, in the only funeral Mackie had received, to her knowledge. "His parents have photos, up in Missouri."

Sarah nodded. Knowing they existed seemed to satisfy her. "But I can't go to Paris. I have to take care of Xochi," Sarah said.

Casey beamed. She was considering it?

"I'll watch her, honey." Grandma reached down to pet the dog. "And don't underestimate us old gals. We're both tough. Xochi'll be here waiting when you get back," she said, before disappearing into the kitchen.

Sarah looked at Casey and nodded. "Then count us in."

CHAPTER 68

Maude would not have recognized Bill if Elż hadn't been standing right beside him in the lobby of the Raffles Le Royal Monceau. The two had secured a table and led Maude there after greetings of kisses. Bill's trademark queenly cackles of glee bounced off the ceiling, recalling for Maude the short Roger had filmed before *The Fix*. That film, *Diary of a Straight Drag Queen*, had documented Bill's wicked drag stand-up and launched the foursome's friendship.

Drinks were quickly ordered.

"I can't believe I am sitting here across from Maude Friendly after so many years!" Bill nestled in an upholstered chair that matched the upholstered loveseat from which she and Elż faced him. A bottle and wine glasses quickly appeared on the gleaming mahogany tabletop between them.

"You look amazing," Maude told him. She and Elż had already had the conversation about changed looks in New York.

"I am fat and awful." Bill laughed.

"You absolutely aren't!" Maude said. "At least no more so than you were twenty years ago."

Bill leaned back with a belly laugh. "I've missed you."

They segued into talk of families as drinks arrived. Like Roger, Bill was on his second marriage. Elż still had just had the one, which kept her ensconced with husband Piotr and their two teenagers in her hometown of Wrocław, Poland, when she wasn't on location. Then they sallied forth into their art. All three had projects going. Elż signaled the waiter for more wine.

"Next I want to do a film without countryside," Bill said. "Nothing that bites."

"I want to shoot one without a serial killer," said Elż.

"I want all my paintings to be free of politics," said Maude.

"Is that possible?" Elż asked.

Maude glanced down at the carpet's pattern of ocher branches against a dusty rose background before answering. "Politics in visual art has always felt contrived to me." She quirked a challenging eyebrow at them.

"Oh, you're spoiling all the fun," said Bill.

But she wasn't. She was creating fun, because arguing was a delight when no one had anything to prove. She might not have the audiences that Bill and Elż had, but she had the fans she needed.

Maude turned to Elż. "I could have sworn when I showed you the new stuff you didn't care for it," Maude said. "Ugh, that look."

She and Bill laughed with recognition. It was so easy to read negativity into someone's reaction to one's art, especially when you went into the encounter thinking your art was the best thing ever created.

"I wasn't sure what I thought of it, to be honest," Elż said. "Your paintings have always been skilled, but it took me a while to notice I was recalling them weeks after. They're memorable. It's what I *shoot* for, talking as a cinematographer. I want to make an impression."

"I'm going simpler and simpler," Maude said. "I take out the extra garbage that sneaks in. That way, I say what I mean. It makes me happier and it seems to make my audience happier as well. I haven't traded up, I traded deeper."

"I'd write that down," Elż said, "but I've had too much wine."

Maude laughed. She knew was stringing words together drunkenly, pompously, happily. "Let me put it this way: I paint what I want and don't worry about what happens to it after."

"And Roger?" Bill said. "What's the boy wonder up to?"

"He's writing a new script," Maude said. "He's carrying a notebook, like his mother."

"Tell me it's not about Sherbeam," Elż said. "I always dreaded the day I would hear that he was doing a documentary about her."

Maude gave that some thought. "I was the one who fell down that hole, not he. Him? He. All this time I've been trying to rescue him when I was the one who needed rescuing."

"Will it be as good as *The Fix*?" Elż asked.

"Oh, God, remember that kid?" Bill asked. "Roger really captured the loneliness of being thirteen: parenting your divorced mom and dad, hoping that falling in love will save you. The earnestness of it still gets to me."

"Everything gets to you, Bill. It's your best quality." Maude refilled her glass.

"He didn't even know what his own movie was about, did he?" Elż asked.

"I think he does now. Love conquers all, oldest trope in the book. The feel-good ending we all hope for," Maude said.

All three grew quiet.

"It doesn't, of course," Elż added.

Bill nodded. "Nope."

"But something doesn't have to be true to be good." Maude sighed, feeling uncommonly joyful, like a bird hopping to the door of her cage, finally fallen open, and leaping into flight.

Bill smiled, but had no snarky comeback.

"So if I promise he's not doing a Sherbeam documentary, can we call him?" Maude asked. "He's in Paris!" This call was a bon voyage she could give Roger before she disappeared from his life, a wave back at the one she'd left standing on the shore.

Elż and Bill traded glances and gave Roger the nod.

CHAPTER 69

Roger watched the train disappear. His daughters were headed to Barcelona and he wasn't. The police kept jabbering at him in French. He checked his phone for a plane ticket to Barcelona. There was not one seat, at any price. He plugged an ear against the police chatter and pressed the other against his phone as he called an airline direct. They laughed at him. Then they explained: all the flights to Barcelona were packed with folk heading south for the big commemoration—Sagrada Familia was finally done.

Roger turned back to the police. "Can you stop the train? Pull them off at the next stop?"

But the next stop was Barcelona and this situation did not qualify as emergent enough to stop it. The Spanish police would intercept them, they assured Roger.

Yeah, sure.

Roger was debating what to do when the phone rang. It was Demmy.

"Demmy!"

"I'm so embarrassed by all the things I said. I love you."

"I love you, too, sweetheart." Roger choked up. "I'm sorry,

too," he said. "For everything. I know these years have been hard."

"It hasn't been that bad. Casey has been great. I really think of her as my mom now. I was such a snot to you both."

"If you and I had just talked more, about your mom, none of this would have happened."

"Yeah."

"I've never really told Casey about what it was like when your mother was sick. I mean, I *told* her, but words can't describe it. It just went on and on, didn't it?"

"Years," Demmy agreed.

"I hope I never see the inside of a hospital again," he said.

"But it's a house of hope and healing!"

They laughed, a joke just between the two of them.

"Can we go for a walk on the beach?" Roger asked. "In Barcelona. Just you and me? And talk, and remember? A phone's not the same."

"Sure, Dad. I'd like that. The hardest part has always been the feeling she's just gone."

"I wanted to talk about her, but the words stuck in my throat. Leave well enough alone, I let myself think. I should've tried harder. But we can start now, okay?"

"Okay."

The phone went silent.

"Dad?"

"Yes, honey?"

"She doesn't seem so gone anymore."

Roger nodded silently. He knew what she meant. Losing someone was a blow. But the blow of loss was distinct from the absence of the person. And once the blow subsided, memories crept back in. You weren't left with a deathbed snapshot; you were left with an epic film.

Roger heard voices in the background.

"What's going on?"

"These two guys who have been helping us got caught on the train. They have to get tickets, but there's only two first-class seats left, and there's a penalty, so it's a lot."

"The bakery guys? I met their mother. Can you get them tickets? I'll reimburse you later. Is it true, um, Casey is coming to Paris today?"

Roger heard a muffled conversation before Demmy's voice came back. "Mom's coming tomorrow, according to Ihsan."

So it was *Mom*, again. "Then I can get her to re-route to Barcelona. You and Abby go to the Barcelona hotel and sit tight till we get there, OK?"

"Sure, Dad."

"Can you put Abby on?"

Demmy did. Abby was nearly silent, but Roger told Abby he loved her and would see her soon in Barcelona. In her little grunts and sighed breaths he thought he heard a response she couldn't articulate yet: she believed him.

Demmy's voice came back on. "Dad?"

"Go take care of the guys' tickets, and I will see you soon. And maybe when we get back, we can make that TikTok–style film we talked about."

"Oh, God, Dad, no. TikTok is dead to me now. And you know that art is the last thing I want to do, right? Do you know how many tropical diseases have no cure? Not just dengue, but Chikungunya, Chagas, even malaria! Tulane Medical School has a program in exactly that. I don't want to focus on loss when the really amazing thing is that people can lessen pain and fight disease. That's what I want to do. I'm going for pre-med. And since all these diseases have already arrived in Brooklyn, I won't count as a White savior."

"Oh," Roger said. There were people who *didn't* want to make films? "How did I miss that about you?" But in truth, it felt like something he knew. Just as it felt true that there was someone he *did* want to make a movie with. "Well, I love you both."

"We love you both, too." Demmy hung up.

Roger dismissed the police, glad to see the end of them, and got back on the phone. He struck out with TGV tickets through the mobile portal, but got himself on a wait list in the station's ticket office. Securing a high-speed rail seat required that he remain present all day, but his Paris hotel agreed to messenger his bag over, so he'd sit tight and make some calls. He got Casey on the first try and told her to go to Barcelona instead of Paris, because Demmy and Abby would be at the hotel there.

"They both miss you. I miss you."

"I miss you too, Roger."

"And did you . . . ?"

"Yes."

"Oh my God!"

"Her name is Sarah now. She lives in Memphis. Has a sweet husband and a sweet dog. Looks like me."

"Oh. My. God."

"*Sarah* looks like me, I mean, not the dog. It's still a big mystery what exactly happened all those years ago, one we may never fully understand, but Sarah's healthy and happy and we found each other. She's so beautiful."

"When do we meet her?"

"If we can all get to Barcelona, tomorrow."

"Then I will do my best. I had a good talk with Demmy. I think we are back to normal. Better than normal, maybe. I think the girls would both like to hear from you."

"Really? I . . ." He heard Casey's voice catch.

"Call them now."

"I will."

They got off the phone, and Roger set about some serious waiting. He didn't get a seat on the next train, five hours later, but did secure an economy seat on the last train of the day and had just planted his butt firmly in a seat traveling south overnight to Barcelona when the phone rang. It was a Polish number.

CHAPTER 70

Sherbeam's new painting was slated to be unveiled at eight, Roger had told Casey, so she had their rideshare driver go straight to the gallery, where her other daughters were waiting. Soon she, Sarah, and Pell—bleary from the flight into Madrid and subsequent train to Barcelona-Sants—stood at the entrance to Galería Les Rambles.

Pau caught them at the door and ushered them into the larger back room, where all eyes turned toward them. Relief flooded Roger's face as he said something to Abby and Demmy, who stood at his side. Roger rested an arm on each girl's shoulder, as though he needed to be touching them. Casey dropped her bag as Sarah and Pell looked goggle-eyed at, well, everything: the bright lights, the international guests crammed inside, the giant nudes.

"Mommy!" Abby rushed Casey and threw her arms around Casey's neck as she crouched. Evidently, Abby now believed Casey wanted her again. Casey gathered Abby up in her arms as Demmy leaned in for a hug as well.

"You're here," Sherbeam sung out when she spotted them. "*Finally*, we can have the unveiling."

Had they been waiting for Casey, Sarah, and Pell? Casey found that unlikely in the extreme. Sherbeam waved everyone over to what was, under its veiling sheet, a huge new canvas. "Come, everyone, come." Sherbeam's *everyone* seemed to include reporters and writers, including the man who had filmed the whole sorry spectacle at the opening and presumably sacrificed the family to the YouTube and TikTok gods. The woman never learned, Casey thought. Or learned the wrong things.

"We'll just be a minute, Sherbeam," Casey said.

"We can't keep everyone waiting, dear." Her tone was more puzzled than demanding, as though unable to comprehend what could be more important than her agenda. And everyone did seem to be there: Nick, Shoshana, Pau, and others who seemed vaguely familiar from the opening, or somewhere. No Maude, though.

"Start without us," Casey said. Sherbeam's dramas no longer seemed compelling. It was not that Casey's skin had become thicker, more that Sherbeam's antics felt like a function of her career and peripheral to Casey. "I need a minute with my daughters. That is, if you'll join us for a quick walk, Demmy and Abby."

Demmy nodded, and Abby stayed tight on Casey's neck as Casey motioned for Sarah and Pell to both come. Roger gave her a quizzical look. "You too," Casey mouthed. They all left the gallery, as Sherbeam called to them.

"Um, hello? Hello? Hello!" Sherbeam's voice faded away.

As soon as they had a modest buffer between themselves and the gallery, Casey said, "Demmy, Abby, this is your sister Sarah."

"Sister!" Abby said. "But you're Black!"

Sarah laughed. "Why, thank you! Not everyone notices," she added, in a conspiratorial stage whisper.

"Is your dad Black?" Demmy asked.

"They're not shy," Casey said to Sarah and Pell. "I think that's the New York in them."

"I don't know what he was," Sarah said.

"He was sort of in-betweenish," Casey said. "But *his* daddy is more what you might call Black."

"Mommy, what are you?" Abby asked.

"You know, we are all going to just have us a sitdown and figure that one out. My mama has said all my life we should decide what we are, once and for all, but what with one thing and another, there's never time."

Sarah laughed. "You are so much my mother."

Casey hugged her. She turned to Abby and Demmy. "We will talk this all out later, for sure. You'll get to meet Sarah's Grandaddy Joe and everyone when we go to Missouri and Arkansas on vacation. Right, Roger?"

Roger nodded, but Demmy made a face. Not revulsion, as Casey had expected, but incomprehension. Casey had some work to do. Her younger daughters barely knew the world beyond New York and Vermont, France and Spain.

"Who's everyone?" Abby asked.

"Well, you know my parents, my granny and my brother already. But you haven't met my aunts and uncles and cousins. And Sarah's daddy's parents, who Sarah hasn't met yet. That's Grandpa Joe and Granny Hank. And Sarah's aunt and uncle, her father's siblings. And then there's Sarah's Grandma, who raised her. And Pell's family, who I haven't even met yet. And then there must be brothers and sisters, right?" Casey turned to Sarah and Pell.

Pell nodded yes. Sarah said, "Nope."

"Except that now that's a yes for you, too, Sarah." Casey indicated Demmy and Abby. "Ta da!"

"Of course." Sarah looked momentarily disoriented. "This will take some getting used to."

"For all of us," Demmy said. She hugged Sarah, and then Pell. "Welcome to the family."

"Back at ya," Pell said.

"I love your accents," Demmy said.

"Love yours, too," Sarah said, with a bit of a bite.

Demmy made a face again. Casey was finding this amusing.

"Who are you?" Abby asked Pell.

"I'm Sarah's husband. So . . ." Pell was playing this for drama. ". . . I'm your brother-in-law!"

Abby's eyes went wide at this new information, then switched gears: "You have to meet *my* friends, too!" Abby grabbed Pell's hand and dragged him toward the gallery. "Ihsan! Nabil!"

Now it was Casey's turn to be confused. But only for a moment. Ihsan. Ethan. *That's* who that vaguely familiar man at the gallery was, the one standing next to the really handsome fellow. He was the man she'd been trading the increasingly detailed emails about collaborating that had her excited about future of her business. She'd seen the two men in the photo with the girls and in the Insta feed Roger had sent her, so she should have known.

They all followed Abby and Pell back into the gallery, ready now to flesh out the explanations of adventures had, to clear up misunderstandings, to reaffirm bonds.

Casey and Roger entered the gallery hand in hand. Sherbeam gave a snort of . . . well, Casey could care less what it was a snort of. Sherbeam could have her moment now, unveiling her latest unrepentant invasion of privacy.

"So gather round." Sherbeam began speechifying as Casey surveyed the crowd, containing all three of her daughters for the first time. She'd never been happier. ". . . and that's how I came to turn my eye to family, for the first time ever. And such riches I've discovered."

Sherbeam pulled a cord. The sheet dropped away.

Before them, larger than life, larger even than the portrait of Roger's late wife Aline, stood a canvas of four figures: a central woman of middle years flanked by two young women with arms about her, and standing in front of her, a child (all mercifully clothed). Here were the last pieces of the puzzle— Casey, Sarah, Demmy and Abby.

What? How?

The room exploded into applause. All four were wonderfully realized in the same almost painfully vibrant color scheme as the Aline painting. Their expressions were dynamic: Sarah was depicted in mid-turn toward Casey, but really looking across to Demmy. Casey was also looking at Demmy, but seemed as though her gaze was about to return to Sarah. Demmy stared boldly at the viewer. Abby, in Casey's draping arms—where she was now and would stay forever if Casey had her way—reached toward Sarah with curiosity.

"But . . ." Casey had never spluttered before. ". . . how could you possibly have known what Sarah looks like?"

Sarah and Pell were looking at each other, the same question dancing across their faces.

"I'd started a painting of you and the girls, Casey, but it didn't have time to properly dry. And nobody touch it now, by the way. I didn't realize how that would appear, my leaving you to the last. So when you said, right here in the Galería, that you had another daughter, I looked for her online," Sherbeam said. "At first I came up empty, so I modeled her on you. But then social media boy tracked your search through the Memphis police, and voila! We found an image. That kid is a genius with search terms."

Demmy high-fived her grandmother.

Casey choked back her surprise. Her mother-in-law had managed this while Casey and Dunne were floundering in Memphis? The woman had her talents, clearly.

"Sherbeam, it's beautiful." Casey no longer felt the need to treat her mother-in-law as a predator, even if she sometimes was. In future, if Sherbeam snarled, Casey would just snarl back.

Sherbeam accepted the compliment with a slight, unquestioning nod and drew closer to Casey but was swiftly sidetracked by her adoring media.

The party rolled on then, louder as voices vied to be heard. Flashes popped; people posed. Soon Casey needed a rest. Her whole family did, and not just from this event, from all of this circus.

Casey suspected Roger would, like herself, embrace a move away from Park Slope, not toward it. And the Planetkiller had to go. She'd trade it for a small electric vehicle and the difference in payments would cover a mortgage on that grand house back in Memphis, and then some. They'd all have a safe haven to go when they needed to escape from Brooklyn, a place to stay when they visited Sarah and Pell. It could be a place to care for, with a legacy to keep going. Rooms for everyone. Even for Ihsan and Nabil, when Ihsan came to the US to strategize about the new partnership Ihsan had proposed and Casey had eagerly accepted.

Roger placed his arm over Casey's shoulder. She placed her hand on his.

"Mommy, Mommy," Abby said in her ear. It felt so good to hear those words. "Come back over to Ihsan and Nabil."

"Thank you so much for taking care of them," she said to Ihsan, yet again.

Ihsan nodded. "Nabil was a great help." His face beamed.

Nabil gave a bow, with a flourish of his arm. The guy clearly liked drama, attention. "Ihsan was in a González Iñárritu movie, you know," Nabil said.

"Of course!" Roger said. "Third kid from the right! The scene where Yussef and Ahmed tell the father about the gun!"

Ihsan looked shocked. "No one's ever recognized me before!"

"I teach that film at NYU. You hardly look changed. Just older. Were you also in the film?" Roger asked Nabil.

"No, I'm the hairdresser, not the actor." Nabil's French accent was heavy.

"And I'm not really an actor," Ihsan said, whispering into Roger's ear, as though he wouldn't mind being thought an actor by the others for just a little bit longer.

Nabil placed his hand on Roger's shoulder and moved Roger's head to the side, inspected the crown of his head. "I can cover that bald spot for you," Nabil said.

"Fuck you," Roger said.

"New York," Casey explained.

Abby started improvising lyrics to a Lizzo tune, about Nabil setting Roger down in a salon chair. Giving him a shampoo and a trim to get that bald spot out of his hair. Demmy and Nabil joined in, then Ihsan, then Sarah and Pell, and soon all were mangling Lizzo lyrics together.

"Quite a tribe we've got here," Roger said as he stood beside Casey.

"Don't you love it?" she asked.

"I really do." Roger kissed her.

She kissed him back, and for the first time since that fog had descended upon her, so many years ago, she knew, well and truly and forever, that she was okay.

EPILOGUE

Demmy was sitting with Jodee in No Woman's Land waiting for Lainie. "I knew you'd get in everywhere, especially Yale," Jodee drawled.

"And I didn't list my legacy connections!" Demmy said proudly, though in the end it hadn't mattered one way or the other.

"Girl, I think an alarm goes off when a legacy application crosses the threshold of Admissions."

Demmy wobbled her head. "Probly right," she said. "More impressively, Abby got into The Hartley. Though she's going to go to some other hipster school." Demmy leaned closer to them. "Less expensive but allegedly decent," she whispered, fighting the feeling that spending less was a social faux-pas.

"I got in, too," Jodee said. "To Yale, not The Hartley."

"Lainie told me. She's waitlisted, unfortunately."

"Ooh," Jodee said, as though stepping in something dirty. "But I'm sure she will get in."

"Oh, she *so* will," Demmy said, though she knew the odds were not good. Her tutee Marie's son—Phillipe or Phil—had gotten in, too. How ironic that Demmy wouldn't be going to school with him; inspired by Marie's stories and the admiration for doctors she'd developed watching her mom's care, she'd declared pre-med and accepted a place at Tulane. The more she found out about it, the more it sounded like the place for her. She'd already made plans to rendezvous with Sarah and Pell in Arkansas over Thanksgiving. Sherbeam had yet to be informed.

Lainie appeared at the backdoor from the main building with two people in tow.

"Delaney-sensei?" Demmy barely recognized him. "That haircut..."

"Isn't it sharp?" the unknown woman with him said. "Lainie convinced Peter to do it."

It *was* sharp, and Delaney-sensei was clearly reveling in the attention, though in a bashful way, as though unaccustomed to it.

"Guys, this is Delaney-sensei's girlfriend, Amanda." Lainie introduced them. "Jodee and Demmy."

"The three terrors," Delaney-sensei said. "Kidding! Three best students."

"And our favorite teacher," Demmy said, realizing with shock that it was true. "Did I tell you all I have a new sister?"

"Abby?"

"No, an older sister!" And she launched into the explanation, right down to Casey's confirming DNA test that in the end had proved superfluous. The looks of interest on all their faces were delicious, and Demmy thought for perhaps the first time that she liked high school and might even miss it.

ROGER WATCHED as his workshop students began reading his scribblings on the screenplay outlines he'd handed back. It was hard to believe the whole Barcelona/Paris/Ozarks escapade had fit almost entirely into spring break. He had been writing like a fiend since he'd returned, and this time there was blood. He was onto a winner.

His students' faces showed no awareness that Roger had been through an inferno, nor did they make any reference to TikTok or YouTube. Had those three million views already blown over? Wait till he told Elż and Bill how fleeting his fame had turned out to be.

His workshoppers' faces showed raw elation and disappointment as they pored over his critiques. Better get used to both rejection and adulation, if they planned to stay on this path. He knew the students were still convinced all criticism mattered, and they weren't wrong, but it was also true that none mattered. So he hadn't got his MacArthur. Big deal. He'd gained a daughter, now back in Memphis, and several new travel destinations he was secretly looking forward to. He'd taken to whistling the banjo lick from *Deliverance* around the house, if only to keep Casey pointing out that the film was set in Georgia, not Missouri.

As his students filtered out of the room, he felt lighter than he had in years. At the tail end of Sherbeam's gallery show, who should show up but the original Niamh, herself. She'd joined them for dinner—the whole gang, almost. (There'd been a recent rumor Maude had been seen in San Francisco.) Niamh had shared the excruciating story of how Roger had called her 'Nyam' for the entire nine months they'd dated (nine!), having read her name off the nametag of the Oxbridge café where she'd worked. She'd corrected him the first time, but it hadn't stuck. He'd also assumed that the café was her year-round job, even though she'd told him early on that she was starting at Oxbridge that autumn as a first year.

"Oh, no," Casey said.

"Oh, yes," Roger said.

"Oops," Nabil said, as Ihsan translated Niamh's words into French.

"She was screaming at me by the end: It's Neeve! Neeve! I'm an Oxbridge student, same as you!"

"God!" Niamh clutched her middle-aged brow.

"I was mortified," Roger said "I felt like the biggest sexist goon."

"You were! But it seems like that has changed."

"Thanks to you all," Roger said. He had loved her back then, though not in the way he loved Casey, his bisexual (so she'd later told him) wife. She'd assured him she was attracted to him, and he had no reason to doubt her. Bisexuality was hardly uncommon; who even kept track? Right? Right? Mostly Casey just sounded honest and happy.

Now young Niamh and Joshua were approaching Roger in the workshop room. They had seemed miffed when they saw their moderately good grades, probably thinking their perfect hair deserved more than what they had earned, but they surprised him by saying thanks and leaving. There was hope for them yet. That left Roger alone in the room with the one who'd earned the top mark: the skinny kid, scruffball dark-horse Sam, who'd brought up colonialism that long-ago day. His outline had been a zingy farce he'd obviously given a lot of thought to. But not too much thought: Roger felt light-heartedness amongst the plot and pinch points. Tropes *ma non troppo*, salted with just the right snatches of dialog to show Roger that Sam could write. Really write.

Sam hovered on the other side of the quadrangle of tables that filled the small room, the last student, seemingly waiting for something. From him.

"How old are you?" Roger asked.

Sam laughed, a short burst, as though caught by surprise.

"Twenty-four. I'm a little older than most."

"That's the age I was when I wrote *The Fix*."

"Are you going to ask me?"

"Ask you what?"

"The perennial question: what am I? I guarantee you'll be wrong."

Like, ask what's his ethnic background? Roger laughed. "The hell I will. I know what you are."

Sam made a stifled sort of face, as though something had gone down the wrong pipe inside. Had he seriously been expecting a guess?

"You're a screenwriter, God help you. And you could be a good one."

"I think so too."

Roger smiled. Confidence was just what he wanted to hear, because this time out, Roger did not want to write alone. For this film, Roger would build his own team of partners, with Sam as his co-screenwriter, if Sam could deliver and getting paid professional wages didn't distract him (assuming Roger landed financing, of course). Maybe he could find roles for the others as well. Roger was not worried anymore about who deserved what. Sam was every bit as talented as Roger, he suspected, but every student in his workshop deserved success, regardless of their use of hair products. Sam just happened to be the one Roger was excited to work with. Really excited.

"So, Sam . . ." (he hated sentences beginning with *so*, but there it was) ". . . how'd you like to make a movie?"

THE END

A REQUEST

Reviews are the lifeblood of independent publishers and authors. If you liked meeting the White clan and following them on their adventures, please leave a review on Amazon or on Goodreads, or both! Please also consider signing up for the Mumblers Press newsletter on https://mumblerspress.com.

Warmest thanks,
Mumblers Press LLC

ACKNOWLEDGMENTS

Thanks to my longtime writing group, the Mumblers, whose love and support have meant and still mean everything: Jan Stites, Wendy Schultz and Melinda Maxwell-Smith, as well as Madelon Phillips, who is no longer with us and is sorely missed. Thanks also to everyone in the San Francisco Writers Workshop—Olga, Judy, Joel, Peng, Monya, Kurt, Tom, Tahirah, Coby, Ken, Mike, Tony, Chiara, Jake and everyone else— for their always insightful advice.

Thanks also to National Novel Writing Month—NaNoWriMo—which gave me the setting, inspiration and motivation to turn a short meta-fiction piece into this novel. Thanks also to Grant Faulkner and Tracy Guzeman for writing such generous blurbs for this novel.

Big thanks to editors Susie Hara and David Groff, who helped whip this book (and other books) into shape by providing both clarity of vision, focus on the details, and an abundance of insight. And to Amy Kenny, for suggesting the cover concept.

And of course, my family, especially my sister and brother, for putting up with me. And good buddy Mookie. If everyone had a whoodle—no, wait, cockapoo, with 4.2% bichon! Darn those DNA tests—in their life, the world would be a better place.

And most of all, my husband, Tom Duffy, who not only provides love and support, but also reads everything, and whose judgment, sense and skill I value immensely.

ABOUT THE AUTHOR

Mike Karpa's fiction, memoir and nonfiction can be found in *Tin House, Foglifter, Tahoma Literary Review, Oyster River Pages* and other magazines. He is the author of *Criminals*, a comic noir set in Tokyo that was selected for Best Books of 2022 (Indie) by *Kirkus Reviews*, and the upbeat post-global warming gay romance *Red Dot*. He lives with his husband and dog in San Francisco.

ALSO BY MIKE KARPA

Criminals

Praise for *Criminals*

Karpa's comic noir has the feel of an Elmore Leonard novel, with colorful grifters and creeps tangled in tawdry machinations in a vividly rendered demimonde. Tokyo is a vibrant setting of traditional niceties and crass modernity ... The mysteries are psychological and spiritual as well as conspiratorial ... Karpa renders amusing action and intricate procedures in spare, observant, and mordantly funny prose that finds meaning in every gesture.

—Kirkus Reviews (starred review)

Best Books of 2022, Kirkus Reviews

Red Dot

Praise for *Red Dot*

Karpa presents a warmly optimistic take on the future in which climate change is manageable and artificial intelligence is soulful rather than sinister, as illustrated in deftly funny sketches ... Mardy's artistic process showcases a similar humanism, and Karpa's attentive, evocative prose revels in the fusion of technical craftsmanship and intuition...

—Kirkus Reviews (starred review)

Mike Karpa is one of those writers whose prose doesn't get in the way. ... a kind of post-apocalyptic maker romance. ... Discovering Mardy's world is one of the delights of reading "Red Dot." It's a wonderful book.

—Queerscifi.com

Mind-blowing, thought-provoking, and emotionally investing ... a must-read post-dystopian mix of romance and sci-fi morality themes made this one of those novels that readers won't be able to put down. The LGBTQ representation that could be found throughout the entirety of this cast of characters was phenomenal to see and more relevant to the world we live in.

—Anthony Avina Reviews

Squirrels-Fall-From-Trees

Forthcoming from Mumblers Press LLC in 2023.